Coastal
CHRISTMAS

Bling!
Romance
An imprint of Iron Stream Media

Bling! is an imprint of LPC Books
a division of Iron Stream Media
100 Missionary Ridge, Birmingham, AL 35242
ShopLPC.com

Cover design by Elaina Lee

This is a work of fiction. Names, characters, and incidents
are all products of the author's imagination or are used for
fictional purposes. Any mentioned brand names, places, and
trademarks remain the property of their respective owners, bear
no association with the author or the publisher, and are used for
fictional purposes only.

Library of Congress Control Number: 2021940368

ISBN-13: 978-1-64526-348-7
Ebook ISBN: 978-1-64526-349-4

DEDICATION

This book is dedicated to my daughter, Hannah.
May all your dreams come true.

Acknowledgments

Thank you to Tom Hurley for lending me your stories and insight into the Vietnam War. Your help was invaluable.

I owe Sue Grimshaw high praise for her expertise in developmental editing. I found the changes difficult at the time but, then again, nothing is more worth the effort than to listen to a great editor. I will be forever grateful to you.

Thank you, Del Duduit, for opening the doors for me to traditional publishing.

And special thanks to my editor, Jessica Nelson, at Iron Stream Media. You saw a vision with this story and made my dreams come to fruition. Thank you for believing in me and launching my career into traditional publishing, and for challenging me to write a better story. Without you, this story wouldn't be what it is today. Thank you!. The journey has been amazing.

Coastal Christmas

This is one of many love letters found in an antique decorated hat box in the attic of an old house. A soldier wrote it during the Vietnam War, a man who missed his beloved wife and young son. He left them behind, in a large farmhouse on the marsh waters of a small coastal town in North Carolina, to serve his country. His grandson and a young lady found the letters some years later.

December 1, 1968

My lovely Shirley,

I'm glad typhoon season is over! Talk about rain. I am so sick of mud, but honestly, the heat and mosquitos were worse. Now it's getting much cooler.

Christmas will be here soon. I know how you love that time of year. I do too. The best thing I ever did was marry you on Christmas Eve. What a celebration we had. I will be home soon enough and I will get to spend the following Christmas with you. I'm sure you'll have the house all decorated like you do. I will sure miss your pecan pie! If I close my eyes I can almost taste it. Like I said, the food here is bad, really bad. They need to hire you to cook for us but I wouldn't want you over here. Besides, someone needs to care for Daniel. How is he? I can see from the pictures you're sending he's really growing. Does he miss me? I miss him almost as much as I miss you.

I have no idea what day of the week it is but I do know that I have 172 days left of this war before I am through with it. Denny leaves here the same day I do, so we will be flying out together. I hope I can last that long!

We have trenches dug around the hospital in case we need to take cover. We learned to mound the dirt we shovel out and pile it along the edges to make the trenches higher. It takes less digging that way. We consider ourselves smart. Then we use sandbags for extra protection from the enemy, but they get old and worn out and need to be replaced too often. If I never have to fill another sandbag or dig another trench I'd be happy. But not as happy as the day I get to see you again and hold you in my arms. I can't stand being away from you so long.

I love you and please kiss Daniel for me.

Love,
Your Robert

Chapter One

"Move here?" I stared at my mom. Was she crazy?

My mother, Nancy McMillan Randolph, shrugged as she leaned back against the overstuffed couch in the town's only coffee shop. "Why not, Terri? I enjoy living in Big Cat, so does your sister. What's not to love?"

I had to admit, something intrigued me about the quaint, coastal town. The serene boats bobbing in the marina eased my jittery nerves. I even admired the pots of colorful mums that decorated the wooden boardwalk along the waterfront. What an interesting idea to relocate, but no one moved here during the dead quiet, off-season.

"Emily would despise me for invading her space," I said, knowing full well my sister would resent the idea. She claimed this town as her newfound safe haven, and Big Cat was too small to deal with her angst. I was already crossing a blurry line by sitting in Coffee Break with Mom and two of my sister's closest friends. But it wasn't my fault, really. I drove to the beach to visit Mom, who insisted she treat me to a cup of the best coffee around. It just so happened Jenni owned the shop and Claire had popped in to visit.

I took a long sip from my mug.

"What would I do for a living?" I asked my mother, more to entertain her than a serious question. Right now my job as an OR nurse at Carolina Raleigh General kept me too busy. Most of my friends were colleagues who I rarely had time to see. If I were lucky I might chat with them briefly in passing during the day. When I managed to have time off, I was often on call, and even quick trips to the beach deemed impossible. I considered it a blessing to be at the coast this weekend for an overdue visit with Mom.

But in Big Cat life slowed down. No one appeared to be in a rush and friends sat around in casual clothes sipping coffee or sweet tea, enjoying conversation.

My mom set down her mug on the little table next to her, raising her eyebrows as if about to make a point. "You were just complaining about your cutthroat boss and the hectic schedule you keep."

She was right. My boss treated people as if they had no life outside of work. She scheduled grueling hours, turned down my vacation time when it better suited her, and severely lacked social skills.

Jenni Botticelli, my sister's good friend and the owner of Coffee Break, leaned forward from her awkward position on the arm rest of the couch. Her short sassy red hair looked like a flame ready to ignite. According to my sister, Jenni thrived on adventure, something I needed in my own stale life.

"My husband's aunt asked me if I know any nurses looking for jobs," Jenni said. "They are hiring for home health care, and apparently nursing positions are difficult to fill."

I smiled while pondering the thought. "Home health," I repeated. I had never given the idea much thought.

"And not only is the coffee in this town unbelievably delicious, the people are friendly." Jenni winked at me.

I closed my eyes and breathed in slowly to inhale the rich aroma that filled the cozy shop, and then exhaled a fraction of my stress in one long sigh.

"Don't forget, Pony Island is nearby with all its glorious wild horses," Claire Rhoades said with enthusiasm laced in her voice. "I'm the local wildlife photographer and my main point of interest is photographing the popular wild horses."

"I have yet to see the horses everyone in this town talks about. They must be amazing."

"Yes they are. Maybe once spring arrives we can ride out to the island on the passenger ferry to see them."

"I'd love that." If I wanted a close-knit group of friends and community, Big Cat fit the bill, except my sister had stamped a large footprint on the town. These were her friends, her people.

Our issues started way back during our parents' nasty divorce. Our dad left us, and as I saw things, my sister, Emily Stallings, grew jealous of my close relationship to Mom. We were a lot alike, so we naturally bonded. Even now, my sister remained jealous. And here my mother suggested we share the same small town?

"Living in Raleigh isn't all that far away," I reasoned. "I can drive three hours to visit without a problem."

Emily had a nasty breakup with her fiancé and was burnt out on just about everything, including family. She started the whole moving-to-the-coast thing to launch a new life. Then Mom remarried, a surgeon nonetheless, and moved here. I now saw why ... the area was beautiful. But after my mom left Raleigh, life grew lonely.

The carefree pace Big Cat offered tempted me more than I wanted to admit.

Even if I considered moving here, I would have to deal with Emily. Deep down I harbored a desire to fix things with her, and we both were trying, but for me to actually move here was preposterous.

"Oh!" Jenni said, jumping up from the armrest and startling me. "I know the perfect house. It's on the edge of the county with a little acreage and a gorgeous view of the Sound." Her expression grew dreamy as she spoke. "They say the house has Christmas magic. The Christmas spirit will bless anyone who lives there with adoration for the holiday. If that isn't enough to convince you, it's rumored whoever lives there will marry their soul mate within the year."

I tossed my head back and laughed because I was the *last* person to believe in myths or fairytales. "Now that would be a true miracle. I barely tolerate Christmas, and I'm not dating anyone, so I doubt the magic will work on me."

"You never know," Jenni said with a grin. "If you buy the house, you may be married before you know what's happening."

I scrunched my face to avoid smiling at her antics. "What if I don't want to get married?"

"Too bad," Claire said, adding her unsolicited opinion. "Sounds like the house has its own ideas." She snuggled deep into the corner of a nearby chair, her fingers wrapped around her mug.

I got the feeling they were teaming up against me.

"I hear the house is listed *For Sale by Owner*," Jenni continued, barely containing her enthusiasm. "What harm is there in looking?"

Again the thought tempted me, as I had a recurring dream lately of finally owning my own house. No more apartments sounded wonderful.

Moving, starting over again, sounded overwhelming but yet appealing. At this stage in my life I wanted to take the next step, wanted to explore other job opportunities. There was no reason to stay. Mom lived here, but so did Emily.

I noticed Jenni watching me with interest as I processed all the information.

"We can call Lynette Cooper," she urged. "She's considered the real-estate guru in this town."

Claire groaned. "I'm not fond of that woman." She pivoted her body toward me and filled me in on the small-town dynamics. "When I first met my husband, Jeff, he had a fiancée … Lynette. I had to deal with rude, nasty behavior and she tried to run me out of town."

"I thought you forgave her?" Jenni asked.

Claire stalled by sipping from her mug. "I did for the most part, but let's just say we have a silent agreement not to hang out in the same vicinity."

I listened to the close camaraderie between my sister's friends and a strange feeling overcame me. I experienced a sense of fitting in somewhere, being accepted. I had always wanted a close circle of girlfriends, sincere women who you could trust and count on. Of course these were Emily's friends and I wouldn't want her to think I planned to steal them away. Growing up as we had, she was always sensitive about that. She had her friends, and I had mine.

My mom had remained quiet long enough. "I love the idea. Let's go see this mysterious Christmas house. There's no commitment if we just look, right dear?" She batted her eyelashes as if she were innocent in all of this.

"I'm pretty sure they say that about puppies," I said, rolling my eyes. "Sure, you don't have to adopt one but cuddle it all you want. No commitment, take the puppy home and return it tomorrow." Yeah, right. Things didn't quite work that way. People ended up falling in love and wanting to adopt the dog. Well, impulsivity didn't suit me well, just like I'd never buy the first house I saw, not that I even planned to buy in Big Cat, North Carolina.

"Don't be so dramatic." Mom chastised me.

Jenni held her cell phone to her ear, chatting full speed ahead in her thick Southern accent. Her sheer excitement entertained me. She disconnected the call and smiled as if she were up to no good. "It's settled. Lynette is calling the owner to see if he's available. She'll call us back."

Curiosity gnawed at me. Secretly, I wanted to learn more about the story behind the Christmas magic and wondered how the house earned such a reputation.

I felt the need to say, "For the record, I'm not planning to buy a home anytime soon, much less move from Raleigh to Big Cat." The town's name had intrigued me from when I'd first heard Emily had moved here, which prompted me to ask, "By the way, how did Big Cat get its unique name?"

Jenni answered first. "Years ago someone spread a rumor about witnessing a cougar running across Front Street. They said they had never seen such a big cat before. Well, the name Big Cat stuck and became the official name of our town."

"The wild horses are another story," Claire added. "Speculation is the Spanish Galleons hit shoals and sank in the *Graveyard of the Atlantic.* The popular theory is the horses swam ashore to the beaches of Pony Island and have survived hundreds of years through several hurricanes and droughts."

I found the history behind the town and the wild horses intriguing.

Just then Jenni's cell phone rang and after a brief conversation she clicked it off and stood. "We are on. We're supposed to meet Lynette in twenty minutes."

"Again, I'm not buying a house, so I'd hate to waste anyone's time." But no one listened to me. They were on their feet, stacking dirty mugs in a bin before they headed for the front door.

"Why don't y'all go without me," Claire said, clearly wanting to avoid seeing Lynette.

I reached out and held onto her arm. "Oh, no you don't. If I have to tour a house I don't want to buy, you need to go along for support." No way did I plan to let her dodge the tour after they practically forced the idea on me.

Claire groaned but didn't put up much of a fight. I speculated that she embraced her own curiosity about the Christmas house.

We piled into my mom's sedan, with Claire and Jenni riding in the backseat. My mind wandered to my sister and I felt guilty intruding on her turf.

As we drove, I stared out the window. Why see a house I didn't want to buy? I thrived living in a city, even though I fantasized about buying a place in the suburbs, but not on the coast. That was Emily's dream.

Fifteen minutes later Mom slowed the car and pointed. "That's the house."

I gasped. A huge, two-story house stared back at me, drawing me in as if I were coming home. Too bad someone had neglected the Southern farmhouse, the paint faded, a shutter hanging on by a thread. Even with all of its flaws, I could see myself owning something like this. But what would I do with an older house in need of a facelift? Oddly enough, something about *this* place took hold of me and gripped my heart, and I knew exactly why.

It tapped into my deepest, most hidden desire to be a foster parent for neglected kids—primarily girls. The oversized pale-yellow house, with its wide lawn, resembled what I had envisioned in my dreams.

"This is gorgeous," Claire said with awe in her voice.

Too stunned to speak, I tried to tell myself I didn't need a country house on the salt marsh. But I couldn't keep my eyes off it.

The towering magnolia tree in the front yard practically called my name. A rope swing with a wooden plank seat hung from an extended thick branch. The tree embraced several sweeping limbs, some twisting low to the ground as if hoping to scoop a lonely kid into one of its wide, welcoming arms. I loved to climb trees as a child and all those heartwarming memories replayed in my mind. The down-home house evoked a plethora of positive emotions in me.

Mom pulled the sedan into the gravel driveway and parked behind a police car and a maroon Camry. A large fenced-off pasture shouldered the left side, presumably for horses. At the end of the gravel driveway stood a rustic cottage, probably an old living quarters for a farmhand. Delicate lace curtains hung in the windows, giving it a Southern look. Curious, I made a mental note to ask about the little house.

We climbed from the car and I inhaled a long, relaxing breath of cool country air. Peace washed through me like a gentle rolling tide.

"Delightful," my mom said, walking toward the backyard while I followed. "I can feel a grandmother's warm touch here."

"I agree," I said as I glanced around. The entire setting soothed me.

The backyard consisted of a wide, unfenced grassy area with a lumbering pecan tree claiming the far rear section. Several misshaped holly bushes grew here and there. And just beyond the yard, where the outlying woods parted, an incredible view of a long slender walkway perched over the marsh. A wooden dock reached into an expanse of sapphire blue water. Standing there, taking in the view, a light breeze tickled my nose with the faint smell of brine and fish.

Near the back door of the main house stood a handsome well-built policeman, his biceps bulging through his fitted uniform. Next to him a woman chatted, her voice cutting through the quiet ambiance, but she glanced our way.

A wave of anxiety danced through me at the thought of wasting these people's precious time. I didn't want to mislead them into thinking I held more of an interest than I did.

The four of us walked together toward them. The stylish woman carried herself in a sophisticated, Southern Belle sort of way and introduced herself with a sweet accent. "I'm Lynette Cooper." She reached out her hand in greeting as we all introduced ourselves.

Everyone except Claire. They barely acknowledged one another, Claire staring out at the water.

The policeman had light-brown short hair and a square jaw. I estimated him to be about my age and tried to ignore his handsome, rugged and sexy way. I noticed he didn't wear a wedding ring, not that it mattered. I wouldn't be living here anyway.

"I'm Matt Baker." He reached forward to shake hands, his strong grip gentle in a comforting way. I immediately felt a connection and then berated myself for my silly notion.

Then I recognized him. "I'm Terri McMillan. You were at my sister's wedding."

He rubbed his chin as if trying to remember me.

Emily's wedding hadn't been a large one, though I wouldn't expect him to recall everyone in attendance. But I'd been guilty of flirting with Matt at their reception, never expecting to see him again.

"My sister married Keith Stallings on his ferry boat," I explained. From what Emily had told me, Keith and Matt were cousins. I couldn't help but shift my weight from one leg to the other, downright uncomfortable with his delicious gaze on me.

His face brightened. "That's right." A knowing grin spread across his face as if he also remembered the flirtatious exchange between us.

My cheeks burned in the awful way only fair-skinned blondes blushed. I hoped his smile indicated his happiness to see me. Or was that just wishful thinking on my part?

My mom stood taller and became animated. "I remember you too. I'm Emily's mother, Nancy."

Emily would kill me fifty times over if she knew I stood here chatting up her husband's cousin, not to mention viewing his house to possibly buy.

A deep clanging sound of chimes catching the light coastal breeze reverberated from the magnolia tree. The peacefulness of the country once again made me wonder if this wouldn't be the perfect place to help troubled teenagers.

Stop that, I scolded myself.

"It's nice to see you again," Matt said to us both.

I felt my cheeks grow warmer. "You too." Out of the corner of my eye, I noticed my mother watching our interaction.

"Come in and see my house," he said. "I inherited it from my grandmother not all that long ago." Matt turned to walk toward the back door, keys jingling in his hand. "Old habits die hard. We never used the front door unless a visitor stopped by."

As we followed him, I had to ask the question. "Curiosity has the best of me and I'm dying to know why you want to sell the house?"

He slowed his step, seeming to weigh his response. "In all truth, I don't want to sell."

My heart skipped a beat. Why did the news disappoint me?

"Excuse me if I sound rude," Lynette said with a drawl. "If you don't want to sell the home, why are you showing it to us, and why is there a *For Sale by Owner* sign out front?"

He grimaced as if the comment struck a painful nerve.

"Don't get me wrong, it's for sale. She asked why I *want* to sell." He drew in a long breath. "I don't want to but don't really have a choice. My renters moved out a few months ago and the house is falling into disrepair. I had bought another one before my inheritance and don't need two, plus my grandmother's place is too big."

But not too big for me and a few foster kids.

He opened the back door and led us into a long narrow but homey kitchen with a huge picture window revealing the same stunning view of the water I saw outside. With a good cleaning it would be even more colorful ... a perfect place for my small tile table.

Stop it.

I glanced around the kitchen. Without seeing the rest of the house I knew I had entered the heart of the home. I sensed a comforting yet protective warmth of a mother's love here. Sure, the aesthetic features needed some help. Maybe a coat of paint, new cabinets and a countertop, along with a generous scrubbing overall. A layer of polish would help the faded heart-pine floors, although even unkept they were still gorgeous. The worn woodwork of years ago made me imagine kids scurrying around their mother as she cooked large family meals for holidays and get-togethers. We then followed Matt into a sunny living room with an oversized stone fireplace on the far wall.

"This takes wood, no gas hookup here, and it needs some repair before it can be used." His square jaw softened, his gaze far away. "I have many happy memories of my family on Christmas Day in this room with all the chaos of opening presents in front of a warm fire."

He smiled but his expression took on a serious look as he made eye contact with me.

"One thing I should have mentioned. There's a stipulation for anyone buying the house. I'm asking the new owner to host one last Christmas here for me and my family. I know it requires some work before a Christmas event is possible, but I'm willing to provide my labor free of cost to make that possible. It's asking a lot, but it's a deal breaker for me."

I nodded and without second thought answered, "I can do that."

Stop. I can't accommodate his request.

I knew next to nothing about hosting a holiday event, let alone a Christmas party. I couldn't imagine how I, Ms. Anti-Christmas, could agree to such an outlandish idea if I did buy the house.

Immediately I thought of the myth Jenni mentioned and wanted to ask Matt about it, but out of fear of sounding ridiculous, I decided to wait.

We followed Matt into the master bedroom suite on the main floor with a view of the water.

My mom clamped onto my arm. "Can you imagine waking up to that gorgeous scenery every morning? You'd never want to climb out of bed."

I groaned in agreement. Against better judgement, the house beckoned me.

I poked my head into the master bathroom. An understatement to say it needed work, the repairs plentiful, but the claw-foot tub and an old-fashioned pedestal sink drew me in. Both added a sense of elegance. And the breathtaking view duplicated the master bedroom.

The cost of repairs, even if Matt provided free labor, would be expensive. At least the asking price of the house came in under my budget, but even with the extra money, I doubted the savings would be enough.

We moved into the large formal dining room, sporting more dirty windows. I peered out the murky pane of glass to admire a lush but misshaped holly bush and the familiar magnolia tree.

Matt led us out of the room to a second bathroom, also in need of a makeover, and then up a flight of faded, wooden steps.

My mom whistled under her breath. "I bet this house made quite a statement many years ago."

I nodded instead of showing my excitement as I struggled with my own complicated thoughts.

The second floor consisted of four large bedrooms and a full bathroom. Once again, the layout of the house tugged at my nurturing side to fill these rooms with foster kids.

Full-sized beds with old wrought-iron headboards and long cedar dressers, in need of refurbishing, welcomed us. With some love and care, each foster girl could have her own perfect bedroom.

My mother wandered down the hall along with Jenni and Lynette. Claire stayed back with Matt and me, I assumed trying to avoid any conversation with Lynette.

"The belongings left in the house will be included with the sale." He shrugged as if pretending the memories of his childhood no longer bothered him. "This room belonged to my father, and later to me when I spent the night."

"When you visited your grandmother?" I asked and he nodded without answering. Matt touched a soft spot in my heart. I related to his pain since I lost my own grandmother recently. Even more than that, although my father hadn't died, he left us when we were so young I suspected it left a scar on both my sister and me.

"You haven't mentioned your grandfather. Were you also close to him?" Call me nosy but I wanted to know.

He shook his head. "No, Grandpa George kept to himself. But my real grandfather died in the Vietnam War when my father was young." He glanced away from me as though uncomfortable sharing his memories with someone. "Too bad I never got to know him. Nana, that's what she insisted everyone call her, used to tell me all sorts of stories about him—well, that was a long time ago." He straightened and headed toward the door as if to end further discussion.

The others joined us in the hallway. I noticed a solid wooden door next to the bathroom. "An attic?" Old attics intrigued me, history intrigued me. Maybe because our family had little of it.

"Yes. We can go upstairs." He opened the door and flicked on the switch to a single bulb overhead. The steep climb up the dimly lit steps made me hold tight to the railing until he turned on a brighter one at the top. Plywood flooring greeted us as well as a narrow path of sunlight from a small circular, sullied window overlooking the front yard. My gaze caught several wooden frames hanging from an overhead joist, likely family photographs.

"Is this your nana?" I pointed to the nearest picture of a couple smiling back at me.

His smile said it all. "And my Grandpa Robert before he went off to war."

I wanted to know more about them, but reminded myself the details weren't my business.

Underneath the small window, a pile of boxes took up residence, but a lone decorated hat box in the center of the floor piqued my curiosity. I picked it up and turned it around in my hands before setting it down.

"You don't want any of this?" While I itched to dig through the neglected items to see what treasures awaited, the number of personal belongings left behind overwhelmed me. Going through all this stuff required copious amounts of time I didn't have.

"We've been through most of it. If it's in your way, I can have it hauled out."

"No way." Again, despite the abundant task at hand, curiosity clawed at me. I looked forward to discovering what secrets the attic held.

Claire explored one corner and pointed to a stack of clear boxes. "These are marked *Christmas*."

Matt laughed. "My grandmother loved the holiday and decorating. I'm sure there are more boxes than just those."

The Christmas lore popped back into my mind. "Are you aware of the myth about this house having Christmas magic of some kind?"

His expression grew serious. "Yes I am, and we very much believe it's true."

I paused for a moment before speaking because I didn't want to insult him, though he didn't strike me as a man who believed in such things. "How so? I mean how do you know it's true?"

He grinned. "Well, so far it's 100 percent accurate." His smile widened to reveal his perfect teeth. "At various times my uncles have lived here with Nana, and all of them were married by the following Christmas. And it proved true for Nana. After my grandfather died, she remarried before the holiday."

I raised my eyebrows. "So you mean if I buy this house, I'll be married in a couple of months?" I didn't want to sound rude but that didn't stop me from speaking my mind. "It sounds like more of a coincidence to me."

He squared his shoulders and averted his gaze.

"Well, it may seem odd to an outsider," Matt said while picking up the hat box only to set it back down. "I've always been curious as to why Nana loved Christmas so much. She always said the holiday reminded her of my grandfather." He opened one of the clear storage boxes and peeked inside. "But I'll tell you, this house comes to life then. You'll see."

Chapter Two

The thought of selling Nana's home almost made Matt nauseous, though he despised seeing it deteriorate the way it had. Her home deserved someone who loved it as much as they had over the years.

Despite being deep in thought, he watched Roy Conner pull into the Good Food's parking lot in his dilapidated truck. Matt often sat in his patrol car near the entrance waiting for speeders and today was no different. He faced one of the busiest intersections on Pelican Lane, a long stoplight notorious for people zipping through before it turned red. He found it to also be the perfect spot to finish paperwork.

When Roy Conner approached his vehicle carrying two cups of coffee, Matt opened the window. "Good morning," he said as he took one of the cups Roy offered him.

"Mornin'." The older man placed his free hand above the car's doorframe as if he planned to chat Matt up a bit. Small town, Southern dynamics.

"How's Kathy?" Matt asked, reasoning a little chitchat never hurt. It kept him abreast of the goings on in the community. Talking with all the lifelong residents made his day, and he couldn't imagine living anywhere else.

"Guess she's doing okay. My wife has a soft heart, though." Roy stepped back and crossed his arms with his coffee cup in one hand. "I need your promise to keep this off record."

Matt downright resented when people compromised his work ethic.

Roy raised his eyebrows as if to await his response.

"Fine," Matt said with reluctance, then took a sip from the steaming cup and almost burned his tongue.

"There's a runaway teen who shows up a couple times a week. My wife brings her inside and offers her breakfast." Roy stopped talking as if to gauge Matt's response. When he didn't answer, Roy continued. "She wants to help the girl by offering her a place to sleep, or to wash up, but she refuses."

Matt leaned forward to rest his forearm on the steering wheel. "How old do you think she is?"

Roy shrugged. "Maybe thirteen."

Matt whistled. "The poor kid." What a tough age, way too young to be on her own. "Just so you know, if she spends the night without the approval of her parents, you *could* open yourself up for charges. Let's just say you'd be better off contacting the police or social services."

Roy stared at him.

Matt didn't want to come off as insensitive, because he did care, too much in fact. Now that he had given his legal spiel, he asked, "What's her story?"

"I dunno." Roy blew on his coffee and took a small sip. "Dang, that's hot." Comfortable silence passed between them as they stared at the cars waiting at the stop light in front of them. "I understand why my wife wants to help, but I'm not sure I like her involved."

Matt decided to probe further. "Why don't you want to call anyone? Help is available."

Roy glanced up. Their eyes met for the first time since he walked up to the car. "She asked my wife to keep a secret. Kathy made a promise."

Matt understood his friend, but the sooner the police got involved the better.

"I don't mind if my wife feeds her but I don't want her to be upset when the girl takes off. And what if by helping, someone comes after my wife?"

Matt knew he'd be equally as protective of his wife if he were married. "It's doubtful Kathy is at risk." Matt drummed his hand on the steering wheel. He wanted to help his friend but didn't want him to take any unnecessary risks. "Like I said, there are programs out there.

It would remove you both from any threat since that's one of your concerns. And the authorities will either return the girl home with her parents, or if it's unsafe, she'll be placed in foster care."

Roy shifted his weight and again leaned against the doorjamb of the car. "My wife is afraid if she reaches out for help, the girl will stop coming by. Right now she allows my wife to give her food and to check on her."

Matt understood Roy's logic. "Where is she sleeping?" With the nights growing colder, he hoped she had some sort of shelter.

Roy shrugged. "I dunno."

Matt rubbed his temples in effort to alleviate a developing headache. "Let me think about how best to handle this situation. What's the girl's name?"

"April."

Matt frowned, doubting the name. "For now I'll check to see if anyone reported a runaway." In the meantime he planned to patrol the area with the hope of finding her. "I'll get together some canned food and warm things to help out." At least he could provide until he found her.

"You're a good man. Keep me posted." Roy backed away from the patrol car and returned to his own vehicle.

The rest of the day, thoughts of April wandering the streets alone haunted Matt's mind. He wondered what happened at home to cause a thirteen-year-old girl to run away. Had she found shelter? He planned to find out.

He patrolled the area around Roy and Kathy's house, the streets nearby, and lastly the back roads. Unfortunately, he came up with nothing.

The rest of the week remained the same, the girl still hiding out, and no reports of a runaway. Matt had gathered a box of general supplies and dropped off the items at Roy's house, so they could give them to April. As luck had it, Kathy Conner agreed to talk to him.

Unfortunately, Kathy hesitated to discuss the teen and he assured her that he wanted to help. He just needed to be patient and wait for her to feel comfortable enough to open up to him.

She brought their coffee mugs to the table and Matt slid one closer to him. "Do you know where she's living?" A loose term, for sure. "Or sleeping, I should say?"

Kathy shook her head in slow motion as if it were an effort to talk. Finally she said, "No, the little girl is frightened and skittish as can be. She won't tell me."

"Does she look healthy?"

"All I can say is she's petite, but from what I can see, she seems a healthy weight for her size."

Good news. She either hadn't been on the street long, or she had another food source besides Kathy. He wanted to offer his services, to talk with April, but feared he would scare her off. He wanted to keep the communication and visitations open with Kathy.

"I want her to be safe." Kathy's eyes glistened from unshed tears as she began to relax and open up more. "She seems like a good kid, maybe a bit rebellious, but what teenager isn't? I think she's afraid of being turned in and that's why she's not willing to confide in me." She fingered the handle of her mug without drinking so much as a sip.

"I want to help too, Kathy," he said, wanting her to know he understood her dilemma. "As winter approaches, she'll need warmer clothes and more blankets." But he doubted she had a place to keep the supplies.

"You can't tell anyone about her," she said with a shaky voice. "I promised and don't want to break what little trust she has with me. She'll run for sure."

Helping April personally without involving the police presented a conflict of interest for him, but he agreed to continue looking for her. Right now he had no leads other than the Conners.

By the end of their casual chat, his frustration grew. He hadn't learned much more about the girl. Kathy didn't really have the information he needed, so he decided to drive around the general area, this time to see what she might be using for shelter. If he were fortunate, he might catch a glimpse of her. No such luck. The girl knew how to stay hidden.

The following day he returned to the usual spot to work on

paperwork, although he had trouble focusing. His thoughts were not only filled with April and her safety, but also with Terri. Matt prayed the sale went through despite his own personal attachment to the house. The home deserved someone else to nurture it by creating their own memories.

Now that they had a signed contract, things were progressing as planned. He had a mental list of items in need of repair, including the chimney, which Nana rarely used except for holiday get-togethers. It needed the usual maintenance, along with patching a thin crack on the back wall of the firebox. Not a huge deal.

Just thinking about the crackling of the fire brought back pleasant holiday memories. His many cousins, their kids, and aunts and uncles used to show up for Christmas at Nana's. Since his grandmother had passed away, Matt had made one failed attempt with his family to recreate the festive holiday at his own small house, but only a handful of people showed up. This year he hoped to rekindle memories by having the festivities at the homestead.

Grateful Terri agreed to the idea, he sensed she wasn't much of a Christmas enthusiast. Not to worry, the magic of the house would take care of any issues she had on the subject. Matt grinned, having seen it firsthand with his own family.

The house chose her, an odd thought, for sure. Maybe he should call it fate, instead. Whatever the reason, he couldn't have picked a better person to purchase it.

He saw Terri as a breath of fresh air—genuine, confident, and sexy as heck. Oddly enough, his thoughts of her apparently summoned Lynette Cooper to call him.

"We have the inspection report," she said with the sound of papers rustling in the background. "Basically the bigger repairs consist of replacing a few windows, a faulty fixture, a water-pipe leak in the crawl space, and repairing the fireplace, which you already know about. Nothing serious."

The repairs aligned with what he'd thought, except the pipe surprised him. He'd stop by there tonight on his way home to check it out. "Doesn't sound too bad. What's next?"

"Now we wait for the bank loan to be approved."

"Very good. Email me the document and I'll take a look at the inspection report." Not that he had much choice but to make the repairs. He needed the house to sell despite any repercussions from his extended family. No doubt they would be upset, but when he inquired if they wanted to purchase the property, no one stepped up. Sure, he experienced some animosity when he inherited the house instead of them. Nana had four sons, Matt's father Daniel being the only child from her first husband, who had died in Vietnam. Matt had been surprised as well when he learned he inherited the house, but then again he had always been closest to Nana. He had spent many nights with her, helping with chores and enjoying her company when no one else had.

Hence the reason he felt the importance to hold a Christmas get-together to pull the family back together.

When a car sped through the intersection, Matt hit the lights and pulled him over. The rest of the day became a whirlwind of issuing tickets and breaking up a domestic dispute. At the end of his shift, he drove past Roy and Kathy's house again in search of April.

They lived in a subdivision near Nana's house, so after his drive around the neighborhood, Matt stopped by to double-check the broken pipe and to turn off the main water source. He then decided to assess the light fixture in question and, indeed, when he flicked the switch nothing happened. He changed out the bulb but no such luck. The fixture provided a major source of light in the hallway and needed to be updated to code anyway, so he might as well do it right. He'd let Terri pick out what fixture she wanted but in general he planned to restore the house back to its original authenticity instead of modernizing it. He just hoped Terri jumped on board with his thoughts because he couldn't imagine Nana's house with a different look.

He checked the windows listed on the report and noticed the seal faulty. Again, an easy enough fix. On his way out, he paused in the kitchen, the room he most sensed Nana's presence. She loved to cook. He always loved when she baked her beloved pecan pies. Come late fall, she always handed him a basket lined with a cloth napkin and sent him outside to the towering pecan tree in the backyard to gather nuts off the ground and low-hanging branches before the squirrels confiscated them.

Collecting a basketful had always been a competitive game for him, and he made sure to harvest enough to fill it to the rim. He found pride in showing her how many he had picked up. They'd sit at the table and search through them, throwing away any nuts with wormholes. Next they'd spread them out on paper towels atop the counter and run a fan to speed up the drying process. Once dried, she mixed her ingredients, adding in the pecans last before she baked the pies. Nope, there was nothing quite like Nana's fresh home-baked pecan pies.

He glanced around. Man, he would miss this old place, and Nana. He knew she lived in his heart, not in the house, but he always felt closer to her here.

When he stepped outside, locking the door behind him, a flash of color from the woods caught his eye. He visually combed the area but saw nothing. Probably an animal, maybe a deer or a dog, but curiosity caught the best of him. He walked to the edge of the lawn and studied the still woods. Maybe his imagination got the better of him. He shrugged and headed back to his patrol car.

His thoughts switched gears to Terri. Although he didn't know her well, from her sister's wedding he pegged her as a genuine, fun-loving person. When she hadn't been dancing, Terri spent a lot of time talking to the groom's grandmother, had even sat at dinner with her. Whenever he thought about Terri, she stole his breath. He had promised to help with the renovations to ready the house for the party, no small feat, and although his intentions were innocent, he hoped their being together would help him get to know her better.

Much better.

Chapter Three

Three men from Helpful Movers carried in a plethora of boxes as I finished cleaning the last bedroom upstairs. My mom had been a tremendous help the past two days and I didn't know what I would have done without her. She excelled at cleaning and decorating, a real superstar, and I heard her downstairs again working. I sensed her pride that I bought my first home. Well, I was proud too.

One of the men called from the bottom of the steps, drawing me out of my thoughts. "This box isn't labeled. Where do you want it to go?"

Apparently there were a few I'd forgotten to mark. "Just put it in my bedroom against the wall," I called down to him. I had no idea where it went and planned to figure it out later.

The house started to resemble a home—my home. Again, I could feel a warm, strong sense of love here. Matt's grandmother must have been a lovely person for I sensed her presence in every room.

I couldn't help but think every few moments how I found the perfect house for me, more perfect than I dreamed possible.

I laughed at my thoughts as I finished wiping out an old cedar dresser. A motion from the corner of my eye caught my attention. Just outside the large bedroom window, I had a partial view of the magnolia tree. There, perched on a long limb, a flock of double-crested cormorants gathered together. A dab of bright orange color splashed the base of their bills and filled me with appreciation for the gangly birds. Whoever had slept in this room was one lucky kid.

I closed the dresser drawer and glanced around to admire my work. The wrought-iron bed just needed a colorful quilt on top, but for the time being, I used a white comforter I'd bought on sale in Raleigh before I moved. My mom excelled at decorating and I planned to utilize her skills by having her add her special touch once I finished cleaning.

Owning a home far outweighed renting an apartment. Looking back, saving large sums of money paid off, in addition to saving my small inheritance from my grandparents when they passed away. It made being approved for a loan so much easier.

I headed downstairs in search of my mother. I knew full well she had convinced my sister to agree to stop by after work this afternoon. Although my mom tried to help, I had mixed feelings about seeing Emily. Understandably so, she'd made it known to Mom about her dissatisfaction that I moved to the outskirts of Big Cat, and I understood why. The small town had been kind to Emily, a healthy move for her, and Mom and I encroached on her territory by relocating here. At Emily's most desperate moment in life, after a devastating breakup, she found supportive friends and the most amazing man. If I allowed myself to really think about it, I might be jealous, but I didn't need or want a man right now. I was in the middle of resurrecting my own life.

"Mom?" I called out.

"In here," she said from downstairs. "I'm cleaning the bathroom."

I found her in the small half bath next to the kitchen. She had her hair pulled up on her head, her long sleeves pushed up to her elbows, and wore rubber gloves. What a sight, but a lovely one.

I loved and adored her. She had done a wonderful job raising us on her own, and I missed her lately, what with her being a newlywed and all.

"I'm going to make a sandwich," I said, leaning against the door jamb. "Want one?"

She swiped the sink with a sponge to wipe off the cleaner. "Sure thing. I'm hungry too and need a rest." She had shown up early this morning before the movers and hadn't stopped cleaning since.

The men had placed my tile table in front of the picture window in the kitchen. I prioritized cleaning the inside of the windows, though the cold weather prevented me from working out there today. I loved the natural sunlight pouring in and the view of the marsh water outside. As I made our sandwiches, my mom and I met at the table to sit and enjoy each other's company for the first time all morning.

I stared out the window and a deep peace washed through me. Country living provided a new level of solace. Few cars drove by my house, and aside from the cries of seagulls, the world stood still.

As I enjoyed my lunch, a flash of movement made me pause. A woman—no, a teenaged girl—ran from my cottage along the edge of the woods. I stared harder, trying to gauge her age and wondering why she didn't attend school today. She wore an oversized blue jacket and her knotted brown hair, long enough to touch the middle of her back, flew wild in the breeze.

"Mom." I pointed toward the woods. "Look."

My mom shrugged. "What?"

"You didn't see that girl running?" The fall leaves were changing color late this year, distorting our view.

My mom leaned closer to the window to peer out and shook her head. "No, I don't see anyone. Are you sure you aren't imagining things?"

I stared at her, unable to resist my next comment. "Maybe I saw the ghost of Christmas, or the magical spirit of this house." I giggled at the absurd thought and finished the last few bites of my sandwich. Mom knew all about the lore and was equally disbelieving, although she adored the Christmas holiday, unlike myself.

Once we finished eating and tossed our paper plates into the trash can, we moved into the living room to check on the movers. I gasped with excitement at the homey scene laid out in front of me.

Two of the men set the love seat down catty-corner from the couch. "Is this where you want it?" the taller man asked me.

"Perfect." The furniture fit in the room with flawless balance to create a warm, inviting atmosphere, with the fireplace the main focal point. Pleased, I sat down on the couch for a moment to embrace the cozy room, to marvel how my belongings complemented the home.

The afternoon slid by as we unpacked and positioned the furniture and accessories in the perfect spots. Our moment of rest didn't come soon enough when we finally stopped to sit down with a glass of sweet tea, just then realizing how exhausted we really were.

"You did well buying this house," my mom said. "I think you'll enjoy living here."

"I hope so." I wondered if one grocery store and no shopping malls within a fifty-mile radius would suffice. But the tradeoff was the coastal water, the smell of the ocean, the scenic marsh, not to mention fresh seafood whenever I wanted. "I think living here will be wonderful."

I had followed up on the nursing job in home health Jenni mentioned. When the new company realized my extensive experience, to my delight, they jumped on the opportunity to hire me.

And I had also started the application process for becoming a foster parent.

A knock sounded on the back door and we glanced at each other. Who would be stopping by? My sister never showed up before the agreed time, and I didn't know many people in town.

I groaned from sore muscles and fatigue as I stood and made my way to the door. To my surprise, Matt peered back at me, his hands buried in his pockets.

Our eyes met for a moment and lingered, the chemistry between us palpable.

I opened the door. "Come in," I offered and stepped aside as a gust of cold air blew inside. "Wow, it cooled off all of a sudden."

"Yeah, the sun went behind the clouds and the temperature dropped." He stepped inside, his gaze pulling away from me and shifting to my mom as she greeted him. He reached out and shook hands with her. "Good afternoon, ma'am."

She smiled but I saw interest in her eyes as she watched us. "An exhausting afternoon at that," Mom said to him, still wearing her knowing smile. I couldn't hide much from her.

He glanced around and let out a low whistle. "I can see you two were busy. It looks as if you've lived here for years instead of hours."

"You are only standing in the kitchen," my mother said.

He shrugged as if he didn't believe her.

Little did Matt know, I made a game out of hiding unpacked boxes because I despised the look of being unorganized. I found it unsettling to see what faced me. "Trust me when I say I have more work than I know what to do with." I had several boxes packed with books and living room items shoved in a nearby large closet, and the kitchen boxes were stuffed in the largest pantry I had ever seen.

My mom glanced at the antique wall clock that used to belong to my grandparents. "Well, kids, I need to run. I want to pick up something for dinner before Clark gets home."

"Married life," I said, laughing. By nature my mother was anything but the epitome of a married woman. She had never answered to anyone, had maintained a busy lifestyle with her friends, and traveled a lot. She gave me hope that people could change and find love.

Matt flashed me a confused glance, obviously wondering what I meant.

"My mom hasn't been married all that long," I explained. "Don't get me wrong, we love Clark. He's a sweetie."

"Yes, the surgeon," Matt said. "We hung out together at Emily's wedding and made good conversation."

"That would be him. Clark can talk your ear off," my mom explained with a huge grin. It made my heart smile to see her happy.

Emily and Keith's small wedding had been most unusual, but very romantic, on his ferry boat. I met Keith's grandmother—Gran they called her—at the wedding reception at the local country club afterward, where a large crowd had welcomed the newlyweds. Gran adored my sister. In fact, Emily had mesmerized everyone in Big Cat, which fascinated me since we had never gotten along all that well. In the past she had her share of difficulties with people in general, especially men. So I was glad she married Keith and could hardly wait until she got pregnant and I became an aunt.

Lately, everyone in my life had coupled up. Perhaps I needed to be more open-minded. I had no idea what caused my skepticism of relationships to begin with, other than listening to my mother complain about my father all my life. But as soon as Mom had let down her guard, she met and married Clark.

I did want to marry one day. I wanted children and a husband, and maybe now more than ever I sensed the possibility. I glanced at Matt and marveled at how easy it was to visualize my life with someone like him.

My mom kissed me on the cheek and said her goodbyes, leaving

Matt and me just standing there, feeling awkward. We both stared everywhere else but at one another.

"Want to see the rest of the house? You know, to prove there are actual unpacked boxes." I risked a glance at him. Dang, I found him handsome and guessed he worked out at the gym several times a week.

"I'd love to see the moved-in look."

We climbed the steps and I stopped at the room he said he had stayed in as a kid, his father's childhood room. I had hidden the unpacked boxes in a spare bedroom facing the back of the house so at least this one looked fairly put together. Since I moved from an apartment, I didn't own a ton of stuff.

My mom had made the bed with fresh sheets and an aquamarine-colored quilt. I had bought a white lamp to sit on the cedar dresser. It was probably a sin to paint such an antique but I envisioned slathering it in white to give the room a beachy feeling. Above the bed, my mom had already hung a colorful painting with an ocean scene I had found at a discount store back home.

His mouth dropped open. "You don't mess around. Never has this room looked so welcoming, even when Nana lived here. Nice job."

I smiled at the compliment. For some reason it really touched me, although I quickly sloughed off the sentiment by saying, "I didn't have much to unpack. It's a guest room requiring few items, so nothing to it." I led him into the next room, the one with the white comforter and another cedar dresser, also without boxes. I was grateful Matt included the furniture with the purchase of the home. In this bedroom my mom had placed several aquamarine-colored pillows and a peach one on the white comforter to pull out the colors in another painting I had bought. I hadn't seen the rooms after my mom had finished working her magic. Impressive.

"The next time I move I'm going to hire your services," Matt said, making us both laugh.

"Or my mother's. I might have bought the items but she is the gifted one, knowing what to mix and match."

"Just curious. What do you plan to do with all these extra bedrooms?"

Before answering him, I led the way down the hall to the room hiding the majority of boxes, except for my own bedroom. Now he would see the truth behind my madness. I opened the door and he tossed his hands in the air with surprise.

"You weren't kidding." His laugh was fun and contagious.

I laughed with him. "Told you." I backed out of the room and showed him the last one filled with a few random boxes.

"Great idea hiding them. Makes sense."

He fixed his sexy gaze on me and I had to fight the urge to fidget. I caught a whiff of his sea-fresh scent and inhaled a long breath, hoping he didn't notice. It had been a long while since I slowed down long enough to smell a man's cologne.

"Exactly," I managed to say. "To answer your earlier question, my dream is to be a foster parent, preferably to help troubled teenaged girls." I pulled the door shut behind us and paused at the stairwell leading to the attic. I itched to snoop around, mostly curious about what was in the old hat box.

"Really? You want to help teenagers?"

I thought about mentioning the girl I saw running from my yard and into the woods earlier, but decided to keep the information quiet for now.

"I've always wanted to help kids who are hurting," I explained, distracted by a wave of excitement flooding through me as I pulled open the old door. A slant of late afternoon sun highlighted the top of the steps and I couldn't help but feel guilty. My bedroom needed unpacking but I wanted to take a break. "You game?"

"Sure." He followed me as I flipped on the overhead lights, eager to dig through the items begging for my attention.

"Where do you want to start?" He glanced around, appearing overwhelmed by the task.

"I noticed an old hat box when I toured the house." I had been too busy to poke around the attic until now. I headed to the section where I thought I'd seen it, but I was wrong. "I swore it was right here."

"I remember seeing that too." He moved a few stray boxes out of the way. No hat box.

Puzzled, I pushed aside more boxes.

"Maybe Nana moved it. She does that."

He had to be teasing me, though the look on his face indicated otherwise.

"Really? You believe a ghost can move objects?" A macho policeman believed in ghosts?

"Not ghosts ... Nana, yes."

"Oh, come on." The short blonde hairs on my arm stood up. I took a step backward, wanting to leave the attic as soon as possible, and tripped over an object. I stumbled and fell onto the plywood floor. There, underneath my legs, was the hat box decorated in red and green crepe paper. I pointed, saying, "How did that end up there?"

Matt's eyes widened, seemingly astonished as well.

I scrambled to stand, Matt's extended arm suddenly there to help me up. I let him assist me, and then bent down and grabbed the box before I scurried toward the steps. I hurried downstairs to the living room in a flash and fought to catch my breath, thankful it took several moments before Matt joined me.

He laughed at the sight of me. "Did you see a ghost or something?"

I stared at him. "Explain that."

He shook his head. "No explanation needed. The box found you."

It took me several minutes to regain my composure. I sat on the couch with the hat box on my lap, telling myself I must have missed seeing it there before I fell over it. Feeling more settled, I said, "This box is old." I ran my finger along the edge of the crepe paper. "What do you think is inside?"

He shrugged. "Christmas things more than likely. The box belonged to my great grandmother first."

But it wasn't placed inside one of the clear Christmas boxes like most of the others. I studied it, turning it this way and that. I noticed faded script on the top, written on a piece of the red paper.

"Look at this. I can't read it, though. Can you?"

He sat down next to me, our knees touching, and I caught my breath.

He pulled the box onto his lap. "Can you turn on that light?"

I flipped on the table lamp next to me.

"My ... precious ..." I strained to make out the last word.

I leaned toward him, practically holding my breath from our proximity. "Hmmm." He squinted, turned the box at an angle. "It reads: *My Precious Items.*" He handed the box back to me. "Go ahead, open it," he suggested, likely giving me the thrill of enjoying my find.

I wiggled the lid and said, "Okay, let's close our eyes. On the count of three we look."

I squeezed my eyelids shut.

"One, two, three." I pulled the lid off and we both gasped. To my surprise, staring back at us was a neatly folded crocheted baby blanket, faded pink, placed atop other items.

He pulled out the delicate object. "I wonder what this is? It's so small."

"It looks like a baby blanket."

He stared at me. "But whose? It's pink, and my grandmother only had boys." He set the blanket on the coffee table, staring at the handiwork as if it held a secret.

Our gazes met, Matt nodding for me to continue. The suspense deepened as I held my breath once again to see what else we'd find. My face remained inches from his as we peered inside the box. A soft, leather-bound diary begged for our attention, along with a Medal of Honor that I handed to Matt, and a stack of yellowed envelopes tied together with a frail and stained rope tie.

He reached inside to remove the stack of envelopes with scratchy writing in black ink. "Wow. I can barely read the postmark but this one is stamped June 1968."

"That would be during the Vietnam War."

He held the letters with care, placing the medal on the table. "These are from my grandfather, addressed to Shirley Baker. That's Nana."

"Are you planning to read them?" I hoped he said yes.

He glanced up at me, his eyes wide from excitement. "I think so, although I have to assume she kept them hidden for a reason."

I believed Nana wanted them read, or maybe that was my own

31

wishful thinking. Regardless, I prompted Matt. "As you said, the hat box found me."

I picked up the diary still nestled inside the box. It held more appeal to me as it was most likely a recount of his grandmother's daily thoughts, her dreams, her struggles while surviving her husband's journey at war. She was a single parent after he left, like many women had become back then. The diary smelled of old leather and when I opened it, I noticed the neat, tidy penmanship, slanted to the left. The art of cursive was lost on the younger generation today. Grateful I had no issues reading longhand, I opened the pages and caught a few glimpses of her thoughts, of the loneliness she felt, the sorrow.

"I'd like to read her diary, if you don't mind."

He shrugged. "I don't see why not."

Matt's Nana blessed my new house with warmth, as if she were sharing the space with me.

Was it disrespectful to read her diary?

"There is a letter at the bottom." Matt picked it up and read it out loud.

> To whoever finds this box,
>
> I have hidden my pain, my memories in my mother's old hat box. I decorated it as a kid and kept it hidden under my bed. Years later I replaced the items with things that meant the most to me. My plan is not to let my secrets, my sorrow, my history die with me. If you are reading this, then you have found the box containing memories of my first husband, the love of my life. Go ahead, read, learn, touch the items, smell them, love them as I have. It was too painful at the time for me to share my thoughts with my family but I assume that time has long since passed. Remember me, remember Robert. My heart will always remain in the house to protect you. If you aren't family, please give them my life's treasures. May they fill you with love also.
>
> Thank you from the bottom of my heart,
> Shirley Baker

Chapter Four

The letters smelled of age, of wisdom, of hope. Matt set the them on his lap and settled back against the couch pillow. What a privilege to hold such a treasure from his grandfather.

With care, he unwrapped the frail twine his grandmother had tied years ago.

"Let's read the diary and letters out loud," Terri suggested. "Reading together sounds fun."

It did sound fun but a bit more intimate than he had planned. The idea should unnerve him, but it didn't.

"Ladies first." He settled back just inches from her to wait patiently.

With care she opened the diary to the first entry and cleared her throat.

Nana's Diary: June 16, 1968

I can't believe my dear, sweet Robert is in Vietnam. Sometimes I receive a letter every day, sometimes three letters, but the worst is when the mailbox is empty. No news is good news. Or at least that's what I tell myself.

I decided to start a diary to help with my loneliness since he left. My grief, my worry is extreme. I try to hide my emotions for Daniel's sake but he is having a difficult time without his father home. It isn't easy for either of us. Everyone is concerned, including my mother, but we all show it differently. I am quiet, my family is verbal and rowdy. Raising a child alone isn't easy.

I even chased Daniel around with a broom to get him to listen to me. How is one woman supposed to manage a wild boy without help? All I ever wanted was a little girl.

Today is Father's Day and I miss Robert more than anything. Daniel is asking where his father is, and why he left. The house is so empty without him. All I pray for is to have my husband return home alive. I miss him.

Enthralled, he listened as she read aloud several more pages of Nana's diary. When she finished, Matt said, "It's a different experience hearing my grandmother's thoughts and learning more about the woman I thought I knew so well." Lost in thought, Matt sat still for a moment before he held up an envelope. "My turn?"

"Please," she said. "I'm eager to hear what your grandfather wrote."

Matt slipped the yellowed paper from the envelope and carefully unfolded it.

June 11, 1968

My lovely Shirley,

We arrived in Chu Lai, about 50 miles south of Da Nang by the coast. It is so hot here. I am miserable. I never wear my shirt anymore, it's just too uncomfortable. We thought summers were scorching at the beach at home. That's almost funny now. I know I signed up for this crazy war because my father fought, but I wish I hadn't. I had a distorted view of combat and a flawed sense of honor for serving my unappreciative country. Why was I so stupid to enlist instead of staying home with you and Daniel? But I'm stuck here. I have to tell myself it isn't so bad. It could be worse. At least I'm not in the bush like some of the other troops.

I'm far enough away from the DMZ (Demilitarized Zone) that I should be safe enough. I don't want to worry you, but I think I'm okay for now. As I said, the worst part is the heat, so that is better than being shot.

Our main job is to protect the hospital. I'm told a French man used to own this old mansion that they've turned into a hospital. I'm not used to filling sandbags and digging trenches in the heat. By the time night hits I'm too exhausted and miserable to sleep much. They are nice enough to let us sleep in the basement of the hospital on bunks sometimes, where it's cooler. We dump barrels of rainwater from the rooftop of a hooch (a shelter) as a makeshift shower. The water is never refreshing, more like a sickening lukewarm from the humid environment, but we manage. At least I'm clean once in a while but it doesn't last long in the heat, even at night.

I love you. Please tell Daniel hi and give him a hug from me.

Love,

Your Robert

P.S. Please send me some of your delicious cookies.

"Amazing," Terri said with awe in her voice. Apparently the romantic story fascinated her too. "They are so in love and separated by too many miles to count. But it makes me wonder if maybe true love does exist."

"Maybe," he said, shrugging. He removed another letter from an envelope. "I'm hooked and need to read more."

She shifted her position on the couch and leaned toward him. "It's a Catch-22. I could devour the letters in a day but at the same time I want to savor them."

"I know exactly what you mean." He unfolded the paper with great appreciation.

June 19, 1968

My lovely Shirley,

I miss you something horrible. The war seems pointless to us. I mean, why are we even here? No one seems to understand. Do people at home even care? Do they think about us, about the young lives being lost? I'll spare you the details but the stuff I see here is horrifying.

On a lighter note, a lot of what I do is fill up sandbags, dig trenches, sweat, and try to survive. The helicopters bring us supplies and food, and wounded soldiers. I have seen more than any person should ever witness. Oh, but I told you I wouldn't get too detailed.

What I can say is that I miss you terribly. My whole existence consists of waiting for your letters. Sometimes I don't get them and I have to wait days, and then several will show up at one time. I never mind the days I receive three at once. It's the times I have no letters that make the hot humid days and nights long and relentless. I never knew heat until I came here.

I want you to know I love you and can't wait to hold you in my arms again. Please tell Daniel I love him and give him a hug from his papa.

Love,

Your Robert

P.S. I can't wait to taste the cookies you are sending.

"I'm almost speechless." Matt placed the letter back into the envelope and turned it upside down on the coffee table to keep them in order. "This is my opportunity to get to know my grandfather, my wish come true."

Terri's eyes widened as she stared at him. "Is the Christmas magic working in more ways than predicted?"

He shook his head a bit too fast.

"I'm happy we found the letters," she said. "Tell me one thing upfront. Did Robert return home from the war? I believe you told me your grandfather died in Vietnam but I can't remember."

Matt sighed long and hard. "No. He never came home." He watched as she swallowed hard, and when she spoke, her words were thick.

She jutted out her lower lip. "Even knowing how things end doesn't make me lose the desire to read the diary and letters. I bet there is a wealth of information in those words, not to mention an amazing love story."

He flashed her a half grin. "Women and romance. I don't get it."

"Me, either." She glanced away as though uncomfortable with the topic. "Will you share the letters with your father and uncles?"

Her big blue eyes searched his, and Matt took a long pause. "I suppose. Right now I just want to cherish them, read them with you. These are a gift." He plucked another envelope from the pile and opened it. "It's our own personal history book. It's all so real."

"What a scary situation to experience firsthand," she said, closing her eyes briefly as if imagining different scenarios. "Fighting in the Vietnam War had to be hard while his family stayed behind at home longing for his return. I can only imagine the horror Robert Baker saw. And your poor grandmother ... How difficult it must have been to raise a son without a father."

"No kidding, I never knew Nana went through all this. I just saw her as a grandmother who baked delicious pecan pies." He shook his head to ward off the disturbing thoughts but held a new respect for her.

They opened a few additional letters and decided to read more later. It amazed him how sharing the letters and diary made them more bonded together. Plus it offered the opportunity for him to learn more about his grandparents on a personal level.

Matt stood to stretch, checking the clock on the mantel.

She slinked off the couch as if tired and said, "My sister is due to arrive soon, but come with me and I'll show you where the real moving mess is."

He couldn't pass up that opportunity, so he followed her into the master bedroom. Her oversized bed dominated the center of the room with its tall, dark wooden posts reaching like arms toward the ceiling. Matt's gaze drifted to the open closet door, which exposed several more boxes. "So you are human," he said, laughing. "This will take a while to unpack."

"Longer than I like," she said, raising her hands as if defeated. "I can't stand feeling disorganized."

"At least let me help you with the sheets." He stepped toward the bed, more than willing for her to put him to work. "I'm sure you'd hate to do this later."

She sighed. "I'd appreciate the help."

She pulled a set of white sheets from a box and a navy blue and white comforter. "I'm thankful I found the linen so easily. Too bad I hadn't asked my mother to decorate my own room. It's in desperate need of her skills."

"All in due time. The house looks amazing to me."

Together they spread out the fitted sheet and folded it around the deep corners, and then added the flat sheet. It felt odd helping her with her bed when they barely knew each other, but then again, it was the right thing to do.

She snatched the comforter off the chair and they straightened it on the bed, working together with ease. He smoothed out the wrinkles as Nana had taught him.

"Thanks," she said. "You're right. I would have regretted having to make it later tonight after an exhausting day of moving and cleaning."

He shrugged with feigned indifference. "Pillows?"

She entered the closet and pushed a couple of boxes off each other in search of the one marked *Master Bedroom Pillows*. Of course it was the last box on the bottom of several but at least she found them. She dragged it from the closet and into her bedroom, found the knife on top of her dresser, and sliced open the packing tape holding the box flaps together.

"Voila," she said, holding up one of the pillows. She tossed it to him and he caught it so he could don the pillow case as she dug out three more pillows and chucked them onto the floor. From another box she removed blue decorative pillows along with two white ones.

"You like pillows," he grumbled.

She tossed one at him, apparently thinking he would see it coming and block it, but he didn't. The pillow landed smack on the side of his face. He glanced up, shocked.

She raised her eyebrows at first as if concerned he would get upset, but when he laughed instead, she rolled her eyes. Retaliation was fair game. When she turned to retrieve the last pillow from the box, he tossed one at her and it landed with a soft thump against the back of her head.

Her mouth dropped open. "You threw one at me!"

Emily chose that moment to stand in the doorway of the bedroom. "What are you doing?" He found the shocked expression on Emily's face somewhat amusing.

Both of them stood there as if caught by the school principal. Busted.

"Ummm," Matt said, all words failing him. "She gave me a tour and I offered to help with unpacking," he managed to say with an awkward lilt in his voice. Whatever. It wasn't like he needed to explain himself.

Terri made no effort to speak and looked so guilty it made him question just how close the two sisters actually were.

Emily didn't move from the doorway. "I'm glad you're getting a lot of unpacking finished."

Annoyance didn't fit her soft-spoken nature.

"When are we going to set aside our past?" Terri asked pointedly. "I understand you aren't overly excited about my impulsive move to Big Cat, but this isn't helping the situation."

Emily said nothing, just continued to stare at the two of them.

Terri tossed a pillow at her. It hit her square in the face.

Emily stood frozen in place and Matt watched with curiosity at the strange interaction unfolding between them. To his surprise, Emily started laughing and picked up the pillow and whipped it back at Terri. Not about to ignore Matt, Terri then chucked one his way. Her poor abused pillows.

The three of them engaged in a massive pillow-throwing contest and apparently Terri angled to win. Before long, she climbed on top of her sister, whacking her with a pillow while Emily shoved one back in Terri's face. They all but smothered each other.

What a relief to see the tension between them release.

Matt roared with laughter, even funnier since no one noticed he stopped retaliating. "This is better than watching comedy on television," he said eventually. "I haven't laughed this hard since I can remember."

Instead of answering him Terri decked him with a pillow to the chest. That dragged him back into the scene. He had no idea how long they engaged in the slumber-party activity but the three of them collapsed on the floor when they were finished.

Matt rolled over onto his back, grateful Terri had placed a large braided rug on the hardwood floor. "Much better than a workout at the gym." He sprawled out near Terri, who stared up at the ceiling, winded.

Emily let out a long dramatic sigh, not an ounce of tension apparent. This was what sisters were supposed to do instead of fight and chip away at each other.

Terri pushed her blonde hair away from her face and smiled with her eyes closed.

The simple motion disturbed Matt. He knew without a doubt he could fall for her ... but he'd been hurt before and wasn't ready to deal with his unwanted attraction toward her. Life was much easier when he remained alone.

Chapter Five

When I woke up later than normal, memories of my old partying days reminded me of when I stayed up until early mornings drinking and dancing at the clubs. I wasn't made for that wild behavior anymore, or for moving, as the case might be.

I groaned and rolled over, not ready to crawl from bed. My thoughts drifted to Matt. He was sexy, sweet, kind—dang, even fun— all rolled into one delicious combination. I pushed the sexy thought from my mind. The last person on earth I imagined myself interested in was a policeman. I respected his job, although a dangerous one, at least from the stories I heard in Raleigh. I didn't know the risk factor in this county.

I rolled off the bed and stood on the cool hardwood floor, taking note to add another braided rug for warmth. I relished the thought of having no plans today other than unpacking the mountain of boxes in my bedroom and closet. My new home health nursing job didn't start for two more weeks.

In the interim, I had decided to start the tedious paperwork and background check to become a foster parent. Training classes started Monday night and lasted for ten weeks. Once I started my new job along with the classes, I imagined it would be daunting but rewarding, nonetheless. I never took the easy road, although sometimes I wished I did. Being such a high achiever often had its drawbacks.

I found a towel from one of the boxes I opened last night, along with my shower essentials, and made my way into the huge master bathroom. I now owned my own claw-foot tub, featuring the gorgeous marsh view, along with plenty of counter space and room for storage.

I just loved it. Despite the need for a makeover, I found the bathroom beautiful.

Once I finished my shower routine, I made a quick breakfast consisting of a protein shake, powdered greens, and a tangerine I plucked from a bowl on the counter. Again, I was grateful for my mother's attention to detail, as she had brought over a few basic food items yesterday and knew my penchant for fruit. I considered her a blessing and didn't know what I'd ever do without her. And I never wanted to find out.

I sat down at my cute little table and absorbed the tranquil view. I found myself searching the yard and its section of woods for the girl I saw yesterday. Why had she been on my property? Not that I really cared, other than for curiosity sake about her lack of attendance in school. The possibility of being my neighbor entered my mind, although they lived at least a quarter of a mile away.

I sat up taller when I saw movement in the woods but it turned out to be a squirrel.

I'd have to explore my yard later, but first I had a lot of work to do. Starting on my chores, I blared my Bluetooth device and bounced around to a Brazilian beat as I pulled out pots, pans, and dishes from the boxes I had hidden in the pantry.

Something caught my attention, and I jumped when I turned to see Matt peering into the kitchen, door ajar, yelling my name.

I turned down the music and waved him in.

"I tried to knock but you were busy dancing. It was fun to watch." Smiling, he stepped inside with his toolbox in hand. He wore a blue baseball cap, old worn jeans, and a grey T-shirt that looked soft to the touch.

I tried not to stare or drool, though my cheeks burned from embarrassment at being caught dancing. "I didn't know you were watching me." I laughed with a light spirit I hadn't felt since my recent trip to Mexico with my mother. Moving here was turning out to be good for my well-being, although I wondered if I'd get used to people stopping by unannounced to visit. I found myself almost liking the drop-ins.

Matt set his toolbox on the counter. "With the intriguing show you were putting on, it's tempting to ignore the house today and watch you dance. But if I want to finish the repairs before the party, I need to get busy."

How had I forgotten the dreaded Christmas agreement? The holidays were the last thing on my mind with unpacking, the upcoming foster-parenting night classes, and starting a new job.

As if he read my mind, he said, "Christmas isn't that far off, you know."

I groaned, not looking forward to the whole festive party-decorating thing, or having a bunch of strangers in my house. However, I had agreed to the stipulation. Owning the home was worth the aggravation.

"Don't look too enthusiastic," he said with a grin.

I immediately felt guilty for being a scrooge. "No disrespect intended, but aren't you supposed to be working today?"

He laughed, his perfect teeth winking at me. "No offense taken. I'm off."

I loved the thought of spending the day with him while we both worked on different projects, pleasant images popping into my mind of how sexy he'd look fixing things. I found the idea of a handyman attractive as heck.

"What all needs to be done?"

He whistled. "Other than the important items from the inspector's report that I already fixed, most everything is cosmetic." He pointed to the stained countertop, the worn cabinets, the dingy floor. "That's just this room."

The entire house needed a makeover. "You plan to accomplish all that before Christmas?"

His gaze locked on mine, as if I challenged his capability.

"Don't take it personally, it was just a question."

He grinned. "Of course, I'll finish it. But first, before I get started in here, we have an adventure to attend to. Priorities." He took my hand and led me out to his truck.

I ignored the fact we were making physical contact, ignored how his touch reminded me of days long ago, of being a school girl with a crush.

"I brought two shovels." He pulled them from the back of his truck and handed me one.

"What are these for?"

He pointed to a hovering tree along the edge of the woods to the right of the path leading to the dock. "Nana's favorite pecan tree. I used to help her harvest the nuts in the fall. We dried them to make her famous pecan pies."

He licked his lips, and I had to turn away and not watch. This man made me feel things I hadn't experienced in almost forever. I didn't need, or want, a guy in my life right now. I had enough to deal with.

"Finding the old hat box yesterday reminded me of a childhood memory." He led the way to the base of a tree and shoved the tip of his shovel into the dirt. "When I was a kid, I dug a fairly deep hole under this pecan tree and buried a wooden box with a few of my own favorite things. I thought we'd dig it up."

"What's in it?" I asked, intrigued by the sense of mystery and adventure.

"Nothing as cool as what we found yesterday, but it's my own time capsule."

I nodded, more than eager to assist him. "What a delightful thought, unearthing your own treasures."

"That it is," he said as he searched the ground. "I forgot where I buried it exactly. The landscape has changed."

"This could be interesting." Surprised by my level of interest, I actually wanted to find a treasure. "What general area do you think it might be?"

He pointed to a spot in the grass. "Maybe there."

In silence we began to dig. I didn't want a bunch of holes in my backyard, but this was too much fun to stop. Plus, I reasoned, the grass would have a chance to grow back in the spring.

We dug in the sandy ground for at least a half hour.

"I know it's here somewhere," he said, clearly frustrated.

I continued to help him, offering support, despite my cold hands.

I should have worn a coat. "We'll find it. The box has to be here somewhere."

"No one else knows about it, so you're right." He smashed his foot against the shovel and tossed aside a good amount of dirt.

We worked in silence for approximately ten more minutes before mine hit a hard object. We both glanced at each other.

Matt hurried over to where I stood. "Bingo."

I scraped enough dirt off the object to reveal the top of a dirty wooden box.

"Yes!" He pumped his hand into the air. "We found it."

We kneeled beside each other, reached into the hole, and brushed aside the remainder of dirt. It was a wooden box all right. From the grin on his face, I figured we'd found *his* box.

"Hand me a shovel," he said.

I grabbed the closest one lying on the ground and passed it to him. He jumped up as if full of youthful energy and dug around the edges until the box loosened enough for us to wiggle it free.

He glanced at me and raised his eyebrows.

"Go ahead, unearth it already."

He touched it and smiled before he lifted it from the ground. The dark wood looked wet, as if half rotten and might fall apart in the process.

"Let's open it on the patio table," I suggested, although I didn't want to mess up the new patio furniture I'd found on sale at a local shop. I preferred not to bring the dirty box inside the house, even though it was much warmer there.

Matt carried it to the table as I grabbed the shovels and followed him. He set it down with a thud and crossed his arms. "I say we delay our self-gratification and do our work first."

I groaned. "No way," I said. "After all this? Patience isn't one of my strong traits."

He raised his eyebrows at me but didn't comment. "I've been taught to work hard first, play second." He grimaced as if he were dying to open the time capsule but feeling guilty.

I chewed on my lower lip. "If that was the case, why didn't we dig it up later?"

He stared at me.

Got him. One point for me.

"Fine." He tugged on the lid but it refused to open. "Be right back."

He hurried inside the house and returned carrying a screwdriver. He then paused before prying it open and exposing his childhood treasure hiding inside.

"I can't stand the suspense. Come on." I nudged him with my elbow while gawking at the box. Out of habit, I pushed strands of loose hair out of my eyes so I could see better. The rest I had pulled up in a messy ponytail, and I noticed he watched me with interest. "Hurry up!"

He laughed. "Okay, okay. I see you're intrigued." He pulled the lid off the container in slow motion as though to torment me more by delaying the surprise.

I nudged him again, and this time he set the lid off to the side. We peered into the box and he reached inside to pull out an old small yellow truck.

His gaze grew distant and a little smile tugged at the edges of his mouth. "I remember when my grandmother gave this to me. It's probably one of my earliest memories." He closed his eyes briefly before saying, "We went to the dime store and she bought me some penny candy, as she called it. I saw this truck on the counter and just had to have it. She said no at first, but I promised her I'd clean the leaves off the patio for her."

I placed my hand on his elbow and envied the magnificent early childhood memories he recalled. Most of mine before the divorce were a blur. It didn't help that my mother had sold our family home early on, and we had moved many times after.

He smiled, appearing to be truly lost in thought again as he removed a red and white, well-worn baseball cap. He flipped it over to reveal a Cardinals emblem on the front. "One of my uncles moved to St. Louis to play for them but his career was short-lived and he returned home. We always played ball in the backyard together, my uncle and me. Nana would make us a pitcher of lemonade and a plate stacked high with sandwiches. Those were good times."

Hearing him speak of his nana made me think of my own grandmother. We used to love to garden, planting everything from flowers to tomatoes to silver queen sweet corn.

Next he pulled out an old fishing lure and turned it around in his hand. "My lucky hook. When I was eight, I caught a huge fish." He held out his arms to indicate a foot-long fish. "Well, unless my memory is wrong."

I laughed, enjoying his playful side.

He held up the last item, a silver dollar. "I remember putting this in here. I thought it would be worth a fortune someday." He laughed and returned the items to the box.

Watching his joy as he reminisced with each item delighted me.

"I need to start on the house but thanks for indulging me," he said, gathering the box in his arms and carrying it with both shovels to his truck. He returned in a flash, ready to work.

Before he walked past me to the door, I touched his arm. "I'm looking forward to fixing up my home but want to make sure we're on the same page." I wasn't sure why, but I had the gut feeling we had different ideas in mind. I preferred to ward off any surprises.

He stiffened as he continued to walk toward the steps. "My plan is to restore the house to original condition. The renters let it fall into disrepair and I blame myself for not paying more attention."

Just like that he opened the door and disappeared inside while I stood there alone. While thrilled that he wanted to make repairs, I heard a little alarm bell in my head. I didn't want to restore the house to original condition, I wanted to update it to my liking. Maybe I was overreacting. Surely he would ask my opinion before making any purchases.

When I entered the kitchen, he had his tool box opened at the counter, hammer in hand.

I had to wonder why, if he cared so much about the condition of the house, had he sold it?

"What are you starting on first?" I asked, prepared to set boundaries in case he had his own agenda, but I didn't want to come across as unappreciative, either.

He glanced up at me with a focused look on his face. "I'm going to fix loose floor boards."

Loose boards I could handle without argument.

He began hammering in the kitchen and making a racket. Despite the noise, I enjoyed having him in my house working. I found it comforting in an odd way.

Once Matt disappeared into another room, I turned up my music. It helped to make the task of unpacking dishes more fun.

A good while later, I sensed his presence behind me and he spoke over my music. "Can you come look at this?"

I turned down the volume and then followed him into the half bathroom at the base of the stairwell.

He shoved his hands into the pockets of his jeans and left me enough space next to him to peer inside the tiny room. "I'd like to replace the sink and toilet as well as refinish the hardwood floor. I think I can fix the stained wood around the toilet."

I raised my eyebrows, impressed. "You want to take all that on?" When he nodded, I asked, "How much will it cost, and how long will it take?" I didn't like the idea of disabling the only guest bathroom on the main floor but loved the thought of him fixing the stain.

He shrugged, frowning as if I were nit-picking the details and needed to trust him more. I probably did.

"That's fine," I said before he answered. Within reason, I decided to let him handle the specifics. The tremendous responsibility of being a floor nurse in a busy hospital for years made it against my nature to sit back and let someone else be in control.

He exhaled a long breath, probably relieved that I agreed to the updates he wanted to make.

I went about my own business until I was hungry, then I went to find him.

"Where's the toilet?" I glanced down the hallway, wondering where he had put it.

He continued to work on removing the sink without looking up. "Outside."

How had he carried it by without me noticing? After all, I had been unpacking dishes in the kitchen. Maybe he was a miracle worker. "Are you hungry?"

"In a bit." He focused on his project with intensity.

I left him alone with his work and made us sandwiches, hoping he'd join me at the tile table.

Eventually he walked into the kitchen and washed his hands. "Thanks for lunch." He sat next to me, making the chair look even smaller due to his bulky size.

"It's the least I can do." I sipped sweet tea from my glass and then asked, "How long has your grandmother been deceased?"

He finished chewing and chased the bite of sandwich with a long swallow of tea before he answered. "Two years and ten days, but who's counting."

I grimaced at the thought of him keeping such an accurate account of the time. I wondered why he still had such difficulty dealing with her death since it had been two years. For some reason I thought she had died recently.

As if he read my mind, he said, "Selling her house bothers me. It's so final."

Understandable.

"Are your grandparents still alive?" he asked.

I shook my head. "My grandma became ill. Her mental health had been deteriorating for close to a year before her physical health declined. She visited the hospital like a revolving door. First she had a cold that wouldn't go away, then she had pneumonia. She never fully recovered, and then she took a nasty fall where she broke her hip. It just went downhill from there until she passed away."

"I'm sorry." He finished the last bite of his sandwich, having practically inhaled his food. "What about your grandfather?"

I shrugged. "He mourned losing my grandmother and within three months after her death, he died. He said he didn't want to live without her."

Matt paused. "I hear a lot of stories where that happens."

"True love, I guess." If only someday I'd find that deep connection with a man. "What do you have in mind for your Christmas party?" I wanted to change the subject off me.

He lit up. "Christmas was a magical time for us, Nana made sure of it. She always decorated this house to the hilt, and Christmas Day she cooked a feast."

I hoped he didn't expect me to create a big spread. That wasn't my forte.

"Everyone usually comes over around 1:00," he continued. "After they have a chance to celebrate in the morning at their own houses. Really, it used to be amazing. Nana usually saved a handful of special ornaments the grandchildren made, so they could hang them on the tree themselves."

I pushed my empty plate aside, a tiny part of me envious at the cozy picture he painted. "Sounds like your family gets along well."

"We used to, before Nana died."

"What happened then?"

He huffed. "No one wants to make time to get together anymore. Back in the day we met here the weekend after Thanksgiving and made a party out of trimming this house." His voice rose with enthusiasm. "The guys hung up the outdoor lights and put them on the holly tree out front, along the gutters, and then lined the driveway with large plastic candy canes. The ladies trimmed the inside, and then they decorated the Christmas tree. For years, Nana had a real one until she got older."

I hid my inner groan. "Decorating." I cringed. "My apartment never so much as saw a wreath. Once I put up a live tabletop plant that served as a Christmas tree without ornaments."

He stared at me in silence for a moment before he asked, "Why?"

I shrugged. "Why go to all the trouble to put up decorations, only to take them down a few weeks later? That's a lot of work." I thought back to childhood when my dad was still around. "I really don't know why things changed, but we used to celebrate more. After my dad left, Christmas became a minimal, formal affair."

"Formal?"

"We sit in a circle to watch each person open their present one at a time, and then place the wrapping paper into a garbage bag when they finish. Even dinner is a stiff event where we dress up and eat off the fine china."

He drew his brows together.

"I know. It's no wonder I can't stand Christmas, or any holiday for that matter."

He remained silent for a long breath as if he didn't know what to say. "I'm sorry, Terri. I hope my family changes things for you."

His words touched me but made me uncomfortable, so I pushed off the sentiment. "Thank you, but enough about me. Tell me more about your joyful experiences."

He hesitated before continuing. "When we were finished with the decorations, the guys always caught a football game on TV and my aunts and cousins usually baked cookies. The smells in this house were mouthwatering. We typically sampled the first batch of each cookie recipe, and the rest Nana froze for Christmas Day."

He was clearly enjoying the memories. I had to admit he painted a heartwarming image.

"The actual holiday get-together ..." He paused to drink the last of his sweet tea. "My aunts, uncles, cousins, older and younger, filled this house. A group of us always played football in the backyard while we waited for everyone to show up. Then we opened presents." He shoved the last bite of turkey sandwich into his mouth. When he finished chewing, he said, "The amount of chaos was off the chart."

I sighed. "My Christmas celebrations are usually quiet. Sometimes we have a few relatives join us, but nothing remotely traditional like yours."

He gaped at me.

"Every year we have an artificial Christmas tree decorated with only blue and white colored balls. My mom places a red candle on the counter and a pinecone wreath on the door. That's it for decorations." My memories disturbed me after hearing what a lively Christmas Matt had as a child. A small part of me looked forward to his big family Christmas.

"That surprises me," he said. "I've seen firsthand how your mother decorated this house, so why the simple Christmas?"

I shrugged.

"You never experienced ripping off paper and tossing it at someone?"

I shook my head. "And now, as an adult, I don't understand the concept of having a gift exchange only to receive a present I requested. Why not just hand someone twenty bucks to get the same amount of money back?"

He shook his head as if my statement bothered him. "When you say it like that, gifts seem pointless."

"Exactly. And it's costly. If I want to treat myself, I just go and buy it." I was glad he understood my perspective.

He didn't speak for a long moment, and still probing for information about what to expect, I said, "Please, continue with your story."

"After we finished cleaning up mounds of wrapping paper, we'd then feast on a buffet of food covering the countertop."

I deserved this crash course in learning just how precious memories actually were. "Did Shirley have to cook everything herself?" What an overwhelming thought, and I wanted to know his expectations upfront.

"No," he reassured me. "Everyone brought a dish. When people arrived, we always had quite the commotion trying to figure out how to squeeze more items into the refrigerator, or how long to heat up their dishes. When my grandparents had the cottage out back finished for the handyman, Old Man Henry as we called him, Nana finally got her extra refrigerator. He never minded if we used it for the holidays, and we always invited him to our get-togethers."

I had barely glanced in the small living quarters when I purchased the house. At some point I needed to check them out in more detail.

"That's pretty much what I imagine the party will be like this year," he said.

"How did your grandmother handle all that?"

He smiled at me with interest. "Are you getting concerned?"

I glanced away. Yes, I was.

"I will do most of it," he said. "Everyone will bring food, so that will help."

Overwhelmed, I tried to absorb his enthusiasm.

"Things will be fine. I promise." He washed off his plate and left it in the dish drainer before he headed back to the bathroom project. I wiped off the table, pushing the chairs back into place. When I looked up, I saw a figure emerge from the woods. The girl I had seen before ran toward the cottage. She glanced my way before she opened the door and slipped into the little house.

With Matt here, I didn't want to call attention to her, and since he was a policeman, I decided not to compromise either of them without knowing more about why she hid out in my cottage. Determined to keep this a secret for now, I pushed my curiosity aside. But I planned to find out the truth as soon as possible.

Chapter Six

Matt patrolled the flat country streets in search of April. Really, how hard was it to find a homeless, hungry teenager?

Apparently, she excelled at hiding.

Up ahead, he saw something run across the road, probably an animal but still worth checking out. When he drove closer, a large dog lifted up his nose from sniffing something in the fall-colored weeds.

Once he found her, DSS, Division of Social Services, would get involved. No teenager deserved to live on the streets without shelter, food, and water. He learned from his father to help kids in need. But from there he differed from his dad.

Growing up, Matt had personally paid a large price for his father's charity. Never would he sacrifice his own kid's safety or future.

He continued to drive through the countryside near Roy and Kathy Conner's subdivision but nothing. No April.

Matt would find her and wouldn't stop until he did.

I paced back and forth in the kitchen in anticipation of getting to the bottom of why the girl decided to hide out in my cottage. I wanted to know more about her, and began to speculate and obsess over her.

Enough already. Without a plan, I snapped the back door shut and headed toward the dark building. Maybe she had left for the day, or for good.

Without knocking, I thrust open the unlocked door and flipped on the lights. The television blared while the girl slept, sprawled out on the couch and wrapped in a lightweight blanket.

She jolted upright and squinted as if momentarily confused as to where she was.

Then she jumped up, ready to bolt, although I happened to block the doorway.

I pushed a strand of hair out of my eyes and stepped inside, admiring the tidy room. She had placed her shoes against the wall by the door, there were no dishes on the counter, and she had stacked a few folded clothes on the farthest arm of the couch.

"Who are you and why are you in my cottage?" The words sounded harsher than I intended.

The girl shrugged, apparently afraid to answer my question.

"Well?" I asked. After working in the psych unit at the hospital, I preferred the no-nonsense approach.

The girl studied the door as if planning her escape. "I've ... been staying here."

The good news was, at least she didn't live under a bridge or under a makeshift cardboard house. The cottage had heat and water, thank goodness, but no shower. I took in her ratty and dirty clothes, along with her knotted long hair, glad she was alive and mostly well.

She probably wondered if I'd turn her over to the authorities, and I didn't blame her. If I had any common sense, I would call them right now.

I fought the temptation to cave in and wrap the girl in my arms. No, I wanted answers. "Tell me more."

She crossed her arms before responding. "Okay, but promise you won't call the cops."

"I will promise no such thing," I said, knowing full well I couldn't keep the secret from Matt for long.

The girl gave up, likely having no place else to go, and sat back down on the couch.

"What's your name?"

She huffed. "April."

I shook my head. "Right. What's your real name?"

"What's so wrong with the name April? It's a real name, ya know." A whirlwind of emotions passed over *April's* face, such as disbelief, anger, resolve.

I relaxed my approach somewhat. "But it's not your real name. When is your birthday?"

Her face contorted and she looked as though she wanted to hide under the pull-out couch. Busted.

"April first."

I raised my eyebrows in amusement.

April added, "No joke."

I restrained from smiling at the girl's sense of humor. "And that's how you came up with the name April. Real name, please."

Her mouth dropped open.

Did she think I was born yesterday?

"Sophie."

I repeated her name to test it out. "Sophie."

She crossed her arms again and grimaced. Maybe I scared her because I now knew her name. Thinking about it, I bet the authorities were searching for her. Sophie had parents somewhere, or at least I hoped she did.

"Spill the story," I said in my feigned, nonchalant attitude.

Sophie pulled her legs up into a tight ball but made no effort to speak.

Patience was difficult for me but I sat down on the opposite end of the couch anyway. "What are you doing in my cottage?"

Sophie squeezed herself into a tighter ball as if I were too close and she didn't want me to accidentally touch her.

"Speak up." My words were direct but my voice held a soft edge.

"I ran away."

She turned her head toward a six-foot teddy bear with a floppy ear propped up in the corner by the TV. I imagined her dragging the bear through the woods and away from the safety of her home. The image struck me right in the heart.

"The bear ..." I tried to encourage her to continue talking.

She stared at it, her gaze unwavering. "My real father gave me Teddy before he died. He's someone to talk to and he doesn't judge me, won't tell anyone my secrets."

I had to wonder all that bear had seen, had to wonder if she had a safe home.

Silence filled the air between us. An oversized coat lay piled in the corner of the room next to Teddy, for which I was grateful, and also happy she had found my warm cottage to sleep in.

"Why did you run away?"

She flinched.

"Pregnant?"

Sophie coughed with animation, and then shook her head.

"What's so bad you'd run away and live on the street?" I shifted my weight and Sophie ducked.

"Someone's been hitting you?"

Sophie didn't answer but shook her head.

I let out a long sigh. If someone had hit her, they would have to deal with my wrath. No one should have to tolerate abuse of any kind, and I had seen enough of that when I worked in the hospital.

I avoided looking at her to make her more comfortable. "Why did you leave then?"

She let out a sigh before she answered me. "My mom got remarried to an alcoholic jerk."

I resisted interrupting her with more questions.

"End of story," Sophie added.

This time I couldn't remain quiet. "An alcoholic man who yells and has laid his hand on you." It wasn't a question but quite the statement.

Sophie stiffened. "He hasn't hit me. Not yet." She risked a glance at me. "How did you get so good at reading kids? You don't have any of your own."

I flinched. How had she known I didn't have kids? It dawned on me that she had been watching my goings-on and I felt somewhat intruded upon. But of course she would observe her surroundings. The kid was smart.

"What's your name so I can stop thinking of you as the woman?"

I smiled. "Fair enough. I'm Terri. In case you haven't noticed, I live here.

An awkward silence passed between them.

"Why *my* cottage?"

Sophie studied me, and to my horror, a tear slid down her cheek. "I don't have anywhere else to go, and it's warm in here." Sophie swallowed hard. "They don't want me anymore."

Terri softened. "Did they tell you that?"

Sophie tried to hide a sniffle and nodded.

"There is support available." I wanted to help, I really did, but also knew I should contact the authorities.

"No! You promised not to tell anyone." She sat up straighter, as if ready to bolt and leave behind what little belongings she owned.

"I didn't promise." I sat perched on the edge of the couch and planned to stop her if she made a move. "For the record, I don't want you to leave."

Was I kidding? I wanted her to stay?

"You heard me. You can live here for now, but I have a few rules." I stood and paced back and forth, trying to make a list. "For one, honesty is a must. I ask a question and you answer. Number two, you keep the place clean, of which you are already doing an excellent job. Number three, you shower at least four times a week in my house."

Sophie raised her eyebrows. I suspected, with the exception of honesty, the rest of my demands were easy.

"I'm not ready to tell you all of the truth."

Sophie likely needed to protect herself in case I changed my mind and called the cops.

I sat back down and sighed. "Okay, but I'm not going to tell anyone, and I can't help if you aren't honest."

Sophie didn't say anything.

"Deal or not?" I asked.

"Deal. Can I take the shower soon, though?"

I relaxed and noticed her scrutiny.

"You're pretty when you smile."

My mouth dropped open. "Um, thank you."

"Is the policeman your boyfriend?" she asked. "Is he going to take me away and lock me up? Or worse, make me go home?"

My heart did a little squeeze. "No, honey. He isn't my boyfriend and he isn't going to lock you up." Not if I could help it. "Let's go." I stood, ready to leave. "If you have laundry, bring it along."

She shook her head, tugging at her dirty shirt. "I only have these clothes. And a few other things."

They could use a washing, for sure.

Sophie scooped up the small armful of items stacked near Teddy and followed me out of the cottage and inside my house. The screen door slapped shut behind us, and I knew she was trusting me.

We made a pit stop at the washing machine, so she could empty her arms and drop the dirty items inside.

"There is a bathroom upstairs," I said as I led the way up the wide wooden steps.

Sophie whistled under her breath. "Your house is more beautiful than I imagined. And it's so clean. No piles of boxes, junk, and clutter."

I slowed in climbing the steps and narrowed my gaze on her. "Boxes, junk?"

She shrugged as if her comment was no big deal. "The more my mom and stepdad clean, the more they mess things up." When they reached the top of the steps she peeked in one of the bedrooms. "But your home is filled with love, like someone wrapping their arms around me."

Her words touched a soft vulnerable spot inside me that I didn't know existed. "I'm not sure what to say, but thank you." Once again, she caught me off guard.

"I thought you just moved in?" Sophie asked, looking confused. "Looks like you've lived here forever."

"Yes, just moved in, but don't be surprised. Most of the boxes are hidden," I explained as I pulled a thick, folded white towel and a washcloth from the linen closet.

Sophie stuck her head inside. "We don't have many towels. I mean we have some but they are never clean unless I wash a load. Half the time the dryer doesn't work, though."

"Oh, honey." What was I supposed to say? I took linen for granted apparently and never thought about not having any when I needed it.

"Well, when it's warmer outside I can hang them on the line, but now it's colder and they stay wet and smell funny. If I hang them inside, *he* ends up using them all before I get a chance."

The poor, sweet child.

Sophie took the soft towel in her hands, rubbing it against her face as if she'd never smelled perfumed fabric softener. She glanced up and noticed me watching her. Thankfully, she didn't say anything more, and instead followed me into the bathroom. With reluctance, she placed the items on the counter.

"I haven't had a chance to unpack the rug and shower curtain yet. If you give me a minute, I'll dig them out of a box. I think I know where they are."

Before Sophie could protest, I hurried off. I wanted to do this for her.

I returned a few moments later with my arms full, dropping an aquamarine rug onto the floor near the tub. Sophie watched as if she couldn't wait to bury her bare feet into its softness. I held a clear shower curtain with fuchsia pink, white, and aquamarine swirls. Together we hung it from the small plastic hoops.

"You're going to a lot of trouble for me."

"It's no problem at all. I have to unpack everything at some point." I hooked the last hole onto the plastic ring and stepped back to admire our handiwork.

"It's been almost three weeks since I've had a shower."

Before I could stop myself, I asked, "Three weeks?"

She nodded. "But I've washed with my hands and a bar of soap. But a hot shower ..." Her face turned all dreamy like.

What a horrifying thought, not to mention her comment made me wonder how long she had been living in my cottage. I forced myself to let it go and not pressure her for details.

"Enjoy." I handed her the fluffy wash cloth. "I'll find my

housecoat, and you can wear that until your clothes are clean." I waited with patience for Sophie to remove her garments, but when she hesitated, I said, "Go ahead and step into the shower and then hand me your things."

She did as I asked and climbed into the tub, closed the pretty curtain, and removed the soiled clothes. She passed them to me, her face peeking around the plastic, as though she were embarrassed by the stench and discoloring.

"I'll be back with the housecoat, so take as long as you want." With that, I closed the bathroom door.

I carried the clothes downstairs and placed them inside the washer with the others. Deciding I better wait to run the water while she showered, I went in search of my robe. Of course it was in the last box I searched through in my bedroom. Thankfully I found it.

When I returned upstairs, I tapped on the door. She didn't answer so I cracked it open. She screeched and the water splashed.

"Sorry about that," I said, wondering why I had scared her. She had turned off the shower but I heard the tub faucet running.

"Hope you don't mind if I take a bath too. I used to get in trouble for using too much water, but it feels so good."

"Honey, take all the time you need." I set the robe on the closed commode lid and turned to leave. "I'm going to heat up some soup. It's not homemade but it tastes good and will warm you up."

Sophie sniffled. "Thank you for your kindness," she whispered.

I paused, once again unsure of what to say, or maybe I was fighting off my own set of emotions. "You're welcome," I mumbled back.

I had a hunch no one had called her honey before and maybe she even liked it, but also my intuition warned me she'd be out of here first thing tomorrow.

Chapter Seven

As I made hot soup for the young lady soaking upstairs in my bathtub, thoughts raced through my head. I had no idea what to do with a runaway teen. If I were approved for foster care I'd be in a better position, and the legal ramifications concerned me.

I had promised I wouldn't turn Sophie over to the authorities, and I wasn't a person who went back on my word. But the tricky part? Matt stopped by my house almost daily, and I had no idea if I could trust him with my secret. Bucking the system by not calling the Department of Social Services, DSS, was probably a bad idea, let alone not calling the police to file a report.

I shouldn't expect him to lie for me. He had a job to do and I didn't need to involve him in this.

More than likely Sophie's family was frantically looking for her. I'd thought about how I would feel if the situation were reversed and she were my daughter. But something made her run and I needed to discover what.

I heard water draining upstairs and suspected Sophie would be down shortly. I made her a hot cup of cocoa, pulled off a large chunk of French bread for each of us, and poured the soup into pottery bowls and set them on the kitchen table. A hot meal always tasted good, even if only canned soup.

A thump upstairs caught my attention. I had to admit, taking in a stranger concerned me a bit. I could hear my mother's words advising me to worry about Sophie stealing things, and maybe I should be, but when I heard footsteps on the old stairs, I knew she hadn't had time to snoop around. When she turned the corner and stepped into the kitchen, she immediately asked, "What smells so delicious?"

"Canned soup." I laughed. "It's not elaborate but will do in a pinch until I can go grocery shopping." I motioned her over to sit at the table. Her presence filled me with an unfamiliar, nurturing desire.

She sat with my robe wrapped around her and stared at the chicken noodle soup.

"Is something wrong?"

She shook her head. "I haven't had a hot meal in a while." She tasted the first spoonful and sighed long and hard.

The dark sky took over the usual peaceful view, and off in the distance a red and green light moved across the dark water, a boat. Living on the marsh and Intracoastal Waterway was a different lifestyle, a blessing I never wanted to take for granted. In comparison to the girl next to me, who I had great empathy for, I also appreciated having a warm, safe house with food.

Sophie used a piece of the bread to absorb the last drops of soup from the bowl. She shoved the entire piece into her mouth.

My heart went out to her. I wanted to offer her one of my guest rooms for the night but my intuition told me, for the sake of her independence and until I got to know her better, to let her continue to stay in the cottage for a while.

The timer beeped on the washing machine, and I excused myself from the table and placed her few items into the dryer. Tomorrow I planned to buy her more clothes. Taking care of people, especially girls in need, resonated with my soul. I never really thought about why I became a nurse but wondered if it was the same reason why I wanted to be a foster parent.

After we cleaned up the dishes, I invited her to stay for Girls' Night to watch a movie in the living room, wishing I had brought some wood inside to build a fire.

It took half the movie for Sophie to relax enough to laugh at the comedy we were watching. She had a beautiful smile. I bet she didn't allow that side to show often and was glad she felt comfortable enough with me to let her guard down.

Sitting here with her reminded me how much I wanted to have

a family someday. If it turned out I fostered kids instead of having a family of my own, I think I'd be satisfied enough. I just knew I needed to have kids around me.

These emotions were not foreign to me but had been buried for years, and this house definitely made me see the possibilities. Whoever built the house definitely designed it for a family.

When the movie ended, we said our goodnights and she let herself out the back door to return to the cottage. I wished I could help her more but knew the situation remained a sensitive topic all the way around. We needed to earn each other's trust as well as to decide how best to handle the situation. Those two things needed to happen before anything else.

I locked the door and strolled into my bedroom, once again thankful for my blessings. As I readied for bed I thought about what else this house planned to offer me. So far it had touched my heart in so many ways that I eagerly awaited more of its goodness.

The following morning the sun streamed through the murky windows. I made a mental note to wash them today while the warm weather blessed us. Fall in North Carolina skipped all over the place, from warm and bright to cold and dreary. This week promised much milder temperatures.

I thought about offering a hot breakfast to Sophie but knew teenagers slept in late. Actually, I hoped she hadn't run off during the night and decided to check on her soon, not wanting to wake her just yet.

I sat at my little table and marveled at the amount of boat traffic while I blew on my steaming mug of coffee. Saturday arrived so fast I had lost track of the days. I'd been busy from morning to night and couldn't believe I'd already been in Big Cat for close to a week.

After I finished my coffee, I decided I might as well get started on my long list of tasks before Matt showed up. I needed to figure out how to introduce him to the idea of Sophie, but in the meantime hoped he'd be busy with his bathroom project. He had buffed out the stain and had refinished the floor. The new toilet and pedestal sink sat in the dining room, and I didn't want to complain, but wished he had asked my preference. Especially since I was the one paying for the repairs. Although I had to admit, the pedestal sink matched the style of the house well, and a toilet was a toilet. I appreciated his hard work, but at some point we needed to have a conversation about how we'd refurbish the rest of the house.

I saw movement from the corner of my eye and I about spit out my coffee when I saw Sophie hauling her oversized teddy bear out of the cottage. She had a backpack swung over one shoulder. Where was she going?

I plunked my coffee mug down so fast the contents spilled on the table. I ran outside, the screen door slamming shut behind me.

Sophie glanced up, her eyes wide from surprise.

"Why are you leaving?"

She shrugged.

I struggled to fight off my disappointment. It broke my heart to think of her on the street without shelter, food, or water.

"Sophie, I want you to stay, so I can help you."

A confused look crossed her face.

"You don't have to run anymore. You are safe here." I didn't know what to say to convince her I wanted her to stay.

Matt chose that unfortunate moment to pull up in his truck.

Sophie glanced between Matt and the woods, and I knew she planned to bolt. Then she glanced down at the huge teddy bear to evaluate if she should drop it or drag it along.

Unsure of what to do, I moved closer to her. "Sophie, he's safe. I promise." Oh, please don't let me tell her a big fat lie. Certainly, if I explained the situation to Matt he'd honor the secret.

She stared at him.

He slammed his truck door and headed their way.

"It's okay," I reassured her. "I give you my word."

She stood frozen, half listening to me and half crazed.

Matt approached, eyebrows raised. When he reached us, he extended his hand as if he knew about her. "April?"

Sophie didn't answer. She had one foot angled toward the woods and one toward me.

"It's okay, Sophie." I needed to repeat myself for her to hear my words. "Matt, tell her she's safe, that you won't report her."

He hesitated longer than I wanted but said the words. "I promise, Sophie." He picked up on the fact her name wasn't April. "I won't turn you in, and you're safe here. You have shelter, warmth, food, and people who can help you."

Sophie's fear visibly eased a few notches.

"I promise. We will help you anyway we can," he said.

I appreciated Matt more than I fathomed possible. He understood teenagers. And without question, he did what I'd hoped and I adored him for that.

"Let's go inside," he suggested.

"I have hot chocolate and can make you eggs," I said, knowing a home-cooked meal tempted her. If she agreed to walk inside to eat, we had a better chance of her agreeing to stay.

She nodded and brought her items back into the cottage.

I had to accept knowing she might disappear during the night, after all the decision belonged to her. All I could do was let her know I cared.

While we awaited Sophie's return, I took comfort in the cries of the seagulls overhead. They filled the air with music. Matt stood close to me but we didn't speak.

Sophie returned empty handed. She followed us into the kitchen, the screen door slapping closed. The wooden sound reminded me of pleasant memories of my grandmother's country house.

The moment of peace zipped away. No sooner than we stepped into the house than my mom's car pulled into the driveway. Before I made for the door to intercept her, I touched Sophie's shoulders. "That's my mom. I promise she's safe too and I'll be right back." I wasn't sure I convinced her, but I left her with Matt and ran outside in time to greet Mom as she stepped from her car.

"Why do you look like you just ran a marathon?" she asked me.

"I feel like I have." My hair fell from its clip and I knew I looked frazzled from all this early morning activity. My life in Raleigh was mundane compared to this.

"I see Matt's truck is already here."

I wished she'd lay off me about Matt but had a more urgent topic on my mind. I waved her comment aside. "There's been a new development. Remember the girl I saw running across the yard the day I moved in?"

"The one I didn't see?"

"Yes, that one. Well, I saw her again. Apparently, she's been living out of my cottage." Not making a whole lot of sense, I needed to inform her as fast as possible because she headed toward the cottage door. I scrambled behind her. "Mom, stop walking and listen to me for a minute. This is important."

She stopped, her body angled toward the cottage as if she were on a mission to see for herself what I was rambling about.

"Sophie is a runaway. I need you to promise to keep this top secret. No one can know, not even Emily." Oh, for sure not Emily.

"Why?"

I inhaled a long slow breath of cool country air to calm myself. "Because I want to help her. If anyone finds out before I can get permission from her parents to stay with me, DSS will take her away." I bent over to inhale another long breath.

"Okay, I promise. But hear me when I say the magic of this house is working. Didn't you say you wanted to help troubled girls?"

I stood ramrod straight and stared at her.

She nodded. "Exactly." Then she pivoted and headed for the screen door of the main house instead of the cottage.

I hurried past her and entered first to keep my mother from saying something awkward to Sophie or Matt. Before she could speak, I said, "Sophie, meet my mom. All is good, and I hope you all are hungry." Without waiting for an answer, I made a pot of coffee, and to my surprise and relief, awkward silence filled the air. That was much better than my mom pelting out a bunch of questions. As I pulled out a carton of eggs from the refrigerator, all eyes remained on me.

I glanced at Matt, who leaned against the counter with his arms crossed.

"Scrambled please," he said with an annoying but sexy grin.

Amazing how he read my mind as to what he wanted to eat, but I just hoped he didn't sense how attractive I found him.

He pushed away from the counter. "I'm going to get busy in the bathroom."

The flirtatious glance he flashed me when he passed by, made me worry he suspected how I felt about him. My cheeks burned hot.

"Scrambled?" I glanced at Sophie, trying to hide my flushed face.

"Please," she answered.

I didn't bother to ask my mom, knowing full well she'd translate my red cheeks. She already questioned my intentions toward him and I didn't want to go there again. She always ordered omelets, so I cracked the eggs in a bowl. Sophie sat at the table, staring out the window and ignoring Mom. I had to wonder if she was figuring out another escape plan.

"Sophie, you have pretty hair. It reminds me of my daughter, Emily's," my mom said, filling the silence.

Sophie didn't respond but a small smile spread from the corners of her mouth. A grin escaped my own lips at my mother's attempt to engage Sophie in conversation.

I melted butter in the pan and cooked the eggs while the bread toasted. More quiet minutes passed slowly, and when the eggs finished cooking, I scooped everything onto plates and placed them on the table. "I wish I had bacon to offer but need to run by the store after I wash the windows." I set a container of strawberry jam between them for the toast.

Sophie practically dove into the food but that didn't stop my mom from trying to strike up a conversation with her. She asked about Sophie's pretty hair again, commented on the view, and questioned if she liked the eggs. Unfortunately, Sophie remained uncomfortable and quiet, just nodding here and there.

While they ate, I made Matt's breakfast, as I had eaten hours ago. I enjoyed cooking for them and found it good practice for when I became a foster parent.

"Sophie, do you like dogs?" my mom asked her, and then turned toward me. "Clark's daughter has a sweet dog that's due to have puppies within a week or two. They should be ready for adoption around Christmas."

Clark was my mother's other half. After years of being single, and at her age, she found the love of her life. She gave me hope someone existed out there for me.

Sophie glanced up from her now empty plate. "Yes! I want to see them," she said, bouncing in her chair.

I tried not to gawk, surprised Sophie had spoken to my mother. Instead, I locked my gaze on Matt's eggs.

From my peripheral vision I saw my mom push her plate aside and pick up her mug of coffee for a long sip. She set it down and said, "I'll let Terri know when they are born."

Who knew how long Sophie would stay with me and hoped my mom didn't make promises we couldn't keep.

"I had a dog once," Sophie said, her voice small. "He used to sleep on my bed every night."

"Me too," my mom added. "Mine was my best friend." She turned toward me with her eyebrows raised. "That's what you need here. A dog."

Another responsibility.

"Oh, I know that look. A dog would give you company and protect you. A watch dog is a good thing when you live out in the country alone."

"Who's alone? I have more company now than I ever have."

My mom rolled her eyes and stood to wash the dishes as I called Matt and set his plate on the table.

"Be there soon," he called back from the bathroom. A muffled grunt wafted down the hallway and into the kitchen, followed by an illegible mumble.

I grabbed a bottle of window cleaner from the cabinet underneath the sink and a roll of paper towels. My mom and Sophie followed me outside, Sophie disappearing inside the cottage.

"Why didn't you tell me about her?" she asked as soon as the teenager was out of earshot.

I shrugged without answer and sprayed the window instead. For one, I didn't want to fully confide in her yet, and for two, I couldn't wait to complete the final process of cleaning the windows to have an unobstructed view of the marsh. It had been too cold outside before now and with the glorious sun shining I needed to grab the opportunity.

"Okay, so you aren't ready to talk about her yet."

"Not really. And I don't know all that much." I would eventually share the information with her once I processed it.

Mom began cleaning what she could reach from the ground, and as I climbed the ladder, I inhaled the salty, fresh air of the Waterway. Country living suited me well.

"Fine then. I'll tell you about Clark, about how much I love moving into his house, and ... about Emily."

I groaned. I almost preferred confiding in her about Sophie.

"You know, Emily's not happy with you," my mother said with an interesting lilt in her voice. "She mentioned something about a pillow fight with Matt."

I rolled my eyes. So she wanted to pry for information about Matt. "Did Emily tell you she joined us?" My mother made an innocent pillow fight sound so intimate.

She stopped washing the window and stared at me. "So it's true?"

I laughed. "Is what true? The pillow fight wasn't intentional and just sort of happened," I said in self-defense.

"He's over here a lot."

I paused mid swipe with the paper towel. "He's here fixing up the house for the Christmas party. Remember the stipulation I agreed to before buying this home?"

My mother sprayed the lower portion of the window and wiped it away before she spoke. "I remember. I'm just saying, he is around a lot."

I closed my eyes and breathed deeply for a moment before I spoke. "He's making repairs. That's all."

My mother didn't answer.

The cottage door shut and Sophie emerged next to us. "Can I help?"

Again, I marveled how I went from such an isolated life in Raleigh, so busy with work I barely had a social life, to having a houseful of friends and family.

"Absolutely." I stepped down from the ladder and handed her the wad of paper towels. "I need to get more window cleaner. Help yourself."

I went inside, thrilled Sophie wanted to be around us, and used the excuse I needed more supplies. I actually did but wanted to check on Matt first. As I headed into the hallway, he stepped from the bathroom and we almost collided.

He reached out and practically held me in his arms, preventing me from stumbling. The pulsating energy running through my body surprised me. Sure, he was handsome but I had no idea his touch would be so electrifying. He must have experienced something similar because he quickly pulled away, but I saw a hint of a smile.

"Sorry about that," he said as he glanced around. "Is Sophie inside?"

I shook my head.

"About her." He hesitated before speaking. "It's not wise to keep her here. You're breaking the law, in case you don't realize, and should turn her over because she is a minor."

I bristled. "You promised." My heart practically broke in two for Sophie because apparently Matt had misled me earlier.

He looked away for a moment and then studied me with such intensity, I held my breath for a moment. "You're putting me in an awkward situation," he said.

I scrunched my brows together, frustrated. "She's a child who needs help. You know how I feel about wanting to be a foster parent. She showed up here for a reason."

His silence unnerved me. And then he said, "But you aren't a foster parent yet."

Ouch.

"Has she been reported missing?" I prodded.

He shook his head. "That doesn't mean anything. I'm sure her parents are looking for her."

"She said they told her not to come back." When he didn't speak, I continued on. "I believe her. I don't want to send her back to an abusive home, that is a real possibility."

He crossed his arms. "Terri, I wish I agreed with you on this but we need to handle it the right way." He waited for my nod, but I didn't comply. "If you want to keep her here, you need to get permission from her parents. Otherwise, I'm required to turn her over to DSS."

I hated this. We stared at each other, neither of us relenting. Unable to stand the tension, knowing he was truly right, I caved in. "Fine, just give me time to find out who her parents are. I need for her to trust me."

He nodded hesitantly. "You need to understand the risk you're taking. I'm sure you are aware that her parents could press charges against you. This is serious, Terri."

"Press charges?" That's all I needed, to have a police record before I started my new job. "I'm just trying to help."

"And you are." He reached out and wrapped me in a delicious hug. "The answer is to get her parents' written permission. If everyone agrees, then DSS won't get involved because Sophie is safe and her parents have given their consent. There are benefits to living in a small town and that is one of them."

I glanced up at him. "You're right, of course, and I just hope it all works out."

But what he said next surprised me.

"And sign her up for a female counselor. That's a must." He played with a strand of my hair and it almost distracted me. "You don't know what Sophie's gone through. That's why DSS is important, because they can help."

Stepping back, I stared into his protective but dreamy eyes, feeling a sense of security. "Okay, I'll look into it."

"Don't worry, it will all work out, Terri." He offered me a reassuring smile. "I can give you a list of names to help."

I fought the urge to fold into his arms again and hug him with gratitude. "In the meantime, I'll work on getting Sophie's parents to agree."

He nodded. "Okay, but you need to hurry. I care about you and don't want to see anything bad happen."

I flashed him a nervous smile but I loved that he just said he cared about me. I had to fight my desire to kiss him.

He waved toward the bathroom as if trying to change the subject. "What do you think so far?"

Glad for the distraction, I leaned around him and poked my head inside. "Wow, you are truly talented." I had no idea the update would make it look so fresh and bright. "And the stain is gone from around the toilet. Thank you!"

He grinned as if proud to show off his work. "Nothing to it. I need to replace the light fixture still."

For the second time, warning bells sounded in my head. "I'd like to choose it, please. And we should also discuss the other changes to the house," I commented, not liking conflict in general, especially since he just remodeled the bathroom and was being so understanding about Sophie. But the situation presented itself and needed to be talked about.

"Sure, where do we start?"

"Well, I know you're planning to paint the exterior of the house too and I'd like a pale yellow with black shutters." Currently, the shutters were an ugly shade of magenta.

He visibly bristled but not everything needed to resemble Shirley's house.

"You don't like the magenta shutters?"

I found it important to set boundaries early on, and I had to be honest. "No, I really don't."

He frowned but didn't say anything.

"Perhaps we need to discuss our ideas in more detail." I didn't plan to argue with him about every change. The house was mine. Period. I considered myself understanding to a point, respected the fact he was the one remodeling, but dang it ... I paid the house payment.

"That's fine, I have time today," he offered. "Neither of us will want to cook after working on the house all day, so we could go in town for an early dinner. My treat."

Maybe he had a good idea to meet outside these four walls. "I'd enjoy that." But what about Sophie? I hated to leave her so soon but she probably preferred some space. I could always bring her a sandwich from wherever we ate.

"Terri?" My mother called from the other room. "You planning to come back out here?"

I had forgotten my mother outside waiting with Sophie. Matt did strange things to my mind. "Be right there, Mom." I nodded in agreement about dinner and hurried back outside, grabbing more window cleaner and towels.

My mom studied me with intensity.

"He's just working on the house, huh?" she questioned.

I nodded without answering, not trusting my voice enough to hide my true, snowballing affection for Matt. I climbed the ladder and got back to work washing the windows.

Sophie stopped and glanced up at me. "You have a thing for the policeman dude?"

"No!" I said a little too abruptly.

"Right," Sophie replied with a little chuckle. "You like him, don't you?" She folded the paper towel in half, sprayed another wisp of cleaner onto the window, and wiped it until the glass sparkled.

Without looking, I knew my mom also waited for me to answer. "Of course, I like him. He's a nice man." Okay, easy enough to admit.

"But do you *like* him?" Sophie pressed.

My mom made some cackling noise from her throat.

Sophie's pointed question disturbed me, but I always preached to be upfront and to own your intentions. Wow, if I didn't find my own self annoying. "Well, I'm attracted to Matt but I barely know him."

She didn't stop there. "He likes you too."

I inhaled a sharp breath. "What makes you say that?"

Sophie laughed. "It's obvious. You both light up like a Christmas tree."

Another reference to Christmas. My inner being grumbled. I had no reply for her so I sprayed cleaner on the window to avoid answering.

"Maybe he's your soul mate."

I stared at her. "I don't even know what a soul mate is."

My mom answered this time. "It's a close friend, someone you are so close to that your souls know when you've found each other."

According to the myth, I would be married by Christmas to my soul mate. *Hardly.* Christmas wasn't all that far away. The lore had to be wrong.

Chapter Eight

I was nowhere near emotionally ready for my dinner meeting with Matt this evening. In general, I despised confrontation but also knew we had no choice but to discuss the renovations, so we both felt at ease with whatever modifications needed to be made. I suspected neither of us embraced change all that well.

The afternoon had passed by swiftly, Sophie and I having raked a few too many leaves after Mom left, and I had barely seen Matt. He took the renovations seriously, maybe too much so.

After a quick shower I slipped into a beige sweater and jeans and managed to arrive downtown at Front Street Café with two minutes to spare. He had suggested we dine at a fancier restaurant overlooking the water but I wanted to stay focused on my agenda. The café was more casual, therefore easier for us to talk.

My mom accused me of ignoring my attraction to him, but I rationalized that he was simply renovating my home for the Christmas party. Nothing else.

And so what if I was in denial.

But if I did fall for Matt, I knew I would worry about his job as a cop, and I'd have anxiety about him not returning home. That brought up another interesting fear. If I cared too deeply for him, I had no idea what I'd do if he left me like the rest of the men in my life. Boom, there it was. The God-honest truth.

A shiver ran up my spine.

I shook it off as I entered the small café, loving its decorative vibrant colors. The bright and cheerful décor paired well with the colorful paintings hanging on the walls. The hostess greeted me with a warm smile and led me to a small square table by the window. Looking around, it was easy to imagine Christmas decorations would soon be hanging throughout the café.

Matt breezed into the diner and spotted me, flashing a half wave and a friendly grin. He said something to the hostess and then approached me.

"Nice spot … my favorite table." And then he bent over to give me a hug. I had to admit, at least to myself, the embrace made me almost melt into him like liquid chocolate. He pulled away, taking off his light jacket and hanging it on the back of the chair.

He pointed to my notebook and pen. "You brought notes?"

How odd. We had discussed the purpose of our dinner, or did he think we were meeting for a date?

In effort to lighten my mood, I smiled. "Thanks to you I have an opportunity to update my house."

He frowned as he tried to fold his buff self into the chair between the wall and the table. I should have taken that seat and left mine for him. He bumped the tabletop, causing the candle to flicker. I pulled the table closer to me to allow him more room.

This was starting to feel awkward and it was because of me and my anxiety-driven agenda. Of course, I was doing what I always do … diving in head first to get things done efficiently, but I needed to slow down. This was a small town. People did things at a slower pace, and I could adjust. Besides, I liked Matt and there was no reason we wouldn't work this out.

A server approached us. According to her nametag, the blonde-haired woman with wild red streaks was named Jane. She set two waters on the table and handed us menus. I'd almost forgotten we were here to eat, my mind so wrapped up in our pending discussion.

Slow down, relax. Breathe. Not everything was fast-paced like working at the hospital in Raleigh.

Jane smiled at us as if she assumed we were a couple. "I'll give y'all time to look over the menu. What do you want to drink?"

We ordered two sweet teas, and then she left us alone with the flickering candle.

No doubt I was attracted to the sexy man sitting across from me. If I could only let my guard down enough to allow myself to get to know him better.

He studied the menu. "So what are you ordering?"

Why did that seem like such a personal question? I needed to get out more and chill. "It's been forever since I've eaten fried flounder. So much for eating healthy. How about you?" I closed my menu and pushed it aside.

"Hmm, sounds good," he said, still glancing over his choices. "But I think I'm going to order the monster rib dinner." He closed his menu, and when Jane returned with our sweet teas, he handed them both to her and placed our orders.

"It won't take too long for your dinner," Jane said, reorganizing the menus in her hand.

Matt winked at me. "Tell Roy to take as long as he wants, we're in no hurry."

Yep, small-town living was a whole new pace.

Matt surprised me when he reached out and placed his hand over mine, his warm, caring touch penetrating through my hand. I had difficulty concentrating on anything else.

"I see you spent some friendly time with Sophie today," he said. "Did you by chance find out who her parents were?"

I shook my head. "No, we're just trying to get to know one another and I didn't want to scare her off. It's too early to ask her."

"Terri, you need to make it a priority to find out."

I sighed. "I don't want to risk the progress we're making with learning to trust each other."

He leaned back against the chair and crossed his arms. "I understand, but like I said earlier today, you're housing a minor."

I frowned. "But we promised her she was safe. Are you going to turn her over?"

"I don't want to, no, but I will have no choice if you don't get permission soon." He glanced toward the kitchen as if to beckon Jane to bring our food, despite his earlier comment.

I didn't appreciate the pressure he put on me. "I'm working on it, but it will take time."

"Okay, but you don't have long. It'd be best if you approach them before they come looking for her." He uncrossed his arms and drummed his fingers on the table.

Nervous habit?

"I'll try to get Sophie to cooperate." I had my doubts. Already I was stressing about having the conversation with her. I fidgeted in my seat, remembering we were supposed to talk about the house. I really wanted to remove my pen from my notebook and click it in and out repeatedly to expel my anxiety.

"If she wants to stay with you, she has no choice but to cooperate. But I have one concern."

I glanced up.

"Just so you know, I'm speaking from experience here. As a pastor, my dad used to take in runaway kids, or anyone who needed a safe place to stay for a while." He hesitated. "They are hurting. Helping them isn't easy."

I wasn't sure what he was trying to tell me.

"Running away is what they do." His expression grew sorrowful. "They leave when you least expect it and take your heart with them."

An awkward moment passed between us. There was a deeper story there but I didn't know him well enough to ask questions. The little flame of the candle flickered in the silence.

He nodded toward my notebook and pen. "Did you have something specific you wanted to discuss?"

I fought to refocus my thoughts. I reached for my notebook and took a moment to look over my notes. "I want to develop a plan for fixing up the house. You know, to make sure our vision is the same."

He frowned. Apparently the subject was touchy.

Leaning back against his chair, he crossed his arms. "What do you mean? The place is in dismal shape. I'd like to give it a facelift to make it look newer, like it was when I was younger."

That little warning bell dinged louder in my head. I shrugged and started with the first item on the list. "I'm okay with the house being painted the same color with the exception of the shutters. Also,

I wouldn't mind the dark cabinets in the kitchen being painted white."

"White?"

"Yes. It's a different look, but it will brighten up the room and give it a beachy feel." At some point he needed to accept I now owned the house.

His face visibly stiffened. "Okay, white. Unfortunately, the countertop probably needs replacing too."

I shook my head. "After hearing the story about everyone lining the countertop with dishes at Christmas, I'm not sure I want it replaced. That memory came alive for me."

He smiled, his expression one of relief.

"The heart-pine floor in the kitchen needs some help," he said as though embracing the negotiations.

"I agree." So far we were working well together. "I'd like to rip down the wallpaper in the hallway and paint the walls a neutral color."

He frowned. "Really? I have to admit I'm nostalgic about the wallpaper."

I didn't want to offend him but the wallpaper was old fashioned, ugly, and had yellowed over the years. I searched for a kinder way to state what I was really thinking. "I'm sure the pattern is no longer available anyway, and I'm sorry Matt, I'm not really a fan of wallpaper."

He remained silent for too long. I refrained from shifting in my seat with impatience. Clearly he had a difficult time adjusting to the idea of remodeling the house.

I was sure I'd come up with a few more modifications along the way that he'd resist but I had a burning question. "Why did you sell the house if you weren't okay with changes being made?"

He cringed. "I get that you're the new owner, but I thought we agreed on restoring the house."

"What exactly does 'restore' mean? Maybe I misunderstood."

He set his square jaw and paused before he spoke. "Point taken, and we'll figure it out."

I wanted to figure it out now, wanted to know if this was going to be an ongoing battle between us.

"Matt, I need to make the house my own," I reasoned. "I don't want to feel as though I'm living in someone else's home." I added with a grin, "It might be more of a girl thing."

He chuckled but didn't comment.

"I appreciate everything you're doing. The bathroom looks great, and if there is something you are uncomfortable changing, just let me know and we'll decide what to do."

"Sounds like a good plan."

Jane approached us with our food and interrupted our conversation. We thanked her and dug in, somehow managing to keep the conversation light while we ate, mostly chatting about the weather and living near the beach. Once we finished, his expression grew playful. "Hey, there is a good old-fashioned oyster roast tomorrow afternoon. If you find out who Sophie's parents are ahead of time and we get permission, we can all go to the get-together. It's always fun."

"An oyster roast?" I wasn't even sure what that was. I cut off a section of fried flounder and savored the bite.

"It's a fundraiser for the fire department. Basically they roast oysters over a fire pit and people stand around and talk, eat, and listen to music," he explained.

"It sounds fun, but I'm not sure about Sophie at this point. She's hiding out for a reason." It really did sound quite charming and was a good opportunity to meet new people and let loose a little bit. I hadn't had much of a chance to get out of the house since the move.

He drummed the table again, definitely a nervous habit of his. "Tell you what, I'll go with you to Sophie's house and we'll get this straightened out. Deal?"

"You're willing to come with me?" Surprised by his offer, I wasn't sure what to say. I found his confidence and willingness to help me heartwarming. "You aren't planning to show up in your policeman uniform to her parent's house, are you?" I asked, half joking. That would be a sure bet for failure.

He smirked. "How inept do you think I am?"

I laughed. "Okay, not that incompetent, I guess."

"You guess?" He frowned playfully. "So is that a yes?" he pressed. "You can't hide out with her forever, and it's time to get you out there.

I'll be able to introduce you to most everyone I know."

He knew me well already. He was right, I couldn't hide away forever. That had been my problem in Raleigh. "I definitely would like to go, but I'll need to talk to Sophie first to make sure she's okay with the idea."

He nodded. "Trust me. I've got you covered, and I understand. Just let me know how it goes with her."

I did trust him, and it was nice to have support. If we were able to obtain her parents' permission, providing what Sophie told me was the truth, then that should satisfy Matt's concerns.

"If we do go, do we need to bring a dish?"

He shook his head. "The Garden Club is preparing side dishes and desserts. We just show up and I'll pay for our plates. It's a fundraiser for the community."

"I've never eaten an oyster," I said, curious about how they tasted.

He stared at me. "Never?"

"Never."

"Then you're in for a treat."

"If Sophie wants to, I'll consider going under one condition." I watched as he tensed, amused that he was concerned by what I might say. "You want the house painted for the Christmas party, right? That's a huge job for one person and there's so much else we need to do before then. And painting needs to be done while the weather is mild."

He raised his eyebrows. "What are you suggesting?"

"I'll call the contractor my sister mentioned and pay him to paint the house. I really don't mind, and that's one big project off our list."

No answer, and his jaw was set in that square, stubborn way again. He shoved a huge bite of rib into his mouth and chewed.

When he didn't offer his opinion, I spoke up. "Matt? You are busy with your regular job too, and Christmas isn't that far off."

He sighed and nodded. "Fine. You're right and I'd hate for us not to have everything done before the holidays. Okay, do what you need to do."

I wasn't sure if he was really all right with my decision to call the contractor, so I decided to push the subject. "You're good?"

"Yep. As you said, there is only so much I can do." His words didn't quite match his tone, but at least he agreed to hired help. He reached forward and placed his hand on top of mine, the smile on his face a relief.

Jane approached and I ordered takeout for Sophie and Matt requested coffee for us both. He mentioned dessert, but I was too full to eat another bite. When Jane brought our mugs and the check, Matt insisted on paying.

"Really, there is no need to pay for Sophie and me," I said, but he wouldn't hear of it.

Matt leaned back against the chair and we drank coffee while he filled me in about the people I'd meet, his job, the guys on the force, and I couldn't hold back my curiosity any longer. "Why did you decide to become a cop?"

He sighed long and hard. "That's quite a story, but basically it was because of my father. Over the years, with him helping several derelict kids, I got tired of the drugs, the anger, the violence I had to deal with. I guess being a cop is my contribution to society."

I detected there was a deeper story behind what he was telling me but didn't want to push him. Given time, I hoped to learn more of his history.

When Jane brought back his credit card, I thanked him for dinner, and we scooted our chairs back to leave. The town's one department store was open until nine, so I had plenty of time to buy a handful of clothes for Sophie. I also planned to dart into the grocery store for a few quick and easy items for her to prepare in the cottage in case she got hungry.

We headed toward the front door and he held it open for me. What a gentleman. Then Matt walked me to my car, gave me a sweet kiss on the cheek, and we held hands for a moment as we said goodbye. In my limited experience, no guys did these things anymore and I loved the gesture.

The department store was virtually empty by the time I arrived. It took me a while to figure out what to buy since I had no idea about Sophie's sense of style. I opted for sensible, comfortable clothes in case she ran off again, including jeans and a cute top if we went to the oyster roast tomorrow. If they didn't fit, we could always exchange them.

When I returned home it was still early in the evening. A light burned from the window of the cottage, and I was relieved Sophie was still awake. I grabbed the bags from the backseat and couldn't wait to see the look on her face, still wondering if I made the right selections. I knocked, waiting for her to answer, juggling the purchases in my arms.

She answered the door as if I startled her, making me wonder if she'd been expecting the authorities.

"Um, hi." She backed away, leaving the door open as an invitation for me to walk inside.

I set the bags of groceries on the counter in the kitchenette, and then placed the others on the couch. "I bought you some things you might need."

Her face brightened as she glanced at everything. "No one has bought me anything in a long time. It feels like Christmas, not that I get much. Thank you."

If she stayed around long enough for the holiday, I planned to buy her all sorts of gifts. Having her here was changing my thoughts on the subject of Christmas.

But the idea of decorating still remained foreign to me. Oh well, I might get there.

I was so pleased Sophie said thank you first before even seeing what I'd bought her. I appreciated her not taking things for granted. The more I spent time with this girl, the more I enjoyed her company. She and Matt were just what I needed at this point in my life. I had the tendency to keep people at a distance, and they were slowly penetrating my emotional protective shell.

Whoa! Slow down there, girl. Where were these thoughts coming from ... I had barricaded my heart for a reason, to protect myself from being hurt again by the people I love.

Shoving my unsettled thoughts aside, I sat on the armrest near her nest of blankets. The television was on, turned to a sitcom I couldn't quite place, but it looked like a good show. At least it wasn't one of those dramatic reality ones.

She sat on the couch next to me and dove into the bags with enthusiasm. I loved catching a glimpse of what she might have looked like as a small child opening gifts.

"Oh! Awesome." She held up the stylish jeans I'd bought her. I even agreed with the sales clerk the frayed holes on them were a trend Sophie might like. "These are super cute." She pulled out the top and wiped a tear from her eye. Seeing her so excited and emotional touched me.

She rummaged in the next bag and removed the short boots. They had a slight heel, which she apparently approved of, because that was what sent her running to me. She wrapped her arms around me half crying, "Thank you, Aunt Terri."

Aunt Terri? I *loved* it.

"You're welcome, honey. You deserve it." I had to choke down my emotions as I tried to remain strong for her, but I was fairly certain my voice gave me away.

Sophie slipped her feet into the boots. "They fit perfectly. How did you know what size?"

"When you were showering that first night, I glanced at your sizes."

She stood to model the pumpkin-colored top as she held it close to her. "I want to wear my new outfit somewhere."

The perfect lead-in to our invitation for the oyster roast as well as finding out who her parents were. "Well, Matt invited us to an oyster roast tomorrow. I recognize your situation and have an idea how we could make this work, but first, are you interested in going?"

Sophie's mouth dropped open. She shook her head.

I said with a soft voice to put her at ease, "You need to be able to go out in public without the fear of being seen. I want to help you with that."

Her eyes grew wider. For a moment, I thought she'd make a run for the door.

I reached out and gently touched her elbow to calm her. "Everything will be okay. I just need to get permission from your parents, so you can stay with me." I needed to make her feel safe.

"No! And he isn't my *parent*," she exclaimed. "He's my drunken stepfather. Big difference." Her excitement earlier transitioned to that of an angry teen, something I wasn't used to dealing with. And I wanted to help kids?

I tried to understand her vacillating emotions, but it also made me wonder how her father died.

"I'm sorry I misspoke." I rubbed her elbow without her moving away from my touch, a sign of improvement in itself. "Believe me when I say I love having you here, but legally I need her permission. I'd like to have your mother's name and phone number, so I can make sure it's okay for you to stay with me."

She pinched her lips together.

"It's okay. Just think about it." I knew better than to push her. In the meantime, I needed to keep Matt from pressuring me about the situation. I knew it wasn't fair to put him in the middle because his loyalty to his job was likely more important at this point than his loyalty to me. And ultimately, I wanted to do right by Sophie.

Questions circulated through my mind. I wondered what area she was from, what school she had gone to, and if anyone would recognize her at the oyster roast? But the last thing I wanted was to put her in danger of someone knowing who she was and calling the authorities. The risk was too great not to get her mom's okay.

If I didn't have her approval before the oyster roast, then we wouldn't go.

If she was allowed to stay with me, at some point I needed to enroll her in school. Of course, I didn't dare overload her with all of this right now. One step at a time.

I needed to earn Sophie's trust, so she'd tell me about her mom. I pointed to another bag of clothes next to her. "Go ahead. I'm dying to know if you like the other things."

Sophie set the shirt she modeled on the couch and sat back down. Just like that her emotions transitioned back to "happy child" as she dug through the remaining items. She unfolded the sweatpants, a sweat shirt, and a casual t-shirt to sleep in. She then placed the bags of underwear next to her and shoved the bra underneath her leg as if embarrassed by the item.

"No one has ever bought me so much stuff at one time," she said, looking as though she might cry.

"Just some comfortable clothes to wear around the house," I said, downplaying the purchases to make her more comfortable.

"Thank you. How did you know my favorite color is blue?"

"A complete guess." But it wasn't really. I had noticed the few clothes she brought from home were mostly blue.

She disappeared into the bathroom and came out wearing the sweats. "It's nice to have new things."

My heart jolted. This girl and Matt were changing me in ways I didn't recognize, from being aloof with my feelings to touching my heartstrings.

"I got lucky finding what I thought you'd like, and they had most everything on sale too." From my purse, I pulled out the small to-go box from the restaurant. "It's a turkey sandwich and a bag of chips."

"Oh!" She opened the box and practically dove in.

My cell phone rang and I quickly answered. "Hey, Em. What's up?"

"If it's not too late, Mom and I are planning to stop by tonight, but I wanted to call you first to make sure it's okay."

"Sure, I'm not doing anything but unpacking and getting settled in, so come on over." The last-minute notice surprised me since it was getting later in the evening. They had never done this before when we lived in Raleigh. Then again, I worked all the time.

I remembered Emily didn't know about Sophie. With hope they wouldn't meet, what with Sophie in the cottage, but it was probably time to tell Emily. She could keep a secret. I hadn't even shared my desire with her to become a foster parent.

I left Sophie to ogle her clothes while I returned to my house but I never got an okay from her about her mother. Of course, there was always the possibility of her running away tonight to avoid it all. The choices I faced were to either obsess and watch her closely, secretly monitoring her, or have faith and let the situation work itself out. For my peace of mind, I chose the latter.

My family showed up and I welcomed them into the kitchen, once again marveling at the increased amount of visitors in my life now.

"Wow," Emily said after I explained the situation. She stood in the kitchen, close to my mom, clearly surprised at my news. "Are you sure you want to take on all that hormonal teenage energy?"

I laughed at her question but said without doubt, "Yes, I do." For the first time in my life, I wanted to make an important commitment to a good cause. However, my family wanted to protect me. So many things could go wrong with this venture, and I knew that, but somehow I needed to explain my passion to help girls in need even if I didn't understand it myself. But the words eluded me. I guessed I feared she would judge me.

I decided to change the focus away from me. "Emily, how is your writing coming along?"

She stood taller and a smile lit up her face. "My book is selling like wildfire," she said with a humble spirit.

"I'm so happy for you." I gave her a hug and ignored the surprised look she gave me.

I even shocked myself. I didn't consider myself a touchy-feely person, but Matt and Sophie were teaching me new ways. I still had room for improvement, for sure, especially with my sister and mother.

Emily pulled her book out of her purse. "I brought this for you in case you want to read it."

I squealed with delight. "Thank you." Why hadn't I thought about buying it before now?

"I have to warn you. There is a scene in there that might trouble you." She sighed and our mother placed her arm around Emily. "Through my writing, I remembered when Dad walked out on us. It's in the book."

I rolled my eyes. "I doubt it will disturb me. I barely remember life with him." Most of my memories included his new family. "I harbor no angry feelings whatsoever." Emily was older and therefore she remembered more details than me about our parents' divorce.

But I couldn't explain the anxiety prickling down my spine.

She said without blinking, "You might be surprised."

Chapter Nine

The next morning I woke up way too early, eager about the possibility of attending the oyster roast later this afternoon. That was, if all went well with finding out who Sophie's mom was. I crawled from bed, showered, dressed, and made coffee. With wishful thinking, I hoped to see Sophie sitting at the table ready to eat. Once again I told myself not to worry. She knew she had a safe place to stay with me and I had to leave the rest up to her.

I decided she was likely still sleeping. After all, teenagers usually didn't wake up at six a.m. But if I didn't hear from her in a couple of hours I planned to knock on the cottage door. I wanted to talk to her more this morning, over hot chocolate and scrambled eggs, with the hope I could wrangle her mom's name from her and her whereabouts.

I brought Emily's book to the breakfast table and the note she inscribed for me inside surprised me. *To my sister, we've been through a lot together and I'm glad it was with you. May you heal through the help of these words as I did. Love, Em.* That short acknowledgment touched me in no way her words ever could. And I had to wonder if she started to let go of her resentment toward me.

I hadn't read anything she had written before, and I quickly became enthralled with her writing style. Curious about the scene she mentioned last night, I read on with a sense of hesitation. I treaded slowly, enjoying living in my naive world as far as my father was concerned. I liked to think being raised without him had no effect on me.

I turned the pages and paused only long enough to carry my mug of coffee into the living room. I chose a sunny spot near the picture window facing the front yard, so I scooted the rattan love seat over and sank into the comfortable blue cushions. It was the perfect reading spot.

Folding my legs underneath me, I became engrossed once again in Emily's novel, *The Long Beach*. It was about a woman trying to find herself after relocating to a coastal town. Aspects of the story were light and fun, but Emily was deep, insightful, and I didn't know my sister to the degree I thought. Before long, and way too soon, I had to extract myself from the book to wake up Sophie. It was already close to ten o'clock.

As I walked toward the cottage, the door opened. Until that moment, I hadn't realized how relieved I was to see her. I needed to get a grip on my anxiety.

"Wow! You look stunning." I adored the outfit with the thin, long-sleeved pumpkin top hugging her body, the stylish jeans with the strategically placed holes lending her hips and legs shape, and the short boots adding a cute flair. My confidence in styling a girl elevated a few notches. But I wondered why she chose to dress up this morning. I decided not to ask and to go along with the moment.

Sophie blushed. "Thank you."

"Have you eaten?" The only breakfast items she had in the cottage were bagels and cream cheese. I planned to buy her more options but really wanted to encourage her to eat in the main house with me.

"Judy Ellis."

Confused, I stared at her, trying to figure out what she was talking about.

"My mom. That's her married name." She headed toward the house and I followed her lead, glad she trusted me enough to confide in me. The screen door slammed behind us as we entered the kitchen. "Mine is Sophie Yates."

Sophie Yates. I don't know why but knowing her full name made our evolving relationship so much more personal.

I tried to keep the mood light by not asking her a bunch of questions, and believe me, it took effort not to interrupt her. I assumed she was hungry and busied myself by gathering items to make scrambled eggs while I listened with what I hoped was a casual ear.

"I'm ready to stop hiding." She sank into the chair at the table and propped up her chin on her hand.

"Good for you, Sophie. I think you're making the right decision," I said to encourage her. I put the hot chocolate pod into the coffee maker, closed the lid, and pressed the button. Then I mixed the eggs in a bowl and dumped them into a pan of melted butter. "Does that mean you want to go to the oyster roast?" I pointed to her cute outfit.

She glanced out the window as if nervous about going out in public, but then she puffed out her chest and looked me in the eyes. "Yes, I want to be brave. Who knows, maybe there will be other kids there I can meet. Sometimes I just want a friend to hang out with."

Her comment jerked my emotions and brought forward a burning question I had dancing in the back of my mind. "Did you go to school here?"

She continued to stare out the window. "I live on the opposite side of town, so I went to Sutherland Middle School."

I had never heard of Sutherland. If she lived on the far side of town, I doubted she'd know anyone at the oyster roast.

Returning to the counter I made a second mug of hot chocolate, handing her the first one, before I made my way back to the stove to check the scrambled eggs. I stirred them around and added a handful of shredded cheese. I could do this. Being a foster parent wasn't going to be as hard as I thought, at least not the cooking part.

"If you want to go today," I said, referring to the oyster roast, "I need to call your mom this morning to get her written agreement. You understand that, right?"

Sophie swallowed hard enough her throat moved up and down.

"And like I said, my dad is dead. A couple of years ago ... a car accident. Thomas Yates."

"Oh, honey." I closed the space between us and wrapped her in my arms. She didn't pull away, so I held her longer. As Matt had suspected, this girl had been through so much. Probably even more than I knew and would find out.

Within a few seconds she pulled away and said, "Okay." She rattled off her mom's phone number and I scrambled to write it down on a nearby pad of paper.

"I'll call after we eat." I also planned to ask Matt to check out the story about her father to verify he was in fact deceased. I scooped the scrambled eggs onto plates and passed her one, then retrieved the mug of hot chocolate from the coffee maker to join her at the table. I wasn't all that hungry, as I wasn't a breakfast eater and already had my protein bar, but I wanted to share a moment together with her.

The oyster roast was going to be fun. I looked forward to getting Sophie out of the house, and to seeing Matt in an environment with friends instead of hanging out on a more intimate level at my home.

Sophie and I sipped hot chocolate and ate together, chatting about clothes, TV shows, and school. Our breakfast was much too short and we cleaned up the dishes. I was hesitant, yet eager, to call her mother, although I had no choice if I wanted to offer my home to Sophie.

I excused myself and went into my room to call.

To my surprise, Judy Ellis answered on the first ring. After some extensive convincing, though seemingly hesitant and a bit angry at Sophie, she relented and agreed to let us come over to talk.

Apprehensive to visit her, I picked up the phone and dialed Matt's number.

"Hey, sweetheart. I'm in your driveway."

"Your timing is always perfect," I said before I hung up, thankful he was here for me. The back door opened and I heard him call out my name.

I met him in the kitchen, and he greeted me with a warm hug and a quick kiss, so close to my lips I could almost taste it. I wished the man would go ahead and kiss me because I wasn't one to make the first move.

With reluctance, we pulled away. "Where's Soph?"

His nickname for her warmed me from the inside out like a melting candle. "She's either in the cottage or in the living room." I wasn't actually sure where she was. "But I just hung up from speaking with her mother."

He raised his eyebrows.

"She agreed to let us come over now if you have time. Sophie wants to go to the oyster roast, so we might as well get this done."

A smile spread across his face. "You bet, let's do it."

A wave of anxiety knotted my belly from the thought of seeing Sophie's unknown living conditions as well as meeting her mother and alcoholic stepfather. I appreciated that Matt was a cop and was thankful he was dressed as a civilian in jeans and a flannel shirt, as promised.

"Any chance you can verify the story about her dad?" I asked, giving Matt the name.

"I'm on it." He left the house to make a phone call.

I pulled out a piece of paper from the kitchen drawer and sat down to write a brief permission slip to allow Sophie to stay with me without repercussions, for as long as her mother agreed. I wanted to protect both of us without overstepping my boundaries.

When I finished, I found Sophie sitting in the living room in front of the television I barely watched. I told her where we were going, and as I suspected, she wanted to stay behind and continue to watch TV. The thought of seeing her mother anytime soon had to be uncomfortable.

In all honesty, I paused for a moment. Up until now I hadn't left her alone in my house. I felt fairly certain I could trust her but there was a niggling concern inside of me that said she could steal me blind. But those were more my mother's words than mine. I really had nothing of great worth, nothing I couldn't replace if that were the case. And if I wanted to foster kids, I better get over that insecurity here and now.

I was about to ask her mother if she could stay with me. If I couldn't trust this kid, then I needed to reconsider because if her mom said yes, I needed to move Sophie into the big house. She was far too young to live in the cottage alone.

It was a big responsibility and I had to ask myself once again, was I ready for all this? Kids were expensive and until DSS approved me as a foster parent, there would be no monetary compensation. I sensed my life changing in ways I never imagined.

I said goodbye to Sophie and joined Matt at his truck. He clicked off his phone and nodded.

"Her story checks out," he said.

"Can you imagine losing your father at her young age?" I thought

I had it bad when my father walked out on us when we were children. It was nothing compared to what Sophie had to deal with.

"Not really," he said as he opened the passenger door for me and then climbed into the driver's side. "I've always resented my dad but losing him would be unfathomable."

I wanted to ask more but now wasn't the time.

"Once I meet her mom, things are going to change. I mean, what if she wants Sophie back?" The thought made me sad. I felt fairly certain Sophie's home life wasn't healthy for her. "I have an overwhelming fear of losing her."

But it wasn't about me or my own abandonment issues. I wanted Sophie to have someone who treated her with love and respect.

I held up the document I had written.

"What's that?" He glanced over at me.

"A document for her mom to sign. I didn't know what to say but did my best." I didn't have the time or desire to get a lawyer involved. The less amount of people who knew about the agreement, the better.

Apparently concerned by my reaction to all of this, he took hold of my hand, his warmth penetrating my cold fingers. "Things will work out the way they are meant to be," he said, his voice reassuring. A long moment passed between us.

"I want to help however I can. And don't let me forget, we need to notarize the document."

I wrapped my fingers around his hand tighter, lingering there to satisfy my own need to know everything would be okay. "How are we going to get it notarized on a Sunday morning?"

He flipped his chin upward as if saying he had my back. "I'm a notary public." His smile pierced my cloudy mood like a ray of sunshine.

I screeched with delight. "You saved the day."

"Not yet, but I hope to." He squeezed my hand. "Later tonight I think we should celebrate by reading Nana's diary and the letters."

That was *if* we had reason to celebrate. I had to believe we would.

"I want to read them regardless." He smiled and it was easy to see how much he treasured them. "Things will be okay." He squeezed my hand again with encouragement, and I appreciated his support.

We turned down a narrow street. "She had quite a walk," I said, amazed at her ability to venture off so far.

"No kidding." Matt slowed and pulled the truck into a gravel driveway. He turned off the ignition but sat still.

An old red Ford truck with huge spots of missing paint sat in front of us in the driveway, along with a dismantled, rusted car parked closer to the house. Parts from the car littered the sparse grass and the backseat tilted against the car, soiled from sitting outside. Near the street, an over-filled trash can had spilled onto the ground, litter everywhere, as if long forgotten by any trashman. Layers of paint peeled off the house, and cracks in the sidewalk were so bad you could twist your ankle.

My emotions clogged in my throat, the overall experience worse than I expected. "I can't imagine Sophie living here."

Matt didn't speak but nodded in answer, as if fighting off his own set of emotions. He probably encountered this sort of situation often, but Sophie stayed here, not a stranger.

"Come on," he finally said. "Let's get this over with." He pushed open the truck door. We met near the base of the sidewalk and he grabbed hold of my hand.

Carefully we picked our way to the front porch. Matt reached out and rang the doorbell, which apparently didn't work. After standing there a few minutes, he rapped on the door.

No one answered, so he knocked again, louder. Finally, a greasy man with long hair and no shirt answered, and I assumed he was Sophie's stepfather. He opened the unpainted wooden door halfway, obviously annoyed by the intrusion.

"Who are ya?" The man squinted in the afternoon daylight.

"I'm Terri McMillan and this is Matt Baker. We are here to talk to Judy," I said. "She's expecting us." I stood with my shoulder touching Matt's arm for emotional support. Something about the man's shifty eyes made me uncomfortable.

He retreated but left the door wide open. Matt and I looked at each other, not knowing if we were supposed to follow him or wait. Who knew if he was even coming back? For a moment we had a distorted view of the inside of the messy house until he returned and said, "She'll be right here."

He left us waiting on the front steps once again.

When a woman with wild frizzy brown hair approached us, I was surprised, as I immediately saw the resemblance to Sophie. Her facial features, the color and shape of her eyes specifically, were a dead giveaway. She wore no make-up, her hair was in desperate need of a good cut, and she dressed in torn jeans and a sweater with holes.

Judy opened the door. "Come on in. Don't mind the mess."

We followed her inside and I noticed the man had made himself comfortable on the couch, watching television.

"Ralph, turn that off. We have company." Either he didn't hear her or ignored her because he continued to watch the screen, laughing occasionally.

There were several piles of boxes stacked high throughout the house and garbage bags cluttered the narrow walkway into the kitchen. She pointed for us to sit in the chairs surrounding the table, full of items such as letters, what appeared to be clean plates, an overstuffed box, and several plastic bags containing canned food. I wasn't sure if they were hoarders or just horrible housekeepers.

She joined us at the table. "I've been too busy working and haven't had a chance to clean up."

I resisted the urge to glance at Matt, as I'm sure we were both thinking about poor Sophie having to live in this mess. And with her scary stepfather.

"About your daughter," I said in a soft voice as not to allow Ralph to overhear our conversation. I wanted her to sign the form without a hitch, so we could leave. "She is doing well and I enjoy helping her. I'd love for her to stay with me longer."

"How long?" The woman lit a cigarette and blew a puff of smoke at me.

I coughed, and Judy laughed.

"As long as she wants." I turned my face away from the next plume of smoke.

"She wasn't supposed to be with you in the first place." Judy crossed her legs, swinging her foot back and forth. "Don't know why she ran away. We give her everything she needs, but she's a spoiled brat."

Hardly. I bit my lower lip to keep from correcting her, my defenses rising. All I wanted was for her to sign the paper.

I decided to try a more direct approach. "Well, is it okay if she stays with me for a while? I'd like to have her spend the school year with me. Of course, I'd cover all her expenses."

Judy stared at me. "School. She hardly went while she lived here. What makes you think she'll go if she's with you?"

That was interesting information to know. "Well, I'd like to give it a try. I do need your written permission, though." I thought about the importance of having the agreement notarized and was grateful Matt was able to authenticate the paperwork.

"I dunno. Sounds very legal. I don't do legal anything." She grunted and my nerves turned edgy. This was not going as easy as I'd expected.

"Judy, this is temporary," I explained. Be patient and let her absorb what I was saying. "I'm not sure why she ran away, but from what little I know, this will give you both time to figure things out." She looked uninterested at my reasoning, so I added, "You can have Sophie back whenever you want." I said the words but my heart ached at the thought. I prayed for the child to be wherever she would thrive. I didn't want to take her away from her family, but I also wanted her to be safe.

Ralph sauntered into the kitchen, adding his two cents. "Heck, sign the thing. She's better off with this woman than she is here. Kids cost a lot. Besides, she was getting snotty and talking back too much anyway."

Judy flashed him a dangerous glare. "You jerk. You never wanted her here in the first place. You wouldn't adopt her when I asked and I understand, but you want her *gone*?"

From the glare in Ralph's eyes, I wanted to get out of here before a brawl happened. What a mess, and poor Sophie.

"Oh, come on. You know it's true. The kid's been a pain in the butt, leaving all the time, mouthing off," he said. "That girl listens to no one. She's too stubborn and it's all your fault."

"Because of you." Judy spat the words at him, heightening my concern. Sophie hadn't mentioned abuse but this situation certainly held many of the signs. If not physical, certainly mental. It honestly broke my heart.

He stormed to the kitchen sink to fill up a glass of water but most of it spilled onto the floor. "You work all the time and she sits here all day long doing nothin'. I try to get her to do things and I get sass. The kid isn't worth anyone's time so if this woman wants her, let her go."

Judy shoved her chair back and ran into the bedroom while Ralph stomped off to the living room.

Matt and I stared at each other, not knowing what to expect. We sat in silence but we were both alert and ready to bolt for the door.

Within a few minutes, Judy returned to the kitchen. Her eyes were red, possibly from crying, and I was shocked when she said, "Okay, let's get this over with."

I held my breath as she signed the paper and Matt stamped it to notarize the document. When we finished, I jumped up from my chair, eager to leave before she changed her mind. I thanked her and made a mad dash to the truck.

Amazing, but we were there just a hint over an hour. We pulled into my driveway, and I said, "Glad to see the painter here. And on a Sunday." The man had his job cut out for him.

"We still haven't agreed on a color for the shutters." Matt pulled in next to my truck and turned off the ignition.

I bristled. My house, my choice. But I didn't want him to resent my decision, either. "I'm thinking black. It's a fresh look to replace the magenta." I despised magenta shutters in general, especially with a pale yellow house. I didn't want to lose the bonding moment we just experienced at Sophie's house, and our relationship had taken on a whole new level of intimacy.

My old, familiar mindset reared its ugly head. What a preposterous thought to let a bonding moment dictate the color of my shutters. I shook my head and hoped he didn't notice me mentally arguing with myself.

"Okay, that would look great. Besides, it's your house anyway."

I paused. He had completely caught me off guard.

Through his actions, over and over again, he continually showed how committed he was to me, to Sophie, and to the house. "You're unlike any other man I've ever met."

"Great. I'll take that as a compliment." He stepped out of the truck and left me sitting there pondering what just happened. When I caught up with him, he was chatting up the painter.

I let them talk and made my way toward the back door when Sophie darted from the house and met me midway. From the tense look on her face, I knew she had been fretting about us visiting with her mother.

"What did my mom say?" She fidgeted with her hands and stared at the ground until I smiled and held up the paper.

"She was hesitant at first but then said yes." I knew all too well how painful it was for a parent to abandon you and wanted to make sure Sophie knew her mother hadn't handed her over to me without thought. At some point, I would encourage her to try to reconnect but for now her safety came first. I hoped I was right by intervening.

Sophie ran into my arms and hugged me. I was pleasantly surprised and my emotions threatened to spill over.

There were still things I needed to know. She had been through a lot but needed discipline too, and there were things we had yet to deal with. She required guidance, counseling, a good education, someone there to support her. I understood now she'd been void of that for far too long.

I wasn't sure how my life went from the busy city to one with a country setting and people I loved, but I was ready to embrace it, one hundred percent. It would about kill me when Sophie's mom decided to reclaim her.

Chapter Ten

The closer they drove to the fire station, the more apprehensive Matt grew. In this small town, everyone knew each other's business, and he did wonder if they knew Sophie. Even though Terri had permission to keep her for now, he hoped no one recognized her as a runaway. He didn't want that for Terri or Sophie.

Helping Sophie remained important to Terri, therefore important to him, even though it stirred up childhood issues with his dad.

He really wanted to share the oyster roast with them.

Besides, it was too late to have second thoughts.

Matt glanced in his review mirror and said to Sophie, "There should be some kids there. Most are younger but I know of one girl your age."

She stared out the window but didn't answer. Maybe she felt a little overwhelmed and he didn't blame her. Change was never easy.

"Sophie?" Terri glanced back at her.

"Hmmm?" She continued to stare out the window.

"You okay?"

"Mmmhmm."

At least she answered Terri. He didn't take it personally, realizing she had a lot on her mind. Teenagers acted hot and cold, after all.

He drove down the street in search of a place to park. To his surprise, cars lined both sides of the road for at least two blocks.

"You weren't kidding when you said everyone would be here," Terri spoke, and in the rearview mirror he saw Sophie stiffen. So she held her own set of concerns about the crowd, people asking too many questions.

"Yep. Wait until you try some oysters, they are the best." Matt found a spot at the end of the street. He glanced again in his rearview mirror at Sophie. "Have you eaten oysters before?"

She puckered her mouth. "No. I'm not sure I want to."

He chuckled. "We'll see about that. They are the best thing other than fried chicken."

"Must be pretty good then," Sophie said, biting her lip as she climbed from the truck. "But I looked up oysters on the Internet and they look gross."

We laughed and walked down to the fire station carrying our folding chairs. As we approached, Terri and Sophie watched a group of men squirting the firehose at the ground.

"What are they doing?" Terri asked with interest.

"Washing mud off the oysters," he explained. "You need good water pressure because they are hard to clean. The firehose is perfect." He made the introductions as Sophie and Terri watched the action, apparently mesmerized by it all.

The smell of muddy oysters permeated the air. Piled on a grate on the ground was a mound of wet shells, steel in color with a hint of cream and sea-glass green.

"They are pretty in their own way," Terri said with awe in her voice.

"But they stink," Sophie complained.

Matt laughed and shook his head. "Welcome to living on the coast," he said, mostly to Terri.

Moving on, they made their way to the nearby small but crowded backyard of Tom and Betty Brown. Classic rock music played from a speaker and filled the air with a welcoming and friendly atmosphere. He hoped they relaxed and embraced the coastal, Southern festivities.

Terry pointed to a rustic table with a long wide board as the top and two saw horses as legs, perched under a tree. "Hilarious but practical and homey," she said, and then turned her attention to a brick firepit with flames shooting upward. Seemingly mesmerized, she watched them in silence.

He explained with enthusiasm. "They dump the oysters on the

grate and fire roast them." His mouth salivated. Man, he loved oyster roasts. Apparently he took get-togethers like this for granted, but seeing the scene from her eyes, small-town living was in his soul. He couldn't refrain from sharing the experience and filling her in on the details. He pointed to the table. "They dump the oysters there and you crack open the shells with a tool."

Terri glanced around as if taking it all in, and Sophie looked like a scared deer ready to run. He nudged her arm. "You've got this, kiddo. Trust me, they're delicious."

Sophie forced a grin and slid her hand around Terri's elbow.

"Love the jar of daisies and the fall-themed tablecloth," Terri said. "You can't go wrong with checkered brown, orange, and white. What's in the jars?" She pointed to a tray holding condiments next to the flowers.

He grinned. Funny, but he never questioned the familiar scene before. "Cocktail sauce, horseradish, Worcestershire, and Tabasco. And a basket of Saltine crackers with a dish of lemon wedges."

"It's all very quaint and country. Lovely." Terri glanced around and her posture relaxed. "I just might love living in Big Cat."

"I know you will," Matt said as the men who were washing off the oysters carried an old-fashioned barrel bucket with ice covering the shells to the firepit. The smell of burning wood filled the air, a reminder it was fall despite the warmer day.

Before they made their way closer to the pit to watch, Roy and Kathy Conner approached them. Matt propped the lawn chairs on the ground, but before he could make the introductions, Kathy grinned at Sophie.

"April, it's so good to see you. I've been wondering where you've been." Kathy wrapped Sophie in her arms. Matt didn't correct her use of Sophie's incorrect name because it wasn't his place. If she wanted to tell Kathy, then she would. Terri stayed back, arms crossed, and watched with interest as the conversation unfolded.

Sophie accepted the prolonged hug as a small smile escaped from her lips. It was enlightening to see how she responded to Kathy and suspected Terri was a bit envious of the loving exchange. Her raised eyebrows and stiff posture revealed her emotions.

Kathy hugged him, and then he turned toward Terri to make the introductions. "This is Roy and Kathy Conner. And this is Terri McMillan."

Terri shook their hands with her eyebrows raised again, as if wondering how they knew Sophie.

Kathy spoke up first. "We helped April when ... let's just say when she came by to visit us a couple days a week. I see she's with you now?"

Here it went. This was what Terri had wanted to avoid, the questions they had all hoped to evade.

"Sophie, that's my real name," Sophie interjected, standing taller.

Kathy placed her hand over her mouth, but smiled.

Matt stepped forward. "All is good now. Sophie is staying with Terri for a while." He didn't elaborate but from their smiles he knew they were happy she had found a place to live.

Kathy then leaned toward Sophie and whispered louder than she probably thought. "I like that name better, honey. Don't be a stranger." She winked and Sophie giggled.

Another older couple strolled up to the Conners and struck up a conversation. Matt nodded toward a girl standing by a set of coolers loaded with drinks and ice. She kept staring at Sophie.

"That's Carley," Matt said. "She's about your age."

Sophie stepped back, so he let up with introducing them. Before they made their way to the pit, other people approached them, and he made a point to make introductions. He loved community get-togethers and despite his earlier concern, so far no one questioned why Terri and Sophie were Matt's guests.

Jenni and Claire arrived with their husbands and kids. The two women took turns hugging Terri as if they were longtime friends. In return, she played with and ogled Jenni's twin boys but Sophie watched with interest. Matt had to wonder if she was jealous of Terri's attention to the babies. Something to watch.

The town of Big Cat just grew smaller and cozier, making me feel as if I belonged to a community for the first time in my life. Everybody knew each other and there was a comfortable sense of welcoming friendship here. Sophie appeared content, and so did I.

We chose to set up the chairs next to Jenni and Claire's crew under a shade tree because it was a bit warm for this time of year. I offered to hold one of the babies and Matt reached out for the other to free Jenni's arms so she could set up camp. Dang, I had to admit he looked sexy holding a baby and I knew I'd be revisiting this memory often. Sophie distracted my thoughts when she made silly faces to entertain the little boy on my lap, her behavior making me wonder if she wished she had siblings.

When my sister and Keith approached us, a shocked expression crossed her face. I guess she didn't expect to see me at a community event, not to mention holding her best friend's baby. She flashed a half wave in acknowledgement, though instead of sitting next to me, she planted herself on the far side of Claire. I knew she was having difficulty adjusting to me moving here, a place she had thought of as her own. While I truly felt she wanted to make amends too, I needed to give her time.

I decided to approach her first. I juggled the baby as I stood and walked over, shifting him onto my hip to face Emily. "Thank you for dedicating your book to me. That was really touching." I offered an honest smile and noticed her facial features soften.

She relaxed in a lawn chair, her interest fully on me now. "So you're reading it." It wasn't said as a question but as a curious statement. "I have to know, have you gotten to the scene I mentioned about Dad?"

"Not yet," I said, apprehensive about what in the world she had written about our father.

"Let me know when you do." A pretty, artsy woman walked up to us and hugged Emily, so we pushed aside our conversation for now.

The woman's loose but thick blonde curls bounced around her shoulders, and atop her head a colorful clip attempted to restrain another batch of wild curls. She wore stylish jeans and a delicate periwinkle knit sweater. I liked her immediately.

"This is Gabbi, your closest neighbor," Emily said to me. "You might have seen her artwork hanging around downtown and in the Front Street Café."

"Yes, your artwork is beautiful." I remembered admiring several bright paintings hanging on the walls of the café when I met Matt to talk about the house restoration. I'd bet most anything Gabbi was the artist. The style fit her free spirit. "And you have the house with all the flower gardens," I said with admiration, having envied the yard several times in passing.

"Thank you. And it's nice to meet you." Gabbi flashed me a friendly, down-to-earth smile and reached out to shake my hand. She nodded at Matt with familiarity.

"You should see Gabbi's view of the marsh." Jenni approached us, her face taking on a dreamy look as she held out her arms to retrieve her sweet baby boy from me. Her husband reached out for the other baby Matt was holding. "Her house is closer to the water," she explained. "And for three seasons a year, her yard is full of colorful flowers. I never want to leave when I visit."

Gabbi grinned at Jenni and then turned to me. "Please stop over anytime."

"Thanks, I just might do that. I'd like to see your flowers up close and personal when they are in bloom."

Someone turned off the music and a group of kids began to sing for us. I returned to Matt and Sophie and sat next to them. It warmed my spirit when Sophie began to sing from her chair along with them. When they finished, Matt said to me, "They are the local kids' choir from the church where my father is pastor."

"They're outstanding," I said, surprised at how sweet their voices sounded.

When they finished, they announced they were ramping up for the upcoming Christmas performance at the town square and were looking for teens to join. Their first practice was this Wednesday night and Sophie practically bounced out of her chair.

She tapped my arm with enthusiasm. "Can I do it?"

I was thrilled she wasn't hesitant to get involved. It was obvious to me she searched for acceptance and a sense of belonging, as I'm sure her life was isolated and tense. I understood her yearning to fit in and find new friends, but ruminated on how I was never brave enough at her age to reach out to join a choir. Kudos to Sophie.

"Can I do it?" she asked again.

I glanced at Matt, who nodded.

"I don't see why not." I wasn't sure how I would get her to choir practice with my foster care training classes but I would figure it out.

A hoopla arose from the firepit. People clapped as they dumped the first batch onto the grate and spread the oysters around.

"Let's go watch," Sophie said with excitement.

We made our way over and found a spot where we had a good view of the action. Sophie ended up standing next to Carley, who turned her back to her, appearing to snub Sophie. Why were kids so mean? I hoped she didn't attend the same school I wanted to enroll Sophie in. She didn't need to deal with such ugly behavior.

When the oysters finished roasting, they dumped them onto the table and we made our way over. Matt showed us how to crack them open with a shucking knife. There were kid friendly options to eat as well, including chicken wings, coleslaw, square buns with butter, and different desserts—chocolate cake for starters, my favorite.

Sophie made a face as we cracked open our oysters. They didn't look appealing to me either, but when I popped a teaser into my mouth, I closed my eyes. Delicious.

A groan escaped my throat, and as I opened my eyes, I saw Matt staring at me. Oh my.

It was Sophie's turn to try one. She wrinkled her face and stared at the oyster.

"You can do it," Matt encouraged.

People pressed in closer around us as they filled their plates.

Sophie ignored everyone and with a deep breath, she stuck the oyster in her mouth. She made a face as she chewed, but then smiled. "That's good, like really good."

Matt clapped his hands together and laughed robustly. "Great. I knew you ladies would enjoy them."

Sophie gleamed at Matt's comment, probably relishing in his praise. I was sure Ralph called her things, none of them complimentary.

We cracked more shells, then made our way to the smaller table to add condiments and to load up our plates with side dishes.

The classic rock music started back up and we talked, laughed, and ate. I couldn't believe how enjoyable the day was, everything about it fun—the music, the people, and Matt. I was beginning to really fall for him.

Everything was going well until a fire inspector and a policeman joined us. Part of me still worried a bit that people might have questions about Sophie.

After introductions, we talked about the popular oyster roast and the great turnout. Then the fire inspector, named Tom Dawson, wanted to know where I lived, where I moved from, and what I planned to do with such a large house. He became interested in my quest to become a foster parent. Unfortunately, the other guy, a police officer named Bob Smith, asked several questions about Sophie. He raised his eyebrows, almost as if he heard about a runaway girl in the area. We brushed it off and I had to remind myself that I wasn't breaking any laws. My paperwork was in order and acceptable, although I was sure he'd ask Matt more on the subject later.

At the end of the day we left the party exhausted but Sophie talked nonstop about what a blast she had.

Once we returned home, Sophie disappeared into the cottage to change clothes. At some point soon, I needed to move her into the big house. One thing at a time, I reminded myself.

I unlocked the back door, but before I made it too far inside my kitchen, Matt pulled me into a hug. We stayed melted into each other's arms for a long moment before he leaned down, our mouths so close, yet not close enough.

"I'm curious," I said as I pulled back slightly to challenge him. "What are we doing here, Matt?"

"What do you mean?"

"We hug each other, spend time together outside of fixing up the house." I raised my hand to include us and the kitchen. "Go to dinner together."

He shrugged. "So if I told you I'm attracted to you, would you be okay with that?"

I swear my heart smiled. "I'm out of practice with this whole attraction thing."

He leaned closer and stared into my eyes. "You're beautiful. I find it hard to believe you don't date much."

I felt my cheeks grow warm. "Thank you." I didn't want to appear as a complete reject when it came to relationships. "I mean, I had a couple of serious relationships but for one reason or another they faltered. I don't think I was ready emotionally."

He leaned closer. "I'm glad I met you now then."

I stared at him, my mouth suddenly parched. I really needed a drink of sweet tea but didn't move.

"Just a couple of relationships?"

I glanced away. "I dated here and there, but after a couple of months I learned we either had nothing in common, or we had serious communication issues. My crazy work schedule didn't help." In all truth, I had given up on meeting the right man and had pretty much stopped dating altogether. I enjoyed my own company, doing my own thing without someone giving me grief. I didn't need the aggravation in my life, although I wished things were different.

"Well, your ex-boyfriends were crazy to let you go."

My cheeks burned hot as I studied him. "What's your story?" I wanted to know everything about him.

"I pretty much dated one girl throughout high school but we broke things off when we went to college. When I came back home, we got back together for a bit but things didn't work out."

"Was it serious?"

He nodded. "It was serious for me but she wasn't ready to take it to the next level."

I figured there was more to the story but sensed he was through with the topic.

Poor timing because the back door opened. With reluctance, I moved away from Matt and noticed Sophie was still wearing the same outfit except she held an armful of clothes.

"I thought you were going to change?" I asked out of curiosity while trying to keep the disappointment from the almost intimate embrace out of my voice.

She stared at the two of us as if curious about catching us so close together.

"I wanted to take a shower to get the fire smell off me."

"Help yourself then," I said as I stepped toward the pantry to preoccupy myself. "Are you all hungry for homemade chicken potpie?" It had been a couple of hours since we ate the oysters, and we had stayed at the party longer to listen to the music. I knew Sophie's answer, as she made a dramatic gesture of pretending to wipe drool from the sides of her mouth. Matt nodded with enthusiasm and I laughed at their responses. "It won't take long to make."

"Sounds amazing," Matt said.

"Are you kidding?" Sophie asked. "Homemade?"

"Of course." This was one of the simple but impressive meals I made from scratch whenever possible. I prided myself in preparing a few easy but healthy meals instead of eating processed food. Besides, when I became a foster parent, I wanted to cook decent meals for the kids.

Sophie scooted off upstairs to shower and Matt busied himself with a project in the living room.

An easy dinner was necessary tonight, but even though I was tired, I still looked forward to reading the diary and letters. I thought about them often and knew Matt did too.

I tossed the few ingredients together, mostly consisting of large-cut vegetables, canned when in a hurry like tonight, creamed chicken soup, and two boneless chicken breasts I sautéed in a pan. Simple really. I mixed everything together in a bowl and spread out a premade pie crust. I scooped the ingredients into it, and then covered the top with another layer of dough.

Sophie reappeared in the kitchen, hair still wet from the shower, and I offered her a butter knife. "Here, this is so you can cut holes into the crust so it can breathe. It's fun to make designs if you want."

Sophie lit up. She bit her lower lip and got to work carving an outline of a pumpkin. When she finished, I stuck it in the oven for forty-five minutes.

"I'll be back in a bit," Sophie said, setting the knife in the sink, and then left the house. I saw a light turn on inside the cottage.

I approached Matt, who was busy removing a corner of the ugly wallpaper in the hallway. I knew I had won the battle about painting the walls instead of leaving the paper. Without thinking, I closed the distance between us and he looked up. His unwavering gaze made my heart beat faster.

As we gazed into each other's eyes there was an understanding between us of what was coming next ... our first kiss. And no sooner had I thought about it then Matt placed his mouth gently on mine.

Our mouths melded together, his breath warm, his scent intoxicating. His hands moved to my arms, holding me close, his right hand sliding down to my waist to the small of my back, making me quiver in its wake. Matt was gentle in his approach but took what he wanted, giving me everything in return.

No one had ever kissed me like that.

So hungrily ...

So eagerly ...

So deliciously.

He pulled away and raised his eyebrows as if to gauge my response. To reassure him, I leaned forward and our lips met again. This kiss was longer, more passionate and loving. Our arms wrapped around each other in a tender embrace.

When he pulled away, I noticed a wide smile on his face.

"Want to read the diary and letters before dinner?" he whispered.

Unable to speak, I nodded. We moved to the couch, but instead of sitting on opposite ends, we cuddled into each other. I leaned forward and handed him the letters and pulled the diary onto my lap.

> *Nana's Diary: July 1, 1968*
> *I won't lie, the past two weeks have been difficult for me and*

I haven't felt well. The last couple of days I have vomited several times. I tried to trace back what I ate but all I could think of was I had chicken salad at my friend Dorothy's house. I know chicken is one of those tricky foods that go bad fast. I can't imagine my reaction has to do with that though. And it's difficult dealing with a wild boy running around while I'm not feeling well, but by the grace of God, I am getting by.

Nana's Diary: July 4, 1968

This fourth of July hardly feels like a celebration with my husband at war. I wonder if the American people appreciate the sacrifices our soldiers are making, the lives lost, and the price we pay for freedom. The holiday is more than shooting off fireworks into the sky.

A bunch of my family members—cousins, kids, parents— planned to sit on the beach tonight to watch the firework display. I'm not sure I want to go. For one, I will be thinking about Robert. For two, I'm still sick to my stomach. If I don't start feeling better soon, I will make a doctor's appointment. I am not a person who likes to visit the doctor unless I have to. It's been at least a year since I've been to his office.

Anyway, I made pasta salad for our picnic on the beach just in case I decide to show up. Maybe I will, maybe I won't. I know Daniel wants to go. Before I do anything else today, I want to write Robert a long letter.

June 25, 1968
My lovely Shirley,

I got two of your letters today. You must have sent them before I asked for your delicious cookies. I guess I have to be patient. I know you have your hands full at home while working and raising Daniel.

I thought it was hot here earlier but now I feel like I'm baking in the heat. The mosquitos are bad and will practically carry you away alive. I'm looking forward to getting a shower tonight, if you can call it that. Shower day is one of my favorites although it doesn't take long to sweat again and stink.

Yesterday we went into a small village and drank. Don't worry, I never drink much because I like to stay aware of my surroundings. Some of the men get rowdy with the women but I think that's just plain crazy. Anyway, it was good to get away for a bit and have some fun with the guys. A person can't work all the time without releasing some tension. I have to go. I am needed.

I love you and say hi to Daniel for me.

Love,
Your Robert

July 4, 1968
My lovely Shirley,

I'm feeling patriotic in a new way. Even though I want to be home with you, the war goes on and it's the 4th of July. We are experiencing our own set of fireworks here, but I would've preferred to be watching them on the beach with you. The heat continues and the mosquitos are bad. I can't wait until the heat breaks and we get a good rain.

Tell Daniel I said I love him, and of course, know I love you more than anything. You keep me going. And I'm still looking forward to more cookies.

Love,
Your Robert

Every once in a while we stopped reading to discuss our thoughts. I didn't enjoy history in general but found it enthralling to read the intimate perspective from real people experiencing the war firsthand.

When the timer on the stove went off, Matt followed me into the kitchen. I opened the oven door and glanced at my creation. A light golden hue covered the top crust, the aroma of a baked pie filling the air.

"Wow, that smells delicious." Matt licked his lips.

I smiled at him before I pulled the pot pie out and set it on top of the stove to settle for a few minutes. As if led by some unprecedented intuition that dinner was ready, Sophie opened the door and entered the kitchen.

"Mmmm," she said, smacking her lips several times.

As usual, Sophie acted as though she hadn't eaten a hot meal in months, although I knew she had because I cooked for her. Nevertheless, her interest in my culinary skills made me feel appreciated. Matt also commented on the idea of a home-cooked meal. As a bachelor, I assumed he didn't cook much for himself.

I had to admit, I was becoming quite the homebody.

We ate mostly in silence because everyone was hungry and too busy shoving food into their mouths. After we finished washing dishes, Sophie excused herself and returned to the cottage. "I think I'll suggest to her tomorrow to bring all of her things inside. I'll set up one of the bedrooms for her."

"What a wonderful idea."

I glanced at Matt as I hung the dish towel on the oven door. "I'd like to add one more item to our remodeling list."

"What's that?" Matt asked without looking up from wiping off the table. He excelled at domestic chores and did them without complaint. I was sure my mother would say he was a keeper.

"I'd like to add a dishwasher to the list. Once I become a foster parent, I suspect I'll have lots of dishes."

He grinned. "I hope you have plenty of young ladies to fill up your house." He tossed the wet paper towel into the trash can. "Just remember, their living here should consist of helping with chores. They need to learn to manage a household to some extent to benefit their future selves."

He was right, and I looked forward to helping the girls to the best of my ability.

Matt and I sat together well into the evening. The more I read, the more I felt as though I knew Shirley and Robert Baker personally. She was almost a celebrity to me now. I knew Shirley watched over my house, protecting the home and even me in her grandmotherly way. I admired her strength as a mother and a loyal wife, the love for her husband apparent. I wished I had met her in real life. She was brave, strong, independent.

After Matt left for the night, I curled up in bed thinking about our goodbye kiss. I never thought it was possible to have intimate feelings to this degree. I always saw a policeman as a rugged hero, not a man I could be attracted to. Boy, was I wrong. It was endearing to see his caring side as he read the letters from his grandfather, his own hero.

Matt was deep and caring, someone I could likely spend my life with.

My mind was too active to sleep, so I picked up my sister's book, curious about the questionable scene she had written. With serious consideration, I continued to read. Then I stumbled on *the* scene.

The family sat down to eat pizza for dinner, except her father was missing as usual. Mom said he worked late nights to put food on the table. She was always home. Without a second car, there weren't many places to visit.

Not having eaten much for lunch other than peanut butter sandwiches, no jelly, both girls dug into the pizza with fervor. Her belly knotted in hunger from anticipation of gooey cheese pizza, not the frozen kind from the oven but the kind where the man delivered it in a box at the door.

She sank her teeth into the first bite, a bite she'd always remember. Her father chose that moment to burst through the door. Without so much as a hello, Princess, he made his way to their parents' bedroom.

The closet door opened with a thud, heavy items removed, drawers opened and slammed shut. All kinds of deafening noises escaped the room like a wild animal attempting to break free of a cage.

Alarmed, Mom followed Dad into the bedroom to check on things. His voice loud, her voice hushed. What were they fighting about?

Without comment, he made his way to the door, dragging overstuffed suitcases, Mom following behind him. Why was she crying? She tugged on his shirt, trying to prevent him from leaving. But he left, without a goodbye, Princess.

Mom spent the evening crying on the phone about not having a job or a car.

What about Thanksgiving or Christmas? Would Santa still come?

Even though that one bite of pizza had tasted so delicious, it now tasted like paper.

Despite wondering if they'd ever eat again, she pushed away the pizza.

I placed the book on my chest and dragged in deep breaths. Emily's nickname was Princess. She was right, the scene bothered me on a gut-wrenching level. I had no recollection of my father leaving, even after I read the scene, but on a deeper level, my subconscious remembered all too well.

Chapter Eleven

Several different emotions surfaced in Matt's mind after finding Nana's old hat box. He was happy to discover it, yet sad because it stirred up the unresolved issues of her death. She had a long, happy life, but they had been extremely close and he still found losing her difficult.

She helped him through a tough time in his life. The many years his father had taken in foster kids were tough, and Matt was often left to his own accord. Sure, disturbed kids needed love and attention, and his dad always had enough for them ... but for Matt? Not so much. But his nana always was there for him.

The letters allowed him a glimpse inside his grandfather's mind to gauge what kind of person he was too. He was every bit the loving, kindhearted man Matt had imagined, maybe even more so. Matt was excited and relieved his grandfather was a devoted husband and father. He was a true hero.

It must have been difficult for Robert to leave his wife and son behind to travel to a foreign country for a war he didn't believe in. His sense of duty to his country had won, not unlike many soldiers of today. Matt had always been interested in history but reading his letters had heightened his curiosity. It made the war more real.

An extra bonus was reading them with Terri.

Although he had concerns about her starting a foster home, mostly because of his own experience, he noticed positive changes in Sophie. She demonstrated more confidence, more trust in Terri and himself, and willingness to participate and help with chores around the house. And Terri's smile and interest in cooking showed how much she enjoyed helping Sophie. She was changing from the reserved, closed-off woman he had first met, and little by little she was letting her guard down.

He wanted to support her dreams but his past kept getting in the way. He didn't dare mention his thoughts to her as he didn't want to ruin her plans.

He had experienced Nana's generosity and caring nature as a child, and he still enjoyed spending every free moment possible in the house. Terri's pleasant company added to the experience. He was happy things worked out the way they did with Terri deciding to buy the home.

He was beginning to have protective feelings over her. From the first day he met her, he knew she was different from anyone he had dated before. Was it love at first sight? For him, maybe. Terri was more reserved but he thought over time things would work out.

A knock on the window of his patrol car jolted him out of his thoughts. "Dad," Matt said, opening the car window. Daniel Baker held a to-go cup of coffee in his hand, probably on his way back from Coffee Break.

"Hey, son." He held up the cup as his way to say hello and leaned on the doorframe to chat.

Matt was on the clock which meant he was unable to invite anyone to sit inside the patrol car. Even though he considered their relationship strained, they still loved one another and looked out for each other. All his life he had tried to earn his dad's approval but he never had. At some point it didn't matter anymore, and he needed to learn to accept it for what it was. People didn't change, nor was it fair for Matt to expect an apology.

His father frowned. "So you sold Nana's house?"

"Yep."

His father shook his head as if he disagreed with Matt's decision.

"Dad, it sat there empty for months after the renters trashed it. No one in the family stepped up to buy it, so I had no choice. The house deserves better than to sit there and rot." Most of Matt's aunts and uncles were older and hadn't wanted to mess with it. He had even extended the offer to his cousins, but crickets.

The sun had moved higher in the sky and out of Matt's eyes, so he flipped the visor away from his face.

His father continued. "I heard the woman who bought it showed up for the oyster roast yesterday."

Gossip in small towns ran as fast as a marathon runner. Not that he was keeping the sale from his family but just hadn't had the chance to mention it yet.

"Yes, Terri McMillan did." Matt couldn't help but smile. "You'll like her. She's a nice lady."

"Some folk are upset you sold the house."

Unbelievable. That was code for "he" was upset about it. "Some folk will have to deal with it, Dad. It was my decision."

His father shifted his weight from one leg to the next, still leaning on the patrol car. He took a sip from his coffee and stared off at the traffic zipping down Pelican Lane.

Matt noticed more wrinkles on his father's face. Time had a habit of marching on for them both and it saddened him their relationship wasn't as it should be.

"But I have good news," Matt said. "Terri, has agreed to host our Christmas gathering there." Matt had mentioned it to his dad once before but his father hadn't commented. Christmas wasn't far off, so it was time to bring up the subject again. Besides, he needed to get the invites out to his family.

His dad blew on his coffee but didn't answer.

"Dad, it's a good opportunity to get everyone back together."

Silence.

"I heard from David," his father said, clearly changing the subject.

It was Matt's turn to frown. David was one of the foster kids they helped. The kid was troublesome and had dragged Matt into the mud with him. What a miserable time in Matt's life.

"He's cleaned himself up. People can change," his dad continued.

Rather than argue, Matt responded, "I'd like to believe they can." He wasn't sure change with David was possible. When it came to troubled kids, it was if his father had more heart for them than he did his own.

"The Christmas party ..." Matt said, trying to keep on topic.

His dad took another drink from his cup and continued to stare off at the road in front of them.

"I've already called and mentioned it to most of the family but I'll be sending out invitations soon." He continued watching his dad take another sip. "Aren't you interested in coming? Being with the rest of the family?" His dad loved Christmas, loved the family gatherings, so his lack of interest was troubling.

"I guess so," he grumbled. "Your mom wants to go. I don't get why we are gathering at Nana's house when you no longer own it."

Matt sat up taller, crossing his arms. "Because, Dad. We've tried a family get-together at my house for the holiday and hardly anyone showed up. And then we had tenants in Nana's house, so having it there wasn't an option."

"Now there is a lady living there. You're sure she doesn't mind?"

Matt shook his head in frustration. "No, she doesn't. She graciously agreed to host our family holiday." Well, sort of. Gracious wasn't quite the right word.

"All right." He backed away from the patrol car. "Good luck planning the party. Let me know."

The house was quiet without Matt. I had a lot of unpacking left, mostly in my room, and I had my foster parenting class tonight. This was also my last week off before I started my job.

It was always nerve-racking to start at a new place, especially since I had worked at the hospital for five years. It was the only nursing job I'd had. For one thing, I didn't know anyone who worked there. Most of my time would be spent on the road as I'd be driving from home to home, wherever they needed me to go. Thank goodness modern technology helped me find my way around. I reminded myself I needed this fresh start, needed to step outside my comfort zone.

I'd been burned out before and hoped this new opportunity was the change I desperately needed.

On my agenda today I planned to have a discussion with Sophie about attending school. I wasn't sure exactly how long it had been since she'd gone, but it was past time for her to return. I needed to broach the subject this morning at breakfast.

I pulled out a large glass bowl and ingredients for banana pancakes, comfort food my mother cooked when Emily and I were kids. The special breakfast was usually reserved for brunch on Sunday mornings.

I whisked the wet ingredients together, diced bananas on a wooden cutting board, and combined the flour mixture slowly into the wet bowl. The griddle was hot and ready, passing the sizzle test when I flicked water on it.

I heard the back door open and Sophie entered the kitchen.

"Good morning," I said with cheer in my voice. I had experienced an unquestionable amount of joy since I moved into the house. Coastal living, the view, and this house all had a positive effect on me.

"Good morning," she said as she joined me at the counter.

I suspected the loving warmth I felt in this home influenced Sophie too.

"Can I help with something?" she offered.

I doled out small portions of pancake batter from a quarter measuring cup onto the griddle. The sizzle and aroma of cooking pancakes and bacon made my stomach growl. "Can you pour two glasses of orange juice?" I asked. The fact she offered to help didn't go unnoticed by me.

Before long I flipped the pancakes and pulled the bacon from the oven to scoop onto a plate lined with a paper towel. I dabbed the grease off and put two pieces on each plate. I slid the pancakes off the griddle and gave us each a small stack. I drank my usual protein shake this morning but loved eating with Sophie. Adding more pancake mix onto the griddle, I turned the dial to a lower temperature to enjoy our breakfast without worrying about the pancakes burning.

Sophie had already dove into hers, and I cut off a large bite and savored it. I stared out the window, appreciating the view in my own backyard, appreciating the wooden walkway leading through golden marsh to the dock. This sunny morning, the water was calm and bright blue with little boat traffic.

"Soon we'll be celebrating the holidays," I said, shocked I was somewhat looking forward to Thanksgiving and Christmas this year. I had two wonderful people to share them with now and that made all the difference. There had been no talk of my own family get-togethers but it was still early.

Sophie shrugged.

"Don't you enjoy Christmas?" I asked, surprised I was actually having this conversation.

She shrugged again. "We never celebrated it much. My mom always worked at the diner." She shoved another bite of pancake into her mouth and chewed as if she enjoyed every bite.

"The restaurant is open on Christmas Day?"

"Yep. Well, they close early but she works until then." She ate the entire piece of bacon in one mouthful. Her appetite always surprised me.

It dismayed me that Sophie hadn't enjoyed the mad ripping of wrapping paper most kids experienced.

As an adult I usually focused on the stressful fighting and arguing that also went hand in hand with the holidays. Now that I met Matt and Sophie, I hoped our holidays would be more festive.

"When my mom remarried, nothing changed with her restaurant schedule," Sophie explained. "My stepfather works on his junky car in the yard, and I usually watch television until my mom returns home." Sophie paused long enough to shove another large chunk of pancake into her mouth. "Mmmm."

I walked over to the griddle, disturbed by Sophie's description of Christmas morning at her house. "You just watched TV?"

She was eating much slower now, probably full from the large amount she practically inhaled. "My mom always made us ham for dinner. I'd get to open a couple of presents, usually clothes." She scrunched her face in distaste.

What teenager didn't want clothes? She'd loved the ones I bought her the other day.

As if she read my mind, she said, "My mom doesn't know what's in style. Still doesn't."

I nodded, realizing the dilemma now.

"Well, this year is going to be different," I promised. "First off, we are going to have a Christmas celebration for Matt's family. That was part of the deal with buying this house."

She set her fork on the empty plate in front of her. "He helps you for more reasons than any dumb party."

I stared at her, wondering what she was trying to say.

"And you like him too, so you can stop pretending." She pushed her chair away and stuck her plate and utensils into the sudsy water in the sink.

I was fast losing ground for the chance to discuss school. I pointed to the chair. "Hang out with me for a few minutes, please."

She looked suspicious but sat down.

"I love having you home during the day ..."

Sophie leaned in the direction of the door as if she wanted to escape.

I reached across and placed my hand on her arm, not to hold her in the chair but to offer support. "I want you to live here as long as you want. That's not what I'm trying to say."

She relaxed a bit underneath my touch.

"You need to go to school, honey."

Sophie didn't respond.

"How long has it been?"

She shrugged.

I sensed she had been out of school longer than I imagined. "I thought we could go talk to them today."

No response.

"Let's go tomorrow then." I wanted to give her a little time to think about it. "I'll be there with you. We can make it fun and go in town for lunch afterward."

She stared out the window.

"You'll be okay. I promise." I squeezed her hand. She didn't pull away from my touch, so I assumed that was a positive sign.

"Fine," she said, standing. She glanced down at her sweatpants. "What do I wear? I only have the one nice outfit and some casual clothes."

She had a good point. "Just wear your nice ones. We'll buy more along with school supplies after we talk to them tomorrow. And we can buy you a cool new backpack." Choosing a backpack was always my favorite part.

She returned to staring out the window. "Why are you doing all of this for me?"

"Because I like you and want to help." Enough said. I just hoped she stayed around long enough to benefit.

She made a dash for the door. Right before she pulled the handle, she mumbled, "Thanks." Off she went, scrambling down the steps and across the yard.

I hadn't even had the chance to mention her moving into the house.

I needed to buy her a new coat, gloves, and a hat. Even though the winters at the coast were mild, we did have some cold snaps here and there. At least that was how the winters were in Raleigh. Occasionally Raleigh got snow but it usually didn't last long. It was a rare season when snow visited the coast.

One thing bothered me, though. She was hesitant about school, that was for certain, but why? I needed to find out the reason her mother hadn't enforced her attendance. And as much as we'd been getting along, she was still a bit skittish. I had seen those moments when I thought she was going to bolt. I needed to speak with her more about that and I had to admit, that was where the counselor came in handy. The one thing I didn't know, and should, was what she faced in her upbringing. Those things had molded her and might be important for me to be aware of while she stayed with me.

As I sighed at the thoughts swirling in my brain, I glanced around my lovely kitchen. I enjoyed how the sun filled up most of the room, illuminating a soft, feel-good glow onto every surface it touched. Without a doubt, the kitchen was the heart of the house. This morning I sensed Shirley stronger than usual, knowing that she'd prepared many a breakfast here.

My cell phone rang from my back pocket and startled me from my thoughts. I wiped my hands on a nearby towel before answering.

"Hi, this is Tom. I met you at the oyster roast. I know this is short notice but I had a cancellation today," the fire inspector said with a deep Southern accent. "Matt asked me to help you out whenever I had a chance."

If I wanted to expedite the foster care process, I needed to accept his offer. Matt had installed additional smoke alarms, placed fire extinguishers in the kitchen and throughout the house, and had taught me how to use them. We even posted a visible evacuation plan. As far as I knew, I was ready for the inspection.

"Yes, what time?"

"In about an hour and a half."

"Wonderful. Please come." I swallowed a lump of panic rising in my throat. Oh, come on. All I needed to do was tidy up a bit and deal with my nervous energy.

I would be one step closer to achieving my dream.

I hurried to finish straightening the kitchen and scurried into my room to shower but my mind stayed busy ticking off my mental checklist. I had stored all flammable liquids outside in a shed and they were clearly labeled. Large numbers marked the house address. Matt even showed me how to use the generator, not that I remembered exactly. In all honesty, I didn't know what I would do without his help. I hoped I never had to find out.

I ran around, straightening up the living room. When I finished, I sat down at the kitchen table and took several calming breaths. Then I remembered the cottage.

I flew out the kitchen door and toward the little building and banged on Sophie's door.

When she answered, she frowned. "What's wrong?"

My intensity probably scared her half to death. I inhaled a long deep breath and let it out slowly. "I have a man coming over to perform a fire inspection, so I can be approved for foster care. He's coming in about fifteen minutes." I hadn't really explained to her in full detail my desire to be a foster parent but now wasn't the time.

She raised her eyebrows.

"I'll explain later but please make sure the cottage is picked up. No clothes lying around."

"Fine," Sophie said with a snarky edge.

Her attitude caused me to pause. Was she confused about my desire to be a foster parent, or did she think I was criticizing her?

I slowed my thoughts down. Reading minds was one thing I wasn't good at. "What's going on here? All okay?" Better to ask straight up than try to guess.

She shrugged, still blocking the door. "So what. I messed up one time." Her voice still held that sharp edge.

Confused, I waited for her to explain. I was in a hurry, but Sophie was important to me. I had to expect snippets of her bruised self to show up when I least expected.

"Sophie, all is good," I said with the intention of downplaying my request. "I'd like to help you straighten the cottage before the fire inspector shows up. That's all." I wanted to reach out to touch her but my intuition warned me against making physical contact. I needed to let her absorb what I was saying without making her feel backed into a corner.

"My stepdad made me keep my room clean even though the house was always a mess. He's too lazy to bother and my mom works all the time. But if my room had one thing out of place, he yelled at me."

"I understand, Soph. I'm not your stepfather."

"It's okay that the place is messy? You aren't going to yell at me?"

Oh, boy. I shook my head. "I'd never yell at you." Her reaction made me realize I had a lot to learn about parenting.

"Well, we need to hurry then." She dove back inside, leaving the door ajar, and began flailing around.

I stepped inside to help her pick up a pair of sweatpants and several socks off the floor by the couch. She folded a blanket and set it on a cushion while I washed several cups she had left behind on the coffee table. Thankfully the place was small and didn't take too long to straighten to my satisfaction.

Within minutes after we finished, a truck pulled into the driveway. This inspection was an important factor to determine my fate as a foster parent. No stress there.

Chapter Twelve

The impromptu fire inspection delayed our shopping adventure for a couple of hours. The clothes and supplies could wait if needed but I wanted Sophie in school as soon as possible. After the inspector left the house, we stopped by the school to sign her up, a bittersweet moment.

"Why haven't you been in school for the last couple of months?" Mr. Dodson, the principal, asked as he leaned back in his leather chair.

Sophie shrugged as if missing school was no big issue.

"I have to wonder if you'll have the same casual attitude about attending here," he said, now thumping his pen against a pile of paperwork on his desk. I wanted to grab the pen and toss it into the trash can. The man made me nervous.

But Sophie came off as unflappable, although I knew she was hiding her feelings.

"I'm curious as to why you stopped going," he pushed further.

When she didn't answer, he turned his stare onto me.

"Give her a chance," I said in my most convincing voice. "New house, new situation." I hoped I was right.

He eventually let her leave, all signed up to start school tomorrow.

As we climbed back into the truck, I decided to probe further about her attendance. "So you mentioned to the principal you haven't been to school in a couple of months. I'm curious as to why you stopped going." I held my breath, unsure if she'd trust me enough to tell me the truth.

She shrugged. "I kept getting kicked out, so why bother."

That brought up another interesting topic. "Why, if you don't mind me asking, did you get kicked out?"

She slammed the door closed behind her and fastened her seatbelt before she answered. "I dunno. The kids were mean and called me names. One day I let loose and told a girl off."

I stared at her before I started the engine. "Anything else?"

Sophie shook her head and stared out the window. "Well, okay. Guess I should tell you the whole story." She paused so long I went ahead and pulled out of the parking lot. "I got into a couple of fights." She glanced at me as if wondering if I were judging her. "It wasn't my fault. They were mean." The defensive edge returned to her voice, the same tone I had heard yesterday before the fire inspector arrived.

"I understand and it's okay. This school is a fresh start." I dropped the subject but Sophie wasn't just a runaway kid. She had baggage, wounds to heal as we all did, but her issues were deeper than most kids her age, thanks to her verbally abusive stepfather and neglectful mother. I had no clue what degree of harm had been done, what level of defensive coping strategies she had developed. I hoped to not only soften her edges but to offer her a chance of healing. Until she returned home and the verbal abuse continued ... unless I had the ability to stop such a thing from happening altogether.

We drove downtown, taking pleasure in hopping from one boutique to the next on Front Street. This small town might not have shopping malls but cute boutiques were plentiful, though a little pricey. Fortunately Sophie was very conscious of what things cost and didn't go too crazy. Regardless, I wanted her to feel good about what we purchased and confident in herself. She found a few sweet tops and a stylish pair of jeans, but the most important thing was we were bonding and having fun together. I was amazed how much I enjoyed being with her.

All these years I had been hiding my emotions, staying safe, missing out on life. Well, no more.

Over a late lunch, I broached the topic of her moving into the house, selecting the room of her choice upstairs. She was open to the idea, even excited about living in the house with me instead of the cottage. I had to admit, the ease to which she adjusted to the idea was a surprise and a relief. It didn't seem right for a thirteen-year-old girl to live alone. And once I got the rest of my residents situated she'd be my right-hand girl to show them the lay of the land.

After we ate we decided to stop in Claire's studio. From the shop window, an oversized canvas greeted us. It was a photo of a wild black stallion.

"Wow!" Sophie gaped at the picture.

"Wow is right." I stared at the majestic horse as he gazed back at me. He perched on a sandy dune with the bright blue water behind him.

Sophie pulled open the shop's heavy door and practically bounced inside.

I gasped as if I had entered a magical shop that existed in one of my wonderful dreams. Wild horses filled the walls. Sure, there were a few colorful photos of marinas, fishermen, and ocean sunsets but they were nothing compared to the wild horses.

"I love horses," Sophie said, staring at the photographs in awe.

There was a lot I didn't understand about her. She came from an entirely different world than me. In a way, we both moved to Big Cat to start over. We were connected on a much deeper level than I imagined. I hoped, prayed even, she would stay with me. I didn't want to keep her from her family, but I wanted her safe.

Her mouth dropped open as she ogled the photograph we had noticed from the shop window.

"Aunt Terri, I love this picture."

It shocked me whenever she called me that because I loved that she felt so comfortable with me.

"I mean, look at the way the wind is blowing his mane. He is so free." She gazed at him for a long minute before she blinked.

Claire approached us. "His name is Magic. He's my favorite stallion on the island."

Sophie glanced up at her. "I can see why. His name fits him."

I stared at the price tag on the photo. It was gorgeous but priced a little more than I felt comfortable paying.

Claire must have read my mind. "I'll give you 40% off for a friends' and family discount."

The offer touched me. "You're very generous." I knew she gave us a deal because of Sophie's situation.

Sophie flashed a quick smile of hesitation at Claire but set the canvas down. When we finished circulating the store, I decided to buy the photo as a present to hang in her new room. "You can have it."

She looked up at me with a sweet expression in her eyes, as if she couldn't fathom the idea. "No, thanks. I can't do that."

I nudged her toward the photograph. "Yes, you can."

She gasped. "For real?"

I nodded. "For real."

"Thank you!" She wrapped her arms around me so tight I had trouble breathing. She stepped away and picked up the photo of Magic, staring at it lovingly.

I paid for the canvas and we carried it along with her bags back to the car. I was glad we parked nearby.

"I'm nervous about starting school tomorrow," Sophie said in the smallest of voices.

She sounded so vulnerable, it made my heart soften more. "It will be okay," I said, but I couldn't imagine how difficult starting a new school must be. "What are you most afraid of?"

She paused for a moment and I saw her swallow hard. "Everything."

My heart did a little squeeze as we climbed into the truck, and I didn't know what to say. "How about if I drive you both ways, so you don't have to ride the bus yet." At least it was something, and I was off this week.

She tilted her head from side to side as if weighing out the options. "That'd be fine." She stared out the passenger window. "Really."

It didn't seem my offer eased her anxiety. "As my parents always told me, they won't know you're nervous if you don't tell them." Maybe that was my mother's wisdom, I couldn't remember. "And I always try to be friendly to everyone. If you can just find that one friend ..."

Actually, I needed to listen to my own advice with starting a new job and having moved to the coast. If it weren't for Matt and Sophie, I would spend most of my time in my home without coming out.

She continued to stare out the window as I drove.

When we returned to the house, Matt stopped by to analyze the painter's work before starting on the trim.

I helped Sophie hang the canvas upstairs, and then we moved her items from the cottage. She picked the very room Matt had slept in as a child when he visited Shirley. For some reason, that felt significant, as if Shirley had a say in helping to welcome Sophie. I didn't feel comfortable enough calling her Nana as Matt did. Besides, I wasn't family.

When we finished, Sophie settled on top of the new quilt on the bed, and I walked outside to the front of the house to talk to Matt. The painter gathered his supplies and disappeared to put the items in his truck. Alone with Matt now, I wrapped my arms around him, sliding my arms inside his jacket.

He turned and embraced me, our lips meeting and lingering like sampling fine wine. Amazingly delicious was an accurate description of him.

"I didn't get a chance to ask you how the fire inspection went?" he asked, holding me in his arms.

I smiled just inches from his mouth. "The house passed."

"Congrats, sweetheart." He kissed me lightly. "You deserve this."

"Thank you," I said in almost a whisper. I appreciated his support, although it was difficult for me to concentrate on his words while so close to him.

The painter waved goodbye to us, and Matt, with me still in his arms, nodded back to him. When the man left, Matt glanced down at me and asked, "Date night tonight?" He kissed my lips again, this time our mouths touching with full, wet warmth.

When he kissed me like that, it was difficult to answer. When I was able to focus again, I said, "I wish I could but I have class tonight."

Instead of answering, he closed his mouth around mine. His lips soft but commanding. The world around me swirled and I was glad I could lean against him.

I sensed someone watching us. I glanced up, parting from his kiss long enough to see the curtain move but Sophie was no longer watching.

Matt noticed too.

"Please take this the right way," he said, pulling back enough to make me feel the cool air between us. He paused as if searching for words. "I love that you want to help kids, but why do you want to be a foster parent? I've never asked you."

I stepped back and stared at him. Why did he want to know? I wondered if he truly supported my dream, but the more shocking realization was I had no idea how to answer him. I was clueless as to why, or where the original urge came from. Interesting though, the question stirred up tense emotion in me and made my belly tighten. I wondered if it had to do with the scene I read in my sister's book.

I ignored his question and asked one instead. "Don't you enjoy Sophie?"

He nodded. "Of course. That's not why I'm asking."

"Then why are you?" Even though he didn't want me to take his question wrong, I had to fight off being defensive.

"Being a policeman, I've seen a lot. Teens start out on their best behavior when they move to a new situation but will show their true colors eventually. They'll start to act out, talk back, get jealous. They will begin to do what they want, instead of what you planned."

I stared at him. "Don't you think I know runaway kids are distressed? I've worked with pediatrics throughout my entire nursing career."

"Living with them is different. Believe me, I know." He glanced back up at the window. My gaze followed his. "Trust me on that."

"I imagine boys are harder." I knew I sounded distrustful of his motives.

"They're both difficult in their own ways." He glanced up at the sky. "It's not supposed to rain but looks like it could pour any minute." His words were clipped as he changed the subject.

"A cold front is supposed to move in tomorrow afternoon. I hope the paint dries beforehand." I considered the weather unusually warm for the season.

He let out a long sigh. "I'm never going to finish restoring this house before Christmas. It's closing in fast."

In all honesty, I wasn't sure he'd complete the enormous project either. "Thanksgiving is around the corner. Just do what you can and try not to worry about the rest," I said. That was the best advice I had. Despite the recent warm weather, winter was approaching, although the colder months were usually January and February.

I was looking forward to spending more time inside, in front of the fireplace, reading Shirley's diary. I wanted to bond with Matt on the couch while we explored the letters and diary again. With my night classes, though, I had no idea when we would have another chance.

"I noticed several pecans on the ground this morning." I couldn't wait to harvest the pecans as Shirley had done. I loved the domestic thought.

His face lit up. "Go find three baskets and line them with linen napkins."

He was including Sophie, despite our conversation. The love in my heart expanded to huge proportions. He never ceased to amaze me. Perhaps it was divine intervention. Whatever the reason, I enjoyed the warm feeling and was excited to share the moment with Sophie. If my intuition was correct, the little girl was in desperate need of affection.

I glanced at the time, then ran inside with lighthearted exuberance.

"Sophie," I called out as I neared the base of the steps. I had a rare flashback to childhood when my father yelled at us from the bottom of the stairwell. Not wanting to repeat the awful memory, I decided to climb the steps and talk to her directly.

"The pecans are ready to harvest!"

Still sprawled out atop the comfy quilt on her bed, she glanced up from reading a book I had loaned her.

"I have a basket for you. Let's go collect pecans!" I wanted to create pleasant memories with her and Matt.

However, she shrugged and buried her gaze back in her book.

"Sophie! Think of pecans on our salads, on top of ice cream, fresh-baked pecan pies." Then a crazy thought occurred to me. "Pecan pies for dessert after our Christmas meal." I didn't recognize myself. I disliked the holidays but I did like pecan pies. "Come on! Let's go harvest them." I practically jumped up and down. I didn't recognize the person I was becoming. "Let's pick them up before it gets too dark."

She didn't speak but in slow motion she set the book aside and sat up. Reluctantly she followed me downstairs. I retrieved three baskets from the top shelf of the pantry, and then opened the cabinet drawer and pulled out three nautical blue linen napkins.

We met Matt underneath the tree. "We have to pick them up off the ground before the squirrels claim them," he said. "Also, if you shake the tree branches the ones that are ready will fall." He demonstrated by jiggling a nearby limb. Several fell to the ground.

"This is awesome." Sophie bent down to pick up a handful and tossed them into her basket.

I smiled, happy she was having as much fun as I was.

Not wanting to rush our bonding moment, having just time enough to indulge myself in harvesting the pecans along with eating a light dinner, but I did have class tonight.

"Did you know that pecans aren't considered nuts?" Matt asked, as he pushed a branch back and forth.

"What? They look like nuts to me," I said, not really believing him.

"It's actually considered a drupe, a stone fruit containing a single seed." He watched me closely to gauge my response. "Seriously. Look it up."

"Guess I believe you," I said, thinking I learned an interesting fact today.

"But I just call them pecans. Drupe sounds so boring."

"Pecans it is," I said, agreeing with him. We collected all of them from the ground. I tried my skill at shaking a limb while Sophie gathered the fallen ones to add to the growing collection in her basket. Then Matt surprised me by climbing halfway up the tree to shake the higher branches.

It was just beginning to turn dark but we had gathered every last pecan we could find. We carried them into the kitchen where Matt lined the countertop with paper towels. I didn't tell him I had called the contractor to install a dishwasher tomorrow, but if I had to move the pecans elsewhere, no harm done. So far I had no plans to replace the countertop, at least not yet. However, I did want to paint the cabinets white, knowing full well Matt struggled with the idea.

"Pick out any rotten ones or those with worm holes," he instructed. We combed through them as we spread them out on the paper towels, glad there weren't many we had to throw away.

"I want to eat one," Sophie said, her voice pitched high with excitement.

"Me too. There is something so down-home about eating pecans off my own tree." Feeling domestic, this summer I wanted to till the ground and plant a garden. I usually claimed to never have spare time to embark on such projects but living in Big Cat had an effect on me.

He plucked two off the paper towels. "This is how we cracked them when I was a boy," he said, folding his hand around two pecans in his palm. "You roll them so they are touching, then you crack them against each other." He demonstrated and the shells broke open with ease.

Our gaze met and lingered. Those eyes ... He pressed two in my palm, touching me longer than necessary. I squeezed my hand closed but the pecans remained whole. I supposed my lack of manly hand strength didn't help.

"Make sure the nuts are touching," he instructed with a hint of a smile, his large hand wrapped once again around mine.

It took several tries before the nuts cracked open, but when they finally did, I held pride from my achievement.

Sophie cracked hers without a problem. "Look! I can do it!"

Her face lit up with joy, giving me a hint of what she might have looked like as a child. My heart ached, wishing I had known her then, yet thankful I knew her now.

She picked apart the shell and popped the meat into her mouth. "Yum! I've never eaten a pecan before."

Matt and I stared at her. Again, I wanted to know more about her childhood, wanted to give her opportunities to experience life to the fullest.

I placed the pecan in my mouth and closed my eyes. "Oh, wow. They are so fresh," I said, my stomach rumbling from hunger. I glanced at the time. "Who wants a quick dinner?"

Sophie shot her hand in the air. "I can help."

"Me too," Matt offered.

For a flash of a second, I had a vision of us as a family.

Together we gathered plates, silverware, and warmed up leftover chicken potpie. "Can you pull out the salad?" I asked Sophie. I always kept a container of fresh lettuce and fixings in the refrigerator where I could place the bowl on the table in a moment's notice for a healthy side choice. I pulled apart two tangerines to top it off.

Sophie's mouth gaped open. "First I get fresh pecans, and now more delicious potpie with a fresh salad?"

Again I wondered about her home life, wondered what kinds of food had she been served for dinner in the past. Did her mother even cook?

Sophie shoved a forkful into her mouth, although she had slowed significantly in comparison to how ravenously she ate when she had first arrived. When she finished, she asked, "Seconds?"

"Of course." I pushed the dish closer to her.

"You're a fabulous cook," Matt said. "When you become a foster parent, the kids will be lucky to have you cooking for them every night."

"Thanks," I said but detected a hint of tension whenever he talked about my dream. At some point, we needed to have more conversation on the topic.

Sophie glanced up. "What's a foster parent?"

I had a feeling she'd resent my dream too. "I want to help give homeless teens a place to live," I explained. As I suspected, a dark expression crossed over her face. "What's wrong?'

She shrugged but didn't answer.

"Don't you like the idea?" I wished she felt safe enough to talk to me.

"Not really."

I stood to rinse off my plate in the sink, grateful that tomorrow I would have a dishwasher. I decided to push the topic further. "Why don't you like the idea?"

She stood and brought her plate to the sink. Without thinking, I took it from her and began washing it.

"What if mean kids come to stay?" She helped by placing the leftover potpie in a container with a lid.

Was she really concerned about mean kids, or about not having enough alone time with me? "I guess there is always that risk," I explained. "My intention is to help kids, to give them a better start in life."

"Aren't I enough?"

I paused. I had imagined helping many kids, not just one. "Of course you are." I wrapped her in my arms. She stiffened against my touch but I hugged her anyway.

She allowed the affection for a brief moment before she pulled back. "I need to organize my things to start school tomorrow."

"Tomorrow?" Matt asked.

I had forgotten to tell him.

"Yes. Aunt Terri and I signed up. We went into town and bought clothes today and supplies." Sophie leaned against the doorway with one foot pointing in the direction of the hallway. "I got a picture of a stallion to hang on my wall too."

"Claire," Matt said. "Everyone loves her photography. Did she tell you her husband is the ranger on Pony Island?"

Sophie flashed a questionable gaze at me.

I stopped washing the dishes. "We can go visit in the spring."

She squealed and jumped up and down. "Yes!" She turned on the heels of her sneakers and darted from the kitchen.

"I have to leave for class in a bit," I said, wishing I could stay with them longer. My mom should be here soon. She agreed to the favor of staying with Sophie while I left.

He frowned and pinched me playfully on my side. "I hoped we had enough time to read the diary or a letter or two. Maybe tomorrow."

I shot a quick glance at the time again. It was tight but I could pull it off. "Maybe we can read one or two."

He planted a quick kiss on my cheek and we made our way into the living room to sit on the love seat together. There wasn't much room but I enjoyed the intimacy. I leaned forward and pulled the items off the coffee table in front of us.

"I think about the letters a lot," he said with a grin in his voice.

"Me too." I handed them to him and held onto the precious diary.

"I want to understand the woman who lived here for years before me. What are you wanting to learn about your grandfather?"

I snuggled into the sofa pillow behind me, lifting one of my legs across his lap to connect with him. Suddenly, I realized just how much I cared for him.

Matt rubbed his hand along my leg, and I felt his touch through my jeans, his fingers leaving behind a tingling trail. He pulled away to remove the delicate, aged string from around the letters.

"I've always wondered why my grandpa left his family. I want to gain insight as to who he was as a person." He held the letters on his lap with such tenderness. "How about you? What do you hope to learn about my grandmother?"

I had to think about his question before I answered. "I want to know the details of her life, about living in this big house while raising a child alone. What feelings did she have as a woman about her husband being away at war? Was she lonely, scared?"

He raised his eyebrows and nodded. "I want to know those things too."

"About your grandmother?"

"Yes." He gave my knee a long, gentle squeeze of affection. "I knew Nana from the standpoint of a boy who slept over at her house, but now I want to know her as a woman."

Eager, I opened the diary and thumbed to the page where I had left off. Together we sat, reading and sharing snippets of the intriguing love story of his grandparents.

Nana's Diary: June 9, 1968

I suspect Robert isn't telling me the full story of what it's like being in the war. I imagine him getting shot at, spending tense hours in a dusty trench at night, trying to stay alive. I can almost hear the metallic thumping of helicopters flying overhead, the shooting of guns off in the distance. Robert makes an effort to keep his letters on a positive note to shield me from the horrors. I have listened to enough news on the radio to understand our young soldiers are getting killed in masses over in 'Nam.

At first Daniel asked a lot of questions about his father and the war but now he goes on with his own simple life. He plays outside, climbs the magnolia tree, plays with friends. I keep him busy helping me with maintaining the garden, harvesting the green beans and tomatoes. It's harder to keep my own mind busy. I can collect the vegetables but my mind is always in Vietnam with Robert.

There is a man down the street. He's even a church man. He is awfully friendly with all the married women who have men off at war. The thought disgusts me. When he flirts with me by offering to help me around the house, does he not think I have integrity? I mentioned this in one of my letters to Robert and he got angry. I fear the time those two men meet again. Robert won't hurt him, but he will give him a good talking to.

I've been sick to my stomach and throwing up for a good month or so now. I pray it's not what I think.

Matt wiped a hand across his face as if Shirley's vomiting bothered him, as if visualizing his grandfather in the trenches took a toll on him.

"You okay?" I asked, reaching for his hand.

He inhaled a long breath and then sighed as he let the air escape his lungs. "I'm fine."

If anything, reading the diary and letters were drawing us closer together emotionally. Matt cleared his throat as he unfolded a letter.

July 8, 1968
My lovely Shirley,

The days drag by. I still haven't received another letter from you or more cookies. I need to know you still love me. I have to tell myself that you do. War is like that. It messes with your lonely mind. I'm sure the mail will arrive soon. For my sake, I hope so!

In your last letter you mentioned you haven't been feeling well. Has that resolved? I hope it isn't the flu and Daniel doesn't catch it. How are you coping? Maybe your brother or cousin can come around so Daniel has a man to learn from. Boys need that, you know. Are you managing to get enough side jobs to help cover the bills? You should be getting paid soon for me being over here.

Last night we had a scary experience with incoming. All is well though and no one died. There were a few shrapnel wounds but we are all okay. No need to worry. We are fine.

I want you to know I love you even more now than when I left. I think about you most of the time unless I'm trying to focus on staying alive.

Love,
Your Robert

P.S. Some scotch would be nice but you'll have to put it in a plastic bottle. Transport is rough on things. Let me know what the doctor says. Kisses.

I set the diary and letters back in the box before I stood. "I need to leave but I can't wait to read these another day."

He frowned. "I'm hooked too, but I need to know everything is okay with my grandparents. But that's the sticking point; things are far from good. Just wish I could change the outcome."

The sorrow in his eyes wrenched my heart. "I agree. It's one of those stories you can't put down, but yet you never want it to end."

Chapter Thirteen

Sophie confessed to me that she despised school. Some kids just didn't do well and apparently she was one of those students.

She said the girls gawked, speculated about where she came from. She had no friends, no one to eat lunch with. She even told me she wanted to erase lunchtime from the day.

"All I do is sit alone, or move from class to class and carry an overstuffed, heavy book bag. There are no available lockers so late in the year. No one talks to me." She pulled an overstuffed pillow into her arms and leaned against the wall of her bed.

It had been a long night and an even longer week. I frowned, unsure of how to help her. "I can talk to Mr. Dodson to see if he can do something about the locker." I tried but nothing I said made her stiff shoulders relax.

She shook her head. "The only thing I have to look forward to are the holidays."

I couldn't relate. Most kids loved time off for Thanksgiving and Christmas, but I never did. I was one of those rare kids who didn't want to spend time with the family because we argued. "I'm sure. Hang in there a little longer," I said in a dry tone.

Sophie sighed and scooted lower in bed. "All the girls do is talk about boys. Yuck. I have no use for them. All they do is grow up and yell and scream at you."

I stared at her. "Did your real father do the same thing?"

She didn't answer me. "Matt doesn't yell. Maybe men who work for the law don't do those things." Her eyes opened wider. "Or do they?"

How was I supposed to answer? "No, Matt doesn't yell, Sophie. If anyone ever shouts at you, I want you to tell me."

Thank goodness for the choir at church. Wednesday nights offered her something to look forward to. Most of the girls were older, kinder. They were busy practicing Christmas carols to sing at the upcoming event called Christmas on Front Street. Sophie said she had never participated in anything like that before, and the youth pastor promised her she had nothing to worry about. Apparently she had to learn the songs, not knowing them growing up.

In the meantime, I focused on helping Matt ready the house for Christmas, my night classes, and starting my new job. Sophie focused on homework and trying to fit in at school.

"When can we go visit Gran again?" she asked one day when I got off work early and picked her up from school. "She is the grandma I don't have." Jenni's rambunctious grandmother lived about a mile down the road from us and we had stopped by a few times. "Plus, I want to see Fran again." Fran used to be a wild horse that the foundation rescued from Pony Island, and Gran fostered several of them. Sophie related to the horses, as she considered herself a misfit. I hoped to change her outlook and to help build her self-esteem and confidence.

"We can visit this weekend," I promised. I had such small snippets of spare time in my busy schedule.

Sophie's face lit up. "Can I adopt one?"

As much as I wanted her to have an animal to love, tending to a horse sent my mind into overload. "Sorry, but with everything going on, the timing is poor."

"You mean the Christmas party that you don't even want to have."

I knew the thought of spending Christmas with Matt's family distressed her. She had never experienced a typical Christmas holiday and said she didn't know what to expect. The Christmas she experienced had almost no presents, no Christmas tree, no fancy meal other than a block of ham, no Santa Claus. She said all through elementary school she had to hear about Santa and what gifts her friends wanted him to bring. Never letting on that she knew the raw truth about Christmas, it separated her from the other kids. No child should have to keep such a secret. She told me she and Christmas weren't friends.

I suspected she planned to run off and avoid Christmas altogether, but she said nothing of the sort. I just had an unsettled feeling. Mostly because I worried about where she would go.

One night, when I asked how her day had gone at school, she started to cry. I swear my insides melted and my heart broke in two. Seeing her cry was too much for me to handle.

I pulled her into a hug, which I loved because usually she shrugged away from my touch. "What happened, Sophie?"

She choked down a sob. "Do you remember the girl we saw at the oyster roast? Carley?"

Of course, I remembered her. She hadn't been very nice to Sophie. "Yes, I do."

Sophie dragged the back of her hand across her wet cheeks. "I was concentrating on opening my locker they finally gave me. Someone pushed into my shoulder, hard."

I listened, barely breathing.

"'Move,' she said after bumping into me. She was strong, more muscular than I thought."

It took so long for her to continue, I asked, "What did you do?"

Sophie shrugged, and a tiny smile flashed across her lips. "I planted my feet onto the floor to make myself more solid. I'm not about to allow some rude girl to boss me around. No way did I dare to move."

While I was proud of her for standing her ground, her safety concerned me.

"She glared back at me." Sophie dragged in a jagged breath. "Some short girl with pretty blonde hair grabbed hold of Carley's arm. She told her to come on and leave me alone."

I pressed my hand to my mouth to squelch a gasp. "Did she leave?"

"She gritted her teeth at me like a bulldog. But her attitude doesn't intimidate me. I'm used to this treatment from the kids at my old school."

The situation was worse than I thought. No wonder she had skipped school all the time.

"I refused to move and didn't throw the first punch. All these people gathered around to watch. You know how kids love a good fight."

I knew no such thing. Aghast, I said, "Oh, Sophie. I'm so sorry you are dealing with this." I played with the back of her hair, and to my surprise, she let me.

"Then I heard this man's loud voice. He said to break it up." Sophie shrank into her bed and pulled up a blanket as if to keep her warm and protected. "The principal raised his voice and told us to take it into his office."

"I never got a phone call," I said, having no clue how to handle this situation and wanting to say the right words.

She shook her head, her hair mushing into a wild mess from rubbing across the pillow. "He threatened to call next time if we didn't knock it off."

"Just know I'm here for you and call if you need me. I can always talk to Mr. Dodson." It sounded like a dumb thing to say to her but I was out of my league here.

She stared at me. "Interfering won't change her behavior. It will make things worse." She chewed on her lip as if something else wrestled with her mind. "Why do you want to help more kids than just me? I mean, aren't I enough?"

"Oh, honey. You are wonderful." I pulled her in close to me, bundle and all.

Sophie looked away. I had to wonder if she was jealous, or bothered by the possibility of sharing my attention with others. The thought gnawed at my mind.

The next afternoon I picked Sophie up from school again. When the bell rang, the kids dispersed like wild animals being freed from their cages. I had arrived later than usual so I parked farther down the line. Sophie didn't see me and stood off to the side to wait. The girl from the oyster roast, Carley, approached her with three other girls. I wanted to climb from the truck to save her but didn't dare. She had to deal with the girl on her own. At least I waited close by if she needed me.

I lowered my window and turned off my music to hear whatever conversation possible.

Carley stepped too close, causing Sophie to plant her feet in place on the sidewalk.

"Go back to where you belong," Carley said, loud enough to attract attention from others, her friends standing close by.

"And where is that?" Sophie raised her voice. I knew her insides were probably quivering and hoped it possible to hide her shaky voice like I had suggested.

Carley stepped even closer but Sophie didn't move.

"Back to hell," Carley spat. The other girls chuckled. A group of kids started to gather around. Where were the teachers?

How did Carley know she had lived in hell?

"I'm going to beat the crap out of you and watch you crawl away."

Sophie stood taller, although she was nowhere near the same size as her aggressor. "Come back when you're alone and your friends aren't here to cheer you on."

Carley paused, apparently not used to someone challenging her.

To my surprise, Carley backed away and laughed. "Chicken. Come on girls, let's get out of here." Carley turned away and her little group followed, just as a staff member started to head their way.

Sophie spotted my truck and casually strolled toward me as if not wanting to attract any more negative attention toward her. She pulled open the truck door and climbed in.

Not wanting to embarrass her, I refrained from commenting. I pulled out of the parking lot when she said, "Wow, much easier than I thought."

I glanced at her. "What do you mean?" It didn't look easy to me.

She stared out the passenger window. "I'm not a chicken. I'm a leader, not a follower like Carley's goons. And I don't hang around bullies."

"You did well. I love how you're viewing the situation from a positive place." I didn't admit how I would have been scared myself.

"You know what, Aunt Terri? I used to think people hated me, but I'm learning from church choir to pray for people like Carley. She seems to be in as much pain as me." She swiveled in her seat in my direction. "Maybe she knows what it's like to start a new school, but I hate to see what lunch brings tomorrow."

Chapter Fourteen

The next day I pulled up in front of Sophie's school. Most of the other cars had arrived and gone, and I still waited for her. Something was wrong.

Motion in my rearview mirror caught my attention. Staring at the ground, she sauntered from the woods toward the truck. I couldn't help but wonder why she was off school property, ambling along as if apprehensive to reach me. My belly knotted with tension. I adored this girl, possibly even loved her, and wanted to protect her.

When she approached the truck, she kept her head lowered. She opened the door without so much as a hello and slid onto the seat with her gaze diverted from mine.

"Sophie?" I touched her arm to physically connect with her. "What's wrong?"

She shrugged but her attention remained on the floorboard.

I leaned over, took in her appearance, and gasped. Gently, I lifted her chin so she would look at me. "What happened?" I asked.

Her swollen face made me shudder. It already showed bruising with the makings of a black eye.

She shrugged.

I turned off the truck's ignition and opened my door.

Her voice raised an octave. "What are you doing?"

"Let's go. We're visiting the principal's office." I kicked my legs out of the truck and stood.

"No!" she cried out.

I slammed my door and headed toward the front of the school. I knew if I didn't stand around and reason with her, she would follow me eventually. With her trailing behind, we entered the school and the main office.

The woman behind the desk inhaled a sharp breath. "Oh, honey. What happened to you?"

Sophie continued to stare at the ground and didn't answer the sweet lady.

"I'd like to talk to the principal," I said.

The lady asked no questions and disappeared into Mr. Dodson's office. Within seconds, the tall man I had only met once before joined us. He flagged us inside and offered us a seat in front of his desk.

"What happened?" he asked Sophie as he sat and leaned back in his oversized black-cushioned chair.

Sophie continued to stare at the ground.

"I understand you've been in a fight, but I expect you to fill me in on the details." He waited for a few moments with patience. "Spill it," he said, more in her language.

Sophie glanced up. "I'd rather not."

I sighed in frustration. How were we supposed to help her if she refused?

"Let me guess," he said. "Does this have anything to do with Carley Davis?"

Sophie flinched, admission enough.

"What happened?" he asked.

No answer.

"Sophie, either way I'm going to find out." He waited. "I know you don't want to rat on Carley, or her friends, but I need to inform you that the consequences for fighting on school grounds are worse if you don't confess what happened."

She shrunk in her chair, giving me sudden insight as to how much I actually did love her. Yes, as in loved her.

"It wasn't on school property," she stated as she leaned back in her chair, arms crossed, head facing downward once again.

"Based on what I saw the other day, and today's incident, I have enough to give you both in-school suspension. I'll expect you to report to my office tomorrow morning." He leaned forward to make a point. "You both will sit in the same room and do your classwork together. It'll be a bonding experience."

He waited for Sophie to answer, but when she didn't, he said, "I'll see you tomorrow morning then."

When we returned to the truck, there were no longer any other cars in the parking lot. We both climbed inside without speaking but the tension could about choke someone.

After she settled in she asked, "Aunt Terri? Do I have to sit in the corner the rest of the night for fighting?"

I turned toward her so fast, she startled. "Sit in the corner?"

She glanced out the window and then back at me as if nervous. "Well, yeah. That's what my mom and stepfather make me do."

No wonder she never wanted to attend school. I struggled to fight off a fit of rage, but when I took in her slumped body and sad, bruised face, the anger drained from me. The poor child.

I reached out and took her hand. "I will never put you in the corner for anything. That's a promise."

She nodded and returned to staring out the window.

My heart went out to her. Taking care of hurting teens required a lot more than I first thought. She wasn't a lost girl but one in desperate need of love. My love.

As we drove home, I asked, "So how does the other girl look?"

A small smile parted her swollen lip. "Worse than me."

I wasn't a proponent of fighting, unless in self-defense, and I felt fairly certain that was the case. "I'm proud of you for defending yourself."

Sophie nodded, her body visibly relaxing. Tomorrow's counseling appointment couldn't have come at a better time.

The house project wasn't coming along as easily as Matt had hoped. Not sure how they were supposed to achieve everything on their wish list before the Christmas party, he grew frustrated. Terri offered to pay a contractor, but call him crazy, he refused. Making the updates himself cleared his conscious about selling the house despite the undue pressure he put on himself.

When Terri's truck pulled into the driveway, he glanced up from reorganizing the old fallen woodpile. Sophie slammed the truck door and hurried down the sidewalk. Terri shook her head with warning and he understood the silent communication not to ask Sophie about the black eye. Instead, he continued restacking the wood.

He gave them time to settle in before entering the kitchen. Terri yanked out an ice pack from the freezer, wrapped it in a clean dish towel, and disappeared into the living room along with a tall glass of water and an orange in her hands. Matt crossed his arms and leaned against the counter. The mouthwatering aroma from the crock-pot distracted him momentarily and smelled like heaven.

When Terri returned, they headed outside for privacy.

As soon as they closed the door, Matt raised his eyebrows. "What happened to Sophie?" Seeing her hurt caused an unfamiliar protective surge inside him.

"That girl at school, Carley, is giving her a rough time."

Matt let out a long, empathetic whistle. "I'd say."

Terri glanced at the pile of logs Matt had stacked. "Looks great."

"Thanks. You're going to need wood for this winter." He sat on the edge of the patio table and reached for Terri's cold hand. He took the other one and rubbed them between his.

She stepped closer and snuggled into his chest, sliding her hands underneath his coat. When she buried her cold face into his neck, he tried not to pull away in surprise.

"I hope I did the right thing by enrolling her in a public school. I can't help but feel guilty," she said, her voice muffled.

He shrugged but stared down at her. Her hair smelled fresh like honeysuckle and made him darn near giddy. He focused his attention on the subject at hand. "Where else would she go? That's the logical option, and she needs to attend school."

"I feel like I failed her." She pulled away enough to glance toward the house, and then back at him. Her expression grew serious. "Do you think I have commitment issues?"

He jerked his head up. "Why are you asking?"

She glanced away from him as she spoke. "Well, first off I could do more for Sophie than I currently am. Plus, I read a disturbing chapter in my sister's book. She wrote a scene that bothered me. These two little girls were eating pizza and their dad came home, packed his bags, and walked out without a goodbye."

Their gazes met and held. "What do you think it means?"

She wrinkled her face and scrunched her shoulders together. "I dunno. But my dad left us when we were little." She paused for a long moment. "I'm pretty sure we're the *kids*."

He wrapped his arms around her to offer comfort but didn't know what to say.

She glanced up at him, her mouth just inches from his. "Thinking back to my own small handful of relationships, I haven't trusted someone enough to develop a deep bond."

He tipped her chin upward. "Do you trust me?"

She looked up into his eyes and nodded.

He kissed her forehead without saying a word. His love, comfort, support said it all.

"How is the house coming?" she asked, and he suspected she wanted to change the subject instead of making him feel pressured to finish the project.

Matt let out a long sigh. "It will take a miracle to finish all this before Christmas."

She closed her eyes briefly as if weighing her words carefully. "The house looks fine. People are just excited to have another get-together here. They won't be comparing the house to how it used to look. Trust me on this."

Even though he found relief in her words, nothing would stop him from completing the repairs on time.

Terri's cell phone rang and broke their intimate moment. She reached into her pocket and said, "It's my sister." She clicked to answer it.

They chatted casually and then she looked up at Matt. "Sure, I'm home," she said into the phone. "Why don't you eat dinner with us. Pot roast and veggies."

Matt's stomach growled.

"See you soon." Terri hung up and snuggled back into him. "Stay for dinner too?"

"I wouldn't miss whatever you have cooking in there, but first I want to finish the wood pile." He gave her a peck, knowing full well he'd want more if he gave her a longer kiss, and turned away.

If Matt were being completely honest with himself, he was starting to have strong feelings for Terri. Okay, more than that. He might be falling in love with her.

And he cared for Sophie, even if he didn't admit his feelings to anyone to protect himself. But it about killed him when Terri brought her home all beat up and hurting. Terri had trusted him, had reached out and he reassured her about the decision she made to sign Sophie up for school. If she developed feelings for him too, he'd count himself one lucky man.

He never pushed her for more, but accepted what she was able to give him. Take it slow and steady, and give her time. He sensed she needed that.

Matt lifted several logs and neatly stacked them on the pile, ignoring the drizzle starting to fall.

When had his emotions toward Terri deepened? He suspected reading his grandparents' love letters and diary had drawn them closer, but that wasn't the only cause. He loved the way she treated Sophie, loved the way she took her in and cared for her.

After he and Julie had broken up, he decided he was better off alone, but he was wrong. He realized now his greatest fear revolved around falling in love, being vulnerable, and having the relationship fail. He'd been thinking of the past lately, his emotionally distant father, his lonely childhood. Now he understood where his fears had originated, and maybe he needed to let the hurt go.

I checked on Sophie, still lying on the couch with the ice pack covering half her face. I sat down near her feet, and to my relief, she didn't move away. As an adult, one never knew a teenager's reaction.

"What are you going to do about this girl?" I asked.

Sophie didn't move but stared up at the ceiling with her good eye. "I don't know. She's had it out for me since the oyster roast."

"I wonder why she's threatened by you?" I leaned back against the couch and put her feet on my lap.

Her uncovered eye stared at me as if she didn't understand my question.

I decided to explain. "In my experience, when someone is angry at you for no apparent reason, it usually has something to do with them personally, not you."

Sophie shrugged. "Like what?"

"I don't know. It helps to remember that, though."

The back door opened. I moved her feet off my lap and got up to see if it was Matt or Emily.

Emily closed the door behind her. "It smells fantastic in here. I'm glad I agreed to dinner."

She didn't enjoy cooking but boy, her husband knew how to make up for it. "Thanks. We're glad for the company." I pulled open the lid on the crock-pot and tested it with a fork. It fell apart with the lightest touch, as did a chunk of potato. Exactly the way I loved it. My belly growled with anticipation.

Not wanting to alarm my sister when she saw Sophie's face, I pointed to a chair at the kitchen table to suggest she relax and hang out with me for a bit. In a lower voice I said, "Just a warning, Sophie got into a fight at school today. When you see her, don't be shocked but it looks worse than it is."

Emily glanced at me with concern. "Is she okay?"

"Sure. Her feelings are hurt more than anything." I walked over to the counter. "Want coffee or sweet tea?"

"Tea."

I pulled out two glasses from the cabinet and set them on the counter, and then retrieved a pitcher of honey-colored deliciousness from the refrigerator. I liked to joke that drinking sweet tea in the South was like drinking diabetes in a cup, laden with serious sugar.

Emily leaned her elbows on the table and stared out at the light rain coming down on the marsh and water. "What a gorgeous view."

"I love it too." I sat down at the table with her as we made small talk for a few minutes, catching up on each other's lives while we drank our iced tea.

"How's your new job going, and your classes?" she asked me, setting her glass on the table.

"I'm loving the job, the freedom of driving around instead of being stuck in one place on a hospital floor." I took a swallow of tea, trying to decide how to tell her about the classes in a positive way. "The classes ... they are tedious. By that time of night I'm exhausted. Between starting a new job, Sophie starting school, and getting the house ready for the Christmas party, it's all too much."

Emily let out a low whistle. "You have a lot on your plate, sis."

"By the way, I read your book." I didn't want to discuss my deep thoughts on the pizza scene but wanted to at least share that I read it.

"What did you think?"

I gazed outside before I looked at her. "I thought it was fabulously written, a real page-turner. Seriously, Em, you have a way with words, and I had a hard time putting it down." Emily smiled, obviously happy I enjoyed it. But I couldn't hold back the truth after all. "I have to tell you the pizza scene disturbed me, like you suspected."

"I thought it might. You always say you don't remember much about life with Dad in the country. I didn't really remember him leaving until I wrote that scene." She brought the glass to her lips, swallowed a long drink.

Life with Dad in the country. I wondered if that subconsciously had anything to do with why I moved to this house.

Emily swallowed hard enough her throat moved. "I didn't understand why it bothered me until I talked to Mom."

Even though I did ask our mother about it, something felt off. "I knew instantly I was probably remembering when he left us. I can't say

I actually recall the memory in detail, but from my visceral reaction I knew the kids were us."

"I can't imagine abandoning us," she said. "I mean, how could he? It took a while before I worked through the painful memories. I couldn't even talk to him for a long while."

I studied Emily's expression, filled with agonizing pain, and held a great deal of empathy for her being the oldest child. She had so many more memories of our childhood than I held.

"Dad came to your wedding," I said, actually surprised she let him attend. "Now that I read your book and know what you were going through, I'm amazed you invited him." I took another long soothing sip of the sweet sugary goodness from my glass.

"I now understand where my abandonment issues came from," Emily said, her voice scratchy with emotion.

"I'm sure I have them too. As I've recently learned, my insecurities show up as fear of commitment." I had a hard time admitting the truth to my sister but to my surprise, a deep sense of relief replaced my anxiety. "I'm afraid of being vulnerable," I admitted. "But I do think I'm overcoming that a bit by living here in Big Cat. Did moving here help you the same way?"

Emily and I had never discussed deep topics such as this and I was happy we were becoming more open with each other. She confessed, "There is something about this coastal town, the water, the people— it's all so welcoming and makes a person feel wanted."

"You are wanted, Em."

She leaned toward me with a soft look in her eyes. "Once you see the truth, the reason behind the fear, you can heal. I did and that's when I fell deeper in love with Keith."

I thought about Matt. My history proved I only fell so far in love before I cut off the feelings or pushed them away before things became too serious.

Actually, I had done the same thing with Emily. I kept her at a distance, but her words of wisdom echoed in my mind. *Once you see the truth and the reason behind the fear, you can heal.*

I swallowed hard despite the tightness in my throat. I drank more tea but instead of helping to ease my tension, I ended up in a coughing fit.

"Thanksgiving is approaching fast." Emily hesitated, knowing full well how I felt about holidays in general. "We're inviting family over and Keith is going to cook."

My mouth watered instantly. I had heard stories about what a chef Keith was, but honestly, I had envisioned a lovely Thanksgiving with Matt and Sophie in this house.

"I know you've been seeing a lot of Matt," she continued, glancing out the window before looking back at me. "Keith and I are hoping the three of you will join us. Mom and Clark will be there too."

I stared at her, unsure of what to say. We hadn't held a family holiday get-together in a while now because ... well, we didn't really get along as a family. Matt knew Clark and was Keith's cousin, so going over there wouldn't be entirely awkward for him, and I respected Emily's attempt to bring everyone together.

"Thank you for asking us, but I envisioned staying here with Matt and Sophie. You know, a cozy day at the farmhouse." I turned from looking at her face, full of disappointment. I wanted to become closer to her, I really did, yet here I was, doing what I'd always done. I excelled at putting up emotional walls. "I'm already hosting a huge family party for Christmas." That exceeded my holiday tolerance. "Why don't you all come over for Christmas Eve? It will already be decorated for Matt's family."

Emily's jaw dropped. "You're actually going to decorate?"

"I know." I laughed and rolled my eyes. "I don't normally do Christmas, but I'm sort of excited about having it." The word excited didn't exactly describe my thoughts, but I was trying to adjust my mindset on the subject. Earlier in the year I had fantasized about skipping the holiday entirely.

With her expression still animated with amusement, she said, "You've always had a problem with Christmas and now you want to host it. Amazing."

Emily's face stiffened and I braced for whatever she dumped on me.

"Christmas is fine, but Thanksgiving ..." She hesitated. "I think you should reconsider."

I bit my tongue to prevent from saying something I might regret. I hadn't talked to Matt yet to see what his plans were, and Sophie never celebrated holidays. She had enough adjustments to deal with. Not to mention, I despised the idea of getting together. My reasoning didn't make a lot of sense to even me, but I didn't want to go over to Emily and Keith's house. Perhaps I just wasn't ready to embrace my family in full yet. As an adult, I enjoyed making my own decisions.

"I know you don't understand," I said.

She shook her head. "You're right. I don't."

That made two of us.

"What about Sophie? I'd think family would be good for her."

She was probably right. "I'll let you know if I reconsider but thank you."

The backdoor opened and in walked Matt. He smiled at Emily. "Good to see you. How's Keith these days?"

"Hope you're doing well, and he's fine," Emily said with a grin. "Talk to Terri about Thanksgiving, will you?" She headed toward the door leading to the living room. "Where's Sophie? I want to say hi."

I had almost forgotten about her. What a great foster parent I'd be.

Emily left the kitchen but reentered in a short minute, her voice hushed. "She's asleep. I need to get going anyway, but thanks for the dinner invite. How about another time?" Without waiting for an answer, she fled the house. A moment later she pulled out of the driveway.

"What was that about?" Matt asked.

Beats me. I had no idea why she had changed her mind other than she was disappointed about Thanksgiving. "Not sure. Maybe Sophie's black eye bothered her. By the way, I invited my family to a Christmas celebration here."

He did a doubletake, grinning from ear to ear. "Really?"

"Yeah, well, the myth also said I would also be married by Christmas." I held my hands up to include the house. "As you can see, I'm far from marrying anyone."

He stuck his lip out in a playful pout as he stepped toward me and wrapped me in a hug. "What about me?"

I knew he was joking and giggled.

He planted a wet kiss just below my ear. "I do have deep feelings for you."

I swallowed hard. Oh gosh, this was the first we'd talked about feelings. "Me too." The words barely escaped in a whisper.

He pulled away. "Let's read more of the diary and letters tonight. I'm hooked."

Chapter Fifteen

What a shame to have some bully beating up on Sophie. And Matt had no clue how to help her. She deserved a happy life. The kid had it bad so far and he wanted to make things better, to make her problems go away. If he could only remember how his own father had handled bully issues with the kids he mentored—though he hadn't done such a good job defending Matt when he needed him most.

Funny how he had spent years resenting his father to now look back in the rearview mirror of time to reflect on how he handled difficult issues. Matt suspected there were good and bad points about his father's parenting skills. To this day his mother remained sweet, the nurturing mom all his friends loved, an elementary teacher all the kids wanted.

After dinner Matt and Terri joined Sophie in the living room. She was still lying on the couch, looking rough. She had only eaten half her food and had pushed her plate to the farthest point on the coffee table.

"Hey, Soph. Need anything?" he asked, and Sophie glowed whenever he called her the nickname. She looked pitiful with that large black eye staring back at him. Her vulnerability drove a little imaginary knife into his soul. This was the reason his dad had helped neglected, hurting kids for years. They touched a piece of you, like seeing a lost puppy standing in the middle of a busy intersection. Sophie might be Terri's responsibility but he cared about her too.

And Matt needed to let go of the anger toward his father that he carried for years. It might take work but he needed to embrace the challenge, for his own good as well as his father's.

"Nope," Sophie said in a feigned tough voice. She pushed the ice pack aside as well, and pulled the quilt up around her shoulders.

"Why don't I make a fire first before we read the letters," Matt offered. "It's a perfect rainy night to have one." Thankful he had carried in a stack of wood earlier and piled it on the hearth as Nana had always kept it, the room begged for warm and cozy.

"Yes!" Sophie's face lit up with animation. "We don't have a fireplace at my mom's house." Matt noticed how she didn't call it home, or her house. Sad, really.

Terri curled into a spot on the love seat, and within minutes, Matt had the living room flickering with flames and a slow, emanating heat.

"Like I mentioned earlier, you're going to need to order firewood before winter sets in," he said, placing the poker into the holder. "Trust me, it will help heat this big room on those cold days." He had given her the name of a man who could deliver and stack the wood for her for a reasonable rate. The fireplace had been a life saver plenty of times. The smudged off-white mantel caught his attention, in desperate need of a paint job, and he added it to the forever growing list of things they needed to fix.

"Warm is good," Terri said. "I love this family room with the big brick fireplace. I can almost imagine your childhood Christmas gatherings here in front of the tree with a decked out hearth."

"They were the best." Staring at the golden blaze, his mind filled with images of Christmas morning. A dusty memory came to mind of a comforting fire glowing in the room along with strands of twinkling Christmas lights on the tree. It was hard to imagine how Sophie had never experienced opening presents from her perch on the couch, ripping through the paper like a small child. Terri's experiences weren't much better either. He intended to create the best Christmas yet for them both. If he succeeded he just might change their opinion of holidays.

These feelings were new to him. Never before did he care about helping two people so much.

Thinking back to Terri's question earlier about fearing commitment, he glanced at Sophie lying on the couch. Talk about a positive commitment. What would Terri do if Sophie's mom reclaimed her? Not if, but when.

Matt sat next to her on the love seat and Terri curled in closer to him. He could get used to this.

"I want to go ahead and dig out the Christmas decorations. I can't wait," she announced. Then her eyes widened and he had to laugh at her surprise. She shook her head. "Honestly, I've never said those words before. I even want to buy more decorations to make Christmas our own."

Matt winked. "It's the magic."

She elbowed him and he gulped. "It's not Shirley or any magic," she said, "but I will say this house does make me feel all loving and snug like a comforting hug."

He winked at Sophie, who remained quiet and watching them with interest. "Why don't we decorate this weekend then? Saturday?" He looked forward to reliving a piece of his beloved youth.

"Yes," Terri said. "Sophie, you in?"

Sophie looked down at the blanket covering her and pushed it off her knees. The warmth from the fire filled the room like the good old days. "Sure. I've never decorated a house for Christmas before, or for any holiday."

Terri's mouth fell open but Matt wasn't all that surprised.

"Then let's make a big deal out of decorating," Terri said with a big lopsided grin on her face. "I was never big on it either. This will be the start of a tradition. We can roast a chicken, bake a homemade pecan pie and cookies, play loud Christmas music, build a roaring fire in the fireplace." She raised her eyebrows and glanced at Matt.

He wondered about the person she was becoming.

"Nana has a Christmas tree in a bag in the attic," he suggested. "We can dig it out and check out what condition it's in."

Terri studied him. "I've never put up my own tree."

"A lot of first-time experiences this Christmas." Matt was glad to witness the change in Terri. "I feel life coming back to this house and love it. My grandmother is here with us in spirit."

Sophie's smile filled his heart with pride. More than anything he wanted the two of them to enjoy Christmas this year. Perhaps the positive changes in Terri were because of Sophie, maybe even because of him.

"I think we should combine your family get-together with mine, instead of having two different ones," he suggested.

Terri stared at him. "I don't want to intrude on your traditional Christmas Day. I mean, I love the idea but your family get-together is important to you."

"No intrusion at all." He squeezed her knee for reassurance and the touch woke up emotions in him that had been lying dormant for many years. Sophie watched them closely but he didn't meet her gaze. If this was going to work, she needed to get used to their increasing affection toward each other. Maybe Terri should have a talk with her, so she understood anything Terri and he felt for each other didn't take away an ounce of how they cared for her. It would have helped had his father told him the same thing when he was young.

"I want to make sure combining our families is the right thing to do," she continued.

"It is, trust me on this. Ready to read the diary and letters?" He couldn't wait to dive into them again.

"What are you reading?" Sophie asked, popping a wedge of orange into her mouth that Terri had cut up for her.

The bruising and swelling of her eye had already improved, thanks to the ice.

"A diary and letters from the Vietnam War," Terri explained. "They are from Matt's grandparents, and we found them in an old hat box in the attic."

Sophie's expression lit up her face, making her look unbruised and youthful again. "I'd be interested in reading those."

"How about we read them out loud like Matt and I do?" At Sophie's nod, Terri removed herself from Matt's arms and retrieved the treasured items from underneath the coffee table. She handed the love letters to him, and then opened the diary to a new entry. "Who wants to read first?"

Matt flagged his index finger at her. "Go ahead." Sophie sat up taller on the couch with her attention focused on them.

Nana's Diary: July 11, 1968

I miss Robert more than I can ever say in writing. Every night I lie in bed wishing he were here with me. I have this sense of underlying worry I can't explain. I worry about how I'm going to pay the bills, worry about him surviving the war and returning to me and Daniel. A boy needs his father, a wife needs her husband. If he doesn't come back home, how will I survive? I love him so much.

I met him in the fifth grade in a tiny schoolhouse down the road. He used to pass me notes and invite me to walk home with him once school was over for the day. Sometimes we met under the large oak tree for lunch. His mother often packed me an apple along with his. Such sweet memories.

But my imagination always takes over. I am so connected to him I have visions of him being shot at in the trenches. I imagine him patrolling the hospital grounds at night, in the rain or heat, to protect the medics inside trying to save lives. I can even hear the choppers flying overhead.

I try not to concern Robert with my health but I'm truly not feeling well. I have a doctor's appointment tomorrow but I suspect I am pregnant. I am excited about the possibility of a baby, especially a girl since we already have a boy. Boys tend to run in both of our families though. My grandparents had five, and each of them had five more. The chance of me having a girl seems unlikely but I never give up hope. If God can move mountains, he can certainly bless me with a baby girl, although in all truth, I'm not sure how well I will handle having another child with Robert in Vietnam. The timing seems off to me but then again, who am I to judge? The man upstairs is in charge.

Terri leaned forward and set the leather diary on the edge of the coffee table. "I want to read more but also want to savor each entry since there aren't too many left. I need to pace out my pleasure."

Matt nodded. "It's like reading a good book. You can't wait to read more but you don't want the story to end."

"Exactly," Terri said.

Sophie was now sitting on the edge of the couch and with her elbows on her knees. "That was amazing. I can't wait to find out if she's pregnant and having a girl."

"Me, either," Terri said. "Her doctor's appointment is the next day. And I really want to peek ahead but don't want to ruin the surprise." She scooted back on the love seat and curled into Matt.

He opened the first letter and unfolded it.

July 16, 1969
My lovely Shirley,

I received three of your sweet letters today. I turned in early so I could read them before it got dark. The mosquitos are something awful over here and will eat a man alive. We have nets over our cots to protect us, so I try not to turn on my light. That's why I'm writing you before dark.

It's so dang hot. I miss home, I miss YOU, I miss Daniel. In my mind I pretend I'm lying on the beach next to you, hoping to trick myself. Have you been to the beach with Daniel lately? Summer here stinks. It hasn't rained in a long while and when the choppers come in, it stirs up dust something fierce. You have to keep your mouth closed and shut your eyes, but then you have a layer of dust on your eyelids. It's better if you can cover your eyes with your hands.

What I wouldn't give to be home with you and Daniel. I even miss something as simple as fishing. Has your brother taken out the boat yet? Someone might as well use it. Tell him not to catch all the fish while I'm gone, though.

How are you handling things? I miss you and need you in my arms. You have a birthday coming up. What will you do to celebrate? I wish I could hug you and give you a kiss. You have no idea how lonely the nights are here without you. The faster I can go to sleep, the faster I can dream about you. I haven't heard what the doctor said yet so let me know. I love you!

Love,
Your Robert

Matt shifted his weight on the love seat. "I can't imagine how hard it is to miss your family so much." Then it hit him. Daniel, his father, grew up without a dad. Maybe that explained his emotional distance from Matt as he was growing up. It made sense. Matt found he was developing more empathy for his father.

Terri leaned away to allow Matt to shift around and find his comfortable spot before she settled in against him. He truly enjoyed reading the words of his grandparents and valued the bonding experience it offered them.

"I'm getting to know my grandfather in ways I never imagined. Prayers do get answered." His eyes turned moist. He glanced away from Terri to avoid eye contact.

"What a sweet love story," she said. "I love the part about the schoolhouse."

"And I want to know about the baby," Sophie added again.

"Me too. I can't wait to hear more," Terri said. "Matt, so Shirley remarried and had four boys?"

"Yep, no girls." Matt cleared his throat.

"So the pink blanket we found in the box ..." Terri's voice trailed off.

Matt cleared his throat, not wanting to imagine the possible scenarios about the pink blanket when there were no girls in the family except Nana.

"Ready?" he asked, changing the subject. His voice sounded raspy as he began to read.

July 19, 1968
My lovely Shirley,

Thank you for the cookies. I shared them with my two friends, Bill and Denny. Bill is a medic and Denny is the one I told you about who is in infantry with me. We ate most of the cookies in one sitting. It rained here most of the day, turning everything into a stream of mud. The ground was so dry and hard the water ran right off the dirt at first and made little rivers. I hear it will start raining more often once we enter the cooler season. I am ready!

I think about you every night as I try to sleep. The nights are still warm but it's cooler than it was when I first arrived. The relief is nice.

How are you feeling? Your last letter said you were going to the doctor. I'm starting to get concerned. I hope you don't push off your appointment as you usually do. I hope it's not something serious.

Can I put in another request for some scotch in a plastic bottle and more cookies? I suppose I could sell them over here for a lot of money, not that anyone here has much money. Speaking of that, how are you handling the finances? I know this is hard on you. Just know I love you. More than you even know.

Tell Daniel I said hi and that I love him too. Please pray for me.

Love,
Your Robert

"Wow." Sophie sat back against the couch and pulled the blanket back over her.

Terri exhaled. "They must have really cared for each other. I don't think our generation loves like that."

Matt turned to look at her. "What do you mean?"

She avoided his gaze and stared at the crackling fire. "I think people are busy doing their own thing. They've all been hurt before and are afraid to open up."

He watched her closely. "Are you speaking from experience?"

She risked a glance his way. "Sure. I'm busy."

He wrapped his arm around her to offer support. "What about the hurt part?"

She lowered her gaze to her lap as if wondering why she brought up the subject. "Yeah, my dad leaving us when I was a kid messed me up for relationships. I didn't realize the extent of my problem until lately."

Matt played with a strand of her soft, fragrant hair. "Love doesn't have to hurt, Terri."

Her gaze slowly met his. He leaned forward and kissed her gently, well aware Sophie was in the room, so he pulled back.

"Believe me, I'm not going to leave you like your dad did," he mumbled, his lips not far from hers.

She blinked several times. "I want to believe you."

"We can work through any issues if we communicate." He played with the back of her hair with his large hand. "The only way I'd leave is if you asked me to."

Sophie climbed from the couch. "I'm out of here. It's getting gross." But she wore a wide grin on her face as she spoke.

"Sorry," Terri and Matt both said. They scooted farther apart from each other as if to behave.

Sophie grinned at them. "I have homework anyway." She darted from the room, leaving her melted ice pack on the coffee table.

Terri said, "I think she actually enjoys seeing us together because she's likely never witnessed a real family setting at her home. You know, that feeling of security or something."

"You might be right," he said. "I know I like it." He ran his lips across her neck.

She flicked her hand at him before she stood and retrieved the pack. "Be right back. I'm going to put this in the freezer in case she needs it again."

"You're good at this and you'll be a great foster parent." He knew he hadn't fully supported her along the way but she held a gift for caring for others.

She stopped dead in her tracks and flashed a wide grin at him. "I appreciate those words more than you know."

After she left the room, he opened another letter. "Terri! You need to read this," he called out.

She hurried back into the living room. "You're reading them without me? I can't believe you." She picked up a pillow from the couch and tossed it at him. He remembered all too well the pillow fight they had when she first moved here.

He buried his gaze back in the letter. "Sorry, but I'm hooked. We can't stop now." He began to read out loud as she snuggled back into him.

> *July 29, 1968*
> *My lovely Shirley,*
>
> *I swear God watches over me. Yesterday we had to defend the hospital. I spent some scary time shooting from the trenches but I'm okay. I have no control over here. Sometimes I feel so tough, and sometimes so afraid.*
>
> *To relieve stress we walked into town for the afternoon to drink and get somewhat intoxicated. A couple of the guys sat at the bar and read their Dear John letters. That's where their girlfriends break up with them. Sad. I'm so glad I have you!*
>
> *Village life is interesting. Some of the pregnant women work the cotton or rice fields to induce labor when they know our medics will be in town. Somehow word gets out they are arriving. They help them with labor and medical treatments, mostly for sexual diseases and prevention. We might as well treat them to protect our men. Many of the women are rather loose around here and some of the guys pay them for sex. Don't worry, I will never do that. The thought is repulsive to me. Besides, there is only one woman for me. That's you!*
>
> *Your last letter sounded sad. I know the distance is hard on you but I can't help wonder if something else is bothering you. You aren't going to break it off with me are you? Not to make you feel guilty but you are the only thing getting me through this war.*
>
> *Please write back to me soon. I can't stand not knowing what's wrong.*
>
> *Love,*
> *Your Robert*

"I have to know more," she said, thumbing through the delicate diary. She stopped and pointed to an entry. "Here! I think I found it."

> *Nana's Diary: July 24, 1968*
>
> *My sorrow has been so heavy I haven't been able to cope with writing Robert much. I know what letters I do write sound depressing. The last thing my loving husband needs to deal with is my heart-wrenching grief. I need him to keep his focus and stay alive. I can't lose two people I love dearly.*
>
> *Turns out all this time I was having morning sickness. I need to find a way to tell him the sad news. I could wait until he gets home, but I can't stand the thought of him never knowing, in case he doesn't return.*
>
> *I lost our baby. They say it's not my fault but tell my heart that. I had spent my evenings making her this beautiful pink blanket, although I didn't know for sure our baby was a girl. In my heart though, I know it was. Now I just stare at the blanket and cry. I know I'm blessed to have Daniel and I need to be cheerful to help him deal with life without his father. But it's so hard.*
>
> *I am going to write Robert tonight. I pray he will handle it well.*

Terri wiped tears from her face. "She lost the baby girl she wanted so badly," she said between sobs.

Matt fought his own emotions to keep Terri from crying more. "That explains the pink blanket we found in the box." It was difficult to talk.

"It's full of her tears. I want to snuggle the pink fluffy blanket in my arms like Shirley did."

It was probably full of years of dust, but he didn't say anything.

"Don't stop reading. I want to hear what happens," she said so quietly he barely heard her.

With shaking hands, he unfolded the next letter.

> *August 5, 1968*
> *My lovely Shirley,*

My heart is breaking in two. I wish I could have been there for you. Why do I have to be away now in this stupid war when my wife needs me? I am so sorry you had to go through a miscarriage alone. Life is so unfair.

I want you to know I love you so much! When I get home, we'll try for another baby. I promise you that.

I look around at all these kids fighting a war we have no business being in. I see so much death that it's almost overwhelming. I don't mind telling you how sad I am. You were brave and I appreciate knowing. If I could get on a plane and return home right now, I would do it. I should never have signed up for the military in the first place.

I know regrets aren't going to help. I'm glad your sister and mother were there for you and I hope they continue to support you. Just know I'm only a letter away and you remain in my dreams every night.

With a broken heart, I'm headed to bed. We have an early morning.

Love,
Your Robert

P.S. See that smudge on the righthand side of this letter? That's my tear. It dripped on the page before I could stop it. Take care, honey. I love you.

Terri's face puckered into a frown. "My nerves are shattered into thin frayed fibers." She sobbed, burying her wet face into Matt's shirt as he held her. His own chest heaved and he suspected she knew he was crying too.

He tried to wrap his mind around Nana's loss. Such a wonderful person, so kind, so loving. She didn't deserve such heartbreak. And except for family support, she had been alone in this big house.

"I already respect her," Terri continued, "but now I appreciate her more. It's an honor to live in her home."

"I'm glad you feel that way," he said, sweeping her into his arms.

"It's a good thing Sophie went upstairs when she did." Terri let out a long sigh. "But it's important for her to know. I'll tell her in the morning about losing the baby."

He nodded. "Probably a good plan."

"We have enough to deal with tomorrow," Terri said with an exasperated sigh. "I have to drop her off at the principal's office for detention."

Chapter Sixteen

Matt unlocked the door to Terri's house. She was working today but had given him the spare key so he could make progress on his day off. He wanted to paint the mantel and then start on the kitchen cabinets. She wanted them painted white, her idea, not his, requiring an attitude adjustment on his end.

She wasn't completely on board with restoring the house to the original style of his grandmother. He understood her argument to update instead of restore, but he was having difficulty with some of the changes. It felt like letting go of Nana. His problem, not Terri's.

She owned the house now, not him, a difficult thought to swallow. It wasn't that he had control issues so much as he had nostalgia issues.

The mantel was easy to repaint. He was finished in no time and crossed it off the long list of things still needing attention. He wanted to replace the screen door, a few rotten deck boards, although staining them would have to wait until spring, and several light fixtures needed replacing. In general, he agreed with her choices for the fixtures but they weren't an original look.

He finished the repairs early morning. After a quick bite to eat, he sent Terri a text offering to make a trip to the hardware store to purchase the supplies needed to start the cabinet project.

Instead of answering the text, she walked inside, the screen door portion opening with ease now and no longer slapping against the wood. A gust of cold air blew inside with her. Bundled up in her coat, she closed both doors behind her.

"I think you brought winter inside with you," he said. She smelled of fresh cold air and saltwater combined. He wrapped her in an embrace, pushing long strands of her windblown hair from her face, and planted a light kiss on her lips. She was the most beautiful woman he had ever seen, lovely from the inside out. He slid his hands inside her coat and around her waist as his kiss lingered.

When they came up for air, she leaned back to meet his gaze. "Let's go to the hardware store together. We can pick out paint, although white is white."

"I get to choose?" he asked, teasing her. They were making progress if they could joke about the changes now, but he needed to let her pick out the color without his input. Like she said, white was white.

He grabbed his coat from the back of the chair. Outside the marsh was blowing from the wind gusts, as well as the tops of the trees. The windchimes from the magnolia tree clanged together in a loud cry for attention. Despite the cold, glorious sunshine filled the cloudless, Carolina-blue sky. He loved weather on the coast.

Once in the hardware store, they compared different variations of white from cooler to warmer, and different brushes and materials. The choices appeared to overwhelm Terri, so he narrowed down the selection by making a couple of suggestions.

Matt checked the time on his cell phone. "It's getting late. Let's get back and start sanding." He was eager to start the project.

As if she had read his mind, she said, "I'm excited to start too. Also, at some point I thought we could drag down the Christmas boxes from the attic."

Matt stared at her in disbelief. "You read my mind. I didn't say anything in front of Sophie but I'm shocked you are so eager to decorate, especially before Thanksgiving."

She laughed. "Eager isn't the correct word."

"Right. The holiday magic is working on you."

She swatted him. "I'm decorating for you, for Sophie too."

"Yep." He dodged her love tap once more and headed toward the checkout counter.

Once they returned to his truck, Terri asked, "Do you mind if we stop off at Sophie's school? It's almost time to pick her up."

"Sure. Will she recognize my truck?" Although things were getting better, he still felt Sophie saw him as a threat, but he hid his concern from Terri. It was possible he was misreading the situation.

"I'm sure she will." Terri stared out the window as if lost in thought.

While they sat in car line Matt brought up the topic of date night. "I'd still love to go out with you. It seems the house project is taking up most of our time."

She smiled as if excited at the thought of alone time outside her home.

"Dinner, maybe a walk on the beach, or downtown?" he asked. "It's decorated for Christmas already." He loved the holiday season, this year especially.

Terri groaned. She tapped her hand on her lap as if uncomfortable with the topic. "Because I love Christmas so much?"

Matt laughed. "That's an old script you are playing. What's the story behind you not liking Christmas anyway?"

She grew thoughtful. "My family always argues. My mom is too formal, I'm too casual, and Emily is too festive." She turned toward him, her expression growing serious. "At least that was the reason I always believed until I read that scene in my sister's book."

"That's no surprise. That was a significant event in your life." The scenario she had shared disturbed him on a deep level. No child should have to deal with their father abandoning ship without so much as a goodbye. "I'm sure that changed your life in many ways."

"No kidding. My mom cried a lot. She spent most of our evenings together talking to her best friend on the phone. I mean, I understand now but as a kid I felt neglected. Some details are coming back." Terri turned to stare out the passenger window.

Matt felt a punch to his gut. "And how does that remind you of Christmas?"

She exhaled before she answered. "He left at Christmastime."

"Oh, wow." It was Matt's turn to glance out at the scenery. The leaves were falling late this year. When he looked back, he noticed a tear sliding down Terri's cheek. He wiped the damp streak off her face with his thumb and placed his hand behind her head.

She dragged in sobs. It was that moment when Sophie surfaced from the building, a frown on her face as she stared at his truck.

Matt lifted his hand to wave, meant to welcome her.

Sophie flashed him a mortified expression as if the simple fact he was there embarrassed her. Without addressing him, she climbed into the back seat and stared out the window.

After Matt pulled the truck away from the curb, Sophie asked, "Why is she crying?"

Her tone of voice implied he was the reason for Terri's tears. "She was sharing something painful with me." He glanced in the rearview mirror. "How was school?"

Sophie continued to stare out the window. "How do you think it went?"

Terri turned around in her seat to face Sophie. "What's going on? Tell us what happened."

Quiet filled the truck. After several minutes, Sophie almost whispered. "I had to sit in a room with Carley all day long." She remained quiet for several moments before she continued. "We didn't talk. It was so quiet I finished my school work in record time, so I sat there and stared at a tree outside the window for hours."

Terri sighed. "What a horrendous day."

Silence fill the truck once again as Matt pulled into the driveway. As soon as he parked, Sophie made a run for the house.

"Poor kid," he said. "I was hoping they'd talk and become friends."

"Me too." Terri climbed from the truck. Together they carried in the supplies from the hardware store.

Terri went upstairs to check on Sophie, and Matt began the daunting task of emptying the cabinets. Eventually Terri joined him.

"Why did I bother to unpack my dishes?" She began to pull them out of the cabinets and stacked them back into boxes. "Good thing I hadn't recycled yet."

Matt grinned. He began removing the cabinet doors and hardware while she finished emptying them. Thankfully he had thought to bring one of the hinges to the hardware store to match it as well as possible.

"Did Sophie open up to you?" Despite her irritation toward him today, he cared about her well-being.

Terri lifted a handful of plates and placed them in a box on the floor. "She's stressed, unhappy with school, and downright miserable. I'm afraid she's planning to run away again."

Matt glanced up at her. "I hope not. I hate to say it but from my experience that's what runaways do. They leave."

She glared at him. "You're biased because of your childhood experiences."

"I hope so. She needs you."

Terri scooted closer to Matt and kissed him on the cheek. "Sometimes I wonder if she needs to return home. But Matt, that place is awful." Tears filled her eyes for the second time today. "I don't want her to leave."

He pulled her in closer. "Me either."

They worked side by side for the next hour without a hitch. In Matt's opinion, a good test for the survival of a relationship was how a couple handled household projects together.

He fought with removing a hinge. The darn thing wouldn't budge. He used his drill to reverse the screws but they were old and corroded. Nothing so far in this house was easy to fix. It was a test of his patience.

"My ex-girlfriend and I fought whenever we attempted to do any project around the house." He slipped the statement in while he was unscrewing hardware.

She looked up. "Were you living with her?"

"No." He set the screwdriver on the countertop and carried the cabinet door into the front dining room where he had piled the other doors. He had marked each one along with individual bags of hardware with a sticky note and a number, so he knew what went together. He learned the hard way to label them, so they aligned easily later.

"Tell me more," she said, pulling out a sheet of sandpaper. She began to work on the frame of the cabinet.

He swallowed hard before speaking.

"I dated Julie off and on for four years. She was dynamic, severely independent, but I grew up traditionally." He drew in a long breath and released it. "My mom stayed home when I was really young and then became a teacher. She cooked seven days a week, cleaned the house. It sounds old fashioned but I loved it."

The screw loosened and he pulled off the door, carrying it into the other room. When he returned, he continued telling her the story of his past. "I thought I loved her more than anything, but looking back, I had a false idea of relationships."

"So you tried to make her into your mother?" Terri asked.

"Pretty much." He began to unscrew another hinge on the next set of cabinet doors. "My mom was the best. She was always busy hanging laundry on the line in the backyard, cooking, gardening."

"Sounds similar to Shirley."

He stilled the screwdriver. "I never made that connection before. Guess I grew up in a sheltered, old-fashioned household. But there's more to it."

"To the breakup?"

He nodded.

"How so? And how long ago?"

Here was the sticking point. "A year. I hoped we would rekindle our relationship, settle our differences, but she has no interest."

He spotted the exact moment Terri pulled away emotionally. She stilled, a blank expression crossing her face.

"So you want her back?"

How was he supposed to be truthful yet not scare her? "I did, but not anymore. We aren't meant to be together."

She crossed her arms. "I didn't realize you are still emotionally involved with someone."

"I'm not." The dang stubborn screw refused to budge. He set the screwdriver down with a thud. It was too difficult to focus on two things at once, especially a topic like this. "I've fallen for you."

He let the words float in the air, so she could absorb what he was saying.

"Me too." She sanded hard and fast at the poor frame as if to ignore the sudden intimacy. "Does she live near here? How long have you known her?"

He was hoping for more acknowledgement about his love for her but guessed she was stuck on trying to figure out if he still had feelings for Julie. "She lives down the street from me. I've known her since fifth grade." Tell her the truth, all of it. "I used to chase her around the playground until she no longer liked me. In middle school I used to wait for her outside her classroom or greet her at her locker until she started avoiding me. She was the only girl I've dated seriously."

"Why me?"

A confused expression crossed his face. "What do you mean?"

"Why are you here, trying to develop a connection with me? Why aren't you running after her?" Terri pulled her arms tighter across her chest.

"I tried for a while but gave up. I'm in love with you." There, he said the truth.

She froze in place.

That wasn't quite the reaction he wanted. In slow motion she appeared to be processing the risk level of being involved with him now that she knew about Julie, and weighing out her feelings toward him. Then she uncrossed her arms and folded herself into Matt. Thank goodness.

"I love you too."

The words were surprising and offered him relief. "I'm one lucky man."

Sophie entered the room. "Why?"

They both turned toward her but remained in each other's arms.

"Why?" Sophie asked again. "What are you talking about?"

Terri let go of him and stepped toward her, but the teenager retreated backward.

"Whenever I think my mom, or you, will finally have time for me, she meets a man." Sophie's facial features hardened. "I know this situation well. You'll pull away and spend all your time with him, and then he starts drinking and yelling at me. Then I'm no longer welcome."

"Oh, honey." Terri moved toward her despite Sophie's likely desire to bolt. "You are always welcome here with me."

Before Sophie escaped, Terri pulled her into a long hug. The teen closed her eyes and wept.

Matt stood there, unsure of what to say or do. The gnawing burn in his belly refused to ease. He wanted to know more about Sophie's family life, know if Ralph had hurt her in anyway before she ran away. Would she be safe when she did return home?

Chapter Seventeen

I was beginning to doubt my skill at foster parenting. If I had trouble with one thirteen-year-old girl, how was I supposed to handle a houseful? The counselor didn't seem helpful, mostly because Sophie said she didn't trust anyone enough to share her thoughts with. I could understand her reasoning to a point, although it helped not to hold all the painful feelings inside your mind.

During my class one night, I decided to ask the teacher about Sophie. She was also my caseworker, helping me with the paperwork and the process of becoming a foster parent, but up until this point I hadn't mentioned Sophie to her.

"She's staying with you? Is DSS involved?" Ms. Phillips focused on legalities rather than answering my questions.

"Yes, she's staying with me. No, DSS isn't involved," I said with impatience. What I wanted was a miracle answer as to how to help manage Sophie. "I have written permission from her mother agreeing to allow her to stay with me." The conversation stirred up my defensive side.

The older woman, her glasses positioned on the far tip of her nose, fixed her pointed stare upon me. I fought off the urge to feel intimidated. My plan was to gather information from her, nothing more.

"What you describe is normal behavior," she said in a sharper than necessary voice. "For one thing she is a teenaged girl who has experienced some unknown level of trauma." She continued to stare down her nose at me. "That's why it's best for the community to utilize DSS and foster parents. You have no idea what Sophie has dealt with at home."

"I'm not trying to hold her back, just simply helping out a child I care about." I fought off a rising wave of panic. The last thing I wanted was for her to make trouble for me and Sophie. I needed to stay calm if I expected advice from her.

There was no response from Ms. Phillips.

I didn't want to divulge too many details, especially about Sophie's detention for fighting. Without a doubt that would increase Ms. Phillips judgment of the situation. No thanks. My worst fear was DSS removing her from my home.

Ms. Phillips pushed her glasses up her nose. "She needs counseling to help her adjust to her new situation. DSS provides what the child needs." Ms. Phillips maneuvered around her desk chair to stand in front of the class again, ready to teach. She leaned toward me. "Sign her up with a female counselor, give her extra love, and listen if she wants to talk."

"She is seeing a female counselor, and I think it's helping already ... I appreciate the advice." Okay, so I glorified the situation with the counselor helping. I turned on my heels and returned to my seat, trying to welcome her insight.

As Ms. Phillips prattled on to the class, my mind drifted to how my life was changing from the aloof, busy career professional to the caring woman who valued quality time with those I loved. Meeting Matt and Sophie had started me down a complicated path of learning some painful lessons, but the reward was my heart filled with a love that I hadn't known existed. In fact it amazed me at what a sheltered, unfeeling existence I had lived. Pathetic really. Instead of relying on my close relationship with my mother to fulfill my social needs, I was learning how to allow people inside my protective bubble.

The once sturdy walls guarding my heart were crumbling.

The following morning I crawled from bed, thankful for a weekend off from work and class. I padded into the kitchen, surprised I had forgotten about the chaotic mess of the cabinet makeover. I had wanted to make homemade pancakes or sausage, biscuits, and gravy but I settled for cereal.

Matt planned to arrive in thirty minutes or so. Our main focus this morning would be sanding cabinets until Sophie awoke. We then planned to switch our attention to decorating for Christmas. In the past, I waited until two weeks before the holiday to put up an undecorated table tree, and then on New Year's Day threw it away.

The quiet of the morning was always my favorite time of day. I ate my cereal at the table and lost myself in the peaceful view of the marsh. I watched as two white birds scurried around in the grass near the dock. A handful of seagulls overhead called out as if lulling me into a tranquil meditation. Every day I valued the blessing of moving to this house on the water.

Sophie popped into my mind. We were a gift to each other. She was a rare and valuable gem other people overlooked. Once I finished my training class I was looking forward to helping a few more girls. This house begged for kids to fill the rooms, though my intuition screamed Sophie wasn't going to appreciate sharing with other girls.

The thought disturbed me on a deep level. I had to decide if I wanted to help only one girl when I had planned to help several. Spreading the gift of love to others appeared a better option, but maybe I was wrong. Perhaps it was detrimental to Sophie by diffusing my attention. I knew Matt wasn't fond of my idea, either, of becoming a foster parent to a number of kids.

I hurried and showered although I knew he would let himself inside. Until I moved here I had been reserved, more private. I was changing.

I heard noise in the kitchen and knew he had arrived. My mood lifted and a sense of peace filled me. I needed to break the habit of overthinking everything and live more in the moment. But here I was doing it again, overthinking things.

Before long I met Matt in the kitchen. He set down his sandpaper to step forward and greet me with a long, delicious hug. His chest felt muscled, his embrace steady and safe. What was I so afraid of? Vulnerability was crucial when building a relationship.

He wasted no time. He handed me the sheet of sandpaper, which I tried to fold in half but it was thick and not cooperating well.

"I figured we could work until Sophie wakes up," he said, "as we had discussed yesterday."

"I'm excited about going through all Nana's things."

He smiled as if all knowing.

I stuck out my tongue at him. "It has everything to do with Sophie. Nothing else." My voice was playful, my heart light.

He reacted with a grin. "Whatever. Whether you choose to admit the truth or not, the house is changing you."

I grumbled but had to admit he might be right. "I agree I'm changing but it's not because of a house." I wanted to wipe the grin off his face.

He kissed the tip of my nose.

Before long, we laid drop cloths atop the counter and were busy sanding the aged brown cabinets in full earnest.

"Let's talk about Thanksgiving," Matt said, bringing up the awkward subject first as we worked.

I paused with the sandpaper in my hand. "I've been meaning to mention it to you. After all, it is next week." I swallowed hard to ready myself for the inevitable conversation.

"I figured we'd spend the holiday together," Matt said without looking up. He rubbed hard at the back corner of the cabinet. "My family gets together at my uncle's house if you're interested. Eating dinner with your family sounds fun too."

Thrilled he wanted to spend the holiday with me and Sophie, I needed to explain to him about my wish to stay here with just the three of us. Maybe enjoy lighting the fireplace, watching movies, reading the letters and the diary. No stress, no family arguments, no awkward conversations.

He paused. "What aren't you telling me?"

I busied myself with sanding the frame of the corner cabinet. I hated to admit my weakness about families and holidays ... most people loved get-togethers. Was there something wrong with me?

"Terri?" He stepped toward me and reached out to still my arm.

I stopped working. "Oh, Matt." His expression was so serious, I touched my fingers to his yummy chest.

"What's going on?"

"I just want to have Thanksgiving here with the three of us. I'm not in the mood for a formal dinner where everyone is prim and proper. I don't want to dress up, and as you can see, I'm casual." I pointed at my ratty jeans with a hole in the knee, and my thin sweatshirt splattered with paint.

Matt laughed. "That's what I like about you. You're down-to-earth and real."

I wasn't sure he was actually giving me a compliment. "Hmmm, if you insist." I laughed and rolled up my sleeves because it had suddenly grown hot. "I just want to stay home with you and Sophie. Is that so bad? I swear I'm not totally antisocial." He deserved honesty.

The corner of his lip scrunched upward and he added an eye roll.

"You don't care?" His reaction surprised me.

He laughed, a low rumble. "I'm all for family get-togethers but sometimes they're difficult. Look at what we're going through for our Christmas party. My dad's not entirely on board either."

Our Christmas party. Surprisingly, I rather enjoyed the sound of those pleasant words.

He went back to sanding the cabinet. "I admit, the situation is a little awkward anyway."

"Why is that?"

"I've mentioned before how I dated the same woman until college. We broke up but when I came home we dated briefly. I discovered we just weren't in the same place." He paused and set the sandpaper down on the countertop. "The piece you might not know is Keith and Emily are friends with her. Keith and I used to hang out together with Julie in high school."

I stared at him. Julie? I hadn't known her name until now. "Wait a minute. Emily is friends with her too?" Why hadn't she said something? I felt like everyone was keeping a dirty little secret from me.

"It's not a big deal. They hang out once in a while."

I wasn't sure why but the fact I was the only one who didn't know this bothered me. Maybe I was jealous a bit and cared for Matt more than I realized.

He laughed again, the same low rumble. "Have faith, sweetheart.

It's nothing." He patted the back of my shoulder.

Apparently I had some work to accomplish in the faith department.

"Let's spend Thanksgiving here," I suggested, changing the subject. "Just the three of us. I'll cook and we can relax by the fire." Holiday cooking wasn't my strength but I planned to make the most delicious turkey ever.

He smiled as he rubbed the age off the old cabinet. "I'd love to spend the day with my two favorite women."

My body filled with a gooey warmth like I'd eaten a brownie square straight from the oven.

Having accomplished a plan to make my first Thanksgiving spread with Matt and Sophie, I turned on my favorite music. The bouncy tune reverberated from my portable speaker as I bopped in place. Without feeling self-conscious, I began to sing in Spanish. From the corner of my eye I saw Matt watching me but I ignored his interest and continued to belt out tunes. I'm sure I was off-key but I was comfortable with him and wasn't bothered in the slightest.

We lost ourselves in the hard, dusty work of the project. Our courtship was unusual in the fact we hadn't dated officially, but yet we were growing closer each day. Originally we had agreed to dinner tonight at a fancy restaurant, but now that we made today a working day along with decorating for Christmas, the date had to wait. My focus was to celebrate Sophie's first decorating experience by roasting a chicken. Certainly that would be similar to baking a turkey. At some point Matt and I would enjoy a dinner date out, so I refused to worry about it. That was proof enough I was changing.

With the two of us working together, we'd made tremendous progress by the time Sophie entered the kitchen. She stretched her arms high over her head and yawned. "No pancakes?" She flashed a look of aggravation at Matt as if he were the cause of the mess. Actually he was, but I was thrilled.

Our plan to spend today together decorating was a wonderful opportunity for Matt and Sophie to resolve their differences.

I pointed to the cabinet mess before me. "It's a cereal day. That's the best I can do."

She shrugged in her usual way and collected the breakfast items I left out for her. She sat in my usual spot at the table. I recognized her gaze as she stared out the window at the peaceful view while she shoveled a spoonful of cereal into her mouth.

When she finished, I set down my sandpaper and washed the dust from my hands. "Ready to embark on the decorating festivities?" I asked her. To my surprise, my voice held enthusiasm.

"Yes!" She came alive with excitement. She rinsed out her bowl and put her dishes in the new, much appreciated dishwasher.

Matt straightened and stretched his back, eyeballing the progress we were making. When he washed his hands, I was practically giddy with excitement.

"Well, let's get started." I spun on my heel and headed toward the stairs with a little extra bounce in my step.

Once we reached the attic, Matt turned on the single bulb and then the main light. I was thankful for the stream of sunlight pouring in through the dirty window I had forgotten to clean.

Sophie tugged on a clear plastic box near the strip of sunshine and sat down on the plywood floor to open it. She poked through the items and held up a long, red velvet bow in desperate need of reshaping. "Can we hang this above the fireplace?"

Matt grew nostalgic, his facial features taking on a faraway look, likely remembering the good old days. He sat cross-legged on the floor next to me. He said in a quiet voice, "Yes, that's where Nana always hung it. Good choice."

Sophie beamed with excitement. "I have good decorating sense. That's what my Aunt Cassidy always said."

Sophie had an aunt? That was news to me. Why wasn't she staying with her aunt then? My belly clinched into a tight mess of knots similar to a tangled wad of Christmas tree lights.

There was so much about her I didn't know.

Matt and I exchanged a glance as if we were both wondering where the aunt was hiding out.

"I thought you never decorated for Christmas before?" I asked in reference to what she said about her aunt's compliment.

Sophie pulled out a yellowed fragile box of blue and white ornaments. "I haven't decorated for the holidays but I've helped Aunt Cassidy with her house."

"I didn't know you had an aunt." I decided I needed to know the truth about what I was up against.

"She lives in Virginia," she said as if the aunt was of no concern to me. "She has her own life, her own kids."

Curiosity was killing me. "Why aren't you with her then?"

Sophie frowned. "My mom doesn't talk to her. She doesn't want me, either."

"Oh, honey." I scooted closer to her and wrapped my arm around her shoulders, and to my surprise, she didn't resist my touch. "I want you."

Matt spoke up. "Correction. *We* want you."

Sophie fidgeted but nodded as she tilted her head down.

I looked away to break the tense moment and leaned toward my box. I couldn't quite reach it, so Matt scooted the container closer to me. I glanced inside. "Check this out." I pulled out a neatly wrapped string of colored lights and sneezed three times. "Years of dust."

"Bless you," Matt and Sophie said in unison.

"Thanks." I sneezed again.

Matt's face took on that now familiar faraway look. "Nana used to decorate the holly bush out front with those."

Two thoughts dawned on me. One, he was having a difficult time sorting through the items. Two, he planned to decorate my house exactly the way Nana had. As usual, I had mixed feelings about the subject. I wanted to be understanding but at the same time this was my first house. I longed to claim it as mine. Was I being unfair? Was he?

He unwrapped an object from crinkled, yellowed tissue paper and held up a blue and white tear-shaped tree topper. Tiny cracks danced through the ceramic as if the antique might fall apart in his hands. "I remember my father climbing onto a step stool to put this on top of the tree. When I got older, I was allowed the privilege." He looked as though he was fighting off tears.

Guilt filled me. The ornament was pretty enough in an old-fashioned way, and by that I was being generous, but not something I imagined placing on my Christmas tree. But I had agreed to host his family party, so I needed to set aside my personal agenda and allow him the honor of decorating. But resentment started to gnaw at my insides.

"Don't you like it?" He turned the tree topper in different directions to showcase the item as if it were for sale.

I was sure the expression on my face revealed my true thoughts on the tree topper. "It was Shirley's and I respect her belongings." My words were true. It still didn't change my opinion.

"We don't have to use it," he said, but his tone of voice sounded contrary to what he was likely thinking.

What pressure. I didn't want to revert back to my usual distaste of holiday decorating and this wasn't helping. I should tell him the truth. Instead, I adopted Sophie's famous, noncommittal shrug.

He wrapped the tree topper back in the tissue paper and placed it inside the box.

I dug through another container and gasped. There before me was the most gorgeous, hand-quilted tree skirt I had ever seen. Several squares were red with darker red swirls, some green with a darker green pattern among an array of cream colored and blue squares. I bet she had stitched this while she waited for her husband to return from the war.

"Did Shirley make this?" I asked in awe.

He nodded as he continued to dig through the ornament box as if he didn't recognize the time required to sew such a fabulous quilted tree skirt.

"Can I see that?" Sophie asked.

I handed it to her.

She turned the skirt over and studied the stitches. "At church there is a group of ladies who quilt for people in hospitals. Maybe I'll sign up to learn how."

My mouth dropped open. I turned my head so she wouldn't notice my surprise. When I recovered I said, "That's a wonderful idea. I'm sure they need help."

Matt picked up another box stuffed full of ornaments and three stockings. "Let's bring all this downstairs."

I nodded but felt compelled to express my need to decorate with my own flair without being locked into how his grandmother had adorned the house. My belly knotted from the inevitable confrontation that was sure to happen when I brought up the subject. I was going to have to say something to him.

Putting off the inevitable, I decided to wait for a better opportunity.

We each grabbed a box, Sophie and I choosing lighter ones, and made our way down the attic steps. The dim lighting made navigating the stairs more difficult but we managed.

We set the boxes on the floor of the family room. Matt lit a fire while Sophie and I pulled items we wanted to use from the boxes.

"Oh, we need music." Not recognizing myself, a person who avoided Christmas music at all cost, I turned on my speaker and connected it to my phone. Christmas tunes floated across the family room like an angel's feather.

"Let's put together the Christmas tree first," Matt said, sounding excited. "Then we can place the ornaments on it as we unwrap them."

Light music filled the entire room with a wholesome warmth as we worked as a team to fit the pieces of the smashed tree together. Once finished, Matt pulled down the branches and fluffed them up. Thank goodness it was a newer tree with the lights built into it, and no dust. We had chosen the corner by the window with the marsh view, and near the fireplace. I approved of the placement, not because it was Shirley's preferred location for years, but because it fit to perfection.

I watched Sophie grin as though her lifelong dream of a festive Christmas holiday was coming true. My heart melted into an unfamiliar liquid puddle next to my feet. My own dreams were materializing.

Matt plugged in the lights and white twinkling dots lit up the room. At that moment, I wanted to be nowhere else but here.

The moment didn't last long because he pulled the misshaped wrapping of the tree topper from the box. With deliberate care, he removed the tissue paper. Now was the time I needed to tell him I wanted to decorate with my own style.

My belly clinched tighter to prepare for the likely confrontation. I swallowed hard. "Matt ... I'd really prefer not to have a tree topper this year." I didn't want to tell him I loathed the family relic.

He snapped his head up from the box.

I reminded myself I didn't need to explain or offer excuses. Stay quiet and let him absorb the information.

"But the tree won't be the same without it." His shoulders slumped with boyish petulance. I'm sure I had a glimpse of his younger years while he sat on the floor helping his nana decorate for Christmas.

Guilt filled me. In the grand scheme of things. it didn't matter if we had a tree topper on the tree or not. I wasn't all that experienced in romantic relationships, but from everything I learned recently, especially from articles on the subject, I recognized the art of choosing your battles. Before I said anything more I needed to decide if I wanted to enforce not having the topper.

Before I responded, he said, "Wow, I'm being self-absorbed." Matt wrapped the tree topper back in the tissue paper. "This is your first house, your first opportunity to decorate your home for Christmas." He released a long sigh. "I've been so busy trying to relive my childhood memories, I didn't take your desires into account."

I was dumbstruck. In my experience, no man had ever validated my feelings to the degree he had, nor had any man empathized with me to this extent. The men in my past would have reacted with defensiveness, anger, or would have walked into the other room without discussion. He threw me off guard and I needed a long moment to gather my thoughts.

When I was ready, I looked into his eyes. "Thank you, but I was being selfish too." I was growing in ways I hadn't imagined. Usually I wasn't one who liked to admit when I was wrong. He challenged me to think about his feelings before my own.

"I do want flexibility in decorating for the holidays," I admitted, "but I agreed to host your family party, so I need to respect your wishes too. Guess we should compromise."

Whatever was happening between us, the level of maturity and commitment we were both showing, caused me to appreciate the significance of taking each other's needs into account first. This was a pivotal moment in my life, where I put aside my own personal agenda for a man I loved. To my surprise, my emotional walls had collapsed into a dusty heap.

He packed the topper into the box. "I appreciate all you are doing for me and my family. A tree topper isn't a huge deal."

I leaned forward and kissed him softly, thankful for having Matt and Sophie to spend Christmas with this year. Magic or not, I was happy.

As I watched them choose ornaments to hang on the tree, I caught a glimpse at the dreamy life possible. All I had to do was be brave enough to push my fear aside. The past was the past ... my future was sitting in front of me.

Chapter Eighteen

I woke up early Thanksgiving morning to put my first turkey I had ever baked in the oven. I researched it online, referred to my rarely used cookbook, and although I had no reason to, I felt confident the turkey would be moist and golden. It was large enough to feed a gathering of ten people but I loved leftovers.

I applied olive oil to a folded paper towel and wiped it over the bird. Next I sprinkled pepper and rosemary across the top. My mother always baked chicken with rosemary, so why not apply the culinary tip to a turkey? The anticipation of the earthy taste made my mouth drool.

My plan was to wash the dishes as I went, a lesson learned from my mother, to keep ahead of the mess. It was easier to hand wash the few items I had already accumulated in the sink. My first holiday dinner was going to be delicious.

I placed the oversized turkey pan in the oven, the rosemary smelling divine and down-to-earth.

Sophie was still upstairs sleeping. Matt would arrive soon enough, offering me plenty of time to shower and fix a few side items on the menu. But for some reason I felt sad.

I had woken up feeling nostalgic. I loved hosting Thanksgiving for the three of us, but not spending today with my family bothered me more than I thought it would. I was actually missing them. Holidays weren't much fun in general, as I spent a lifetime trying to avoid them, but now I faced my first Thanksgiving without my mom and sister.

The absence gave me an unwanted vision of what life might be like if something dreadful happened to either of them. I tried to shake off the thought, but it held fast.

I attempted to tap into the cozy atmosphere I had tried so hard to create. Today was a blessing, after all, and I was spending it with Matt and Sophie. The progress Sophie had made so far in her personal journey at school, with the choir at church, with allowing me to touch her, was fulfilling on its own.

After I showered, I performed a once-over on the house. Then I returned to the kitchen to prepare the side dishes. I chopped vegetables for the veggie tray, put homemade cookies I baked yesterday on a tray and covered it with wrap, and began chopping potatoes, slow cooking them in a pot of water to prevent them from turning brown. The more I prepared early, the more I was able to enjoy Matt and Sophie.

"Good morning," Sophie said from the doorway, her hair the worst case of bed head I'd yet to see. I greeted her with warmth and offered her a bowl of cereal as not to ruin her appetite even though it was noon.

"Something smells delicious."

"Turkey," I said, proud of myself. The possibility dawned on me that if she hadn't celebrated Christmas before, she might not have experienced the mouth-watering taste of a roasted turkey. I wanted to ask but didn't want to make her uncomfortable.

"Makes my belly rumble." She shoveled a spoonful of cereal into her mouth.

The back door opened, startling me. I wondered when I'd get used to people walking into my house unannounced. But in all honesty I didn't mind too much, especially when it was Matt.

His arms were full of goodies including a home-baked pecan pie from the nuts we had collected. He winked at me and turned to Sophie. "Good morning, Soph. I'm surprised to see you up so early."

She groaned in response.

He set the items down on the counter and scooped me into a hug. His lips met mine and lingered, making me want to stay in his arms longer.

He felt safe, secure … familiar yet enticing. I was starting to accept this feeling. I'd had my share of dysfunctional and noncommittal relationships. I was guilty of being too guarded and was just beginning to understand how my past played a part in that. But I had to say I was changing for the better.

"The turkey smells divine," he said. He made a show of sniffing in the direction of the stove.

"Thanks. It's my first time making one." I smiled wide as if I had just been told I was an exquisite chef. I hoped the turkey tasted as delicious as it smelled.

He opened the oven door. "It appears you're a pro."

I laughed. "Hardly but I could get used to the compliments."

"You deserve them." He left the kitchen as if on a mission. I heard him in the living room stacking wood in the fireplace to create a festive ambiance.

I had forgotten to order more wood but planned to call tomorrow. Who knew? Maybe this winter would be a harsh one and I didn't want to run out.

My family would have enjoyed the food and atmosphere. I wondered what they were doing at Emily's house. I imagined them standing around in the kitchen, snacking on appetizers, the divine aroma of Keith's cooking filling the air. They would be drinking wine, talking, laughing. Did they miss us? Why did I care?

Matt returned to the kitchen. "How much longer before we eat? I didn't have breakfast."

"An hour and a half," I said, confident I knew what I was doing.

He scrunched his face as if disappointed he had to wait so long to eat.

"You can pull out the veggie tray and snack a bit," I offered. "Or we could read more of Shirley's diary and the letters while the turkey finishes baking. I have the side dishes ready but it's too early to start cooking."

He nodded, but I got the feeling he was uncertain about the baking time. He was a gentleman and didn't question me on my culinary skills. I hoped I was correct with the time frame.

After Sophie rinsed out her cereal bowl and stacked it in the dishwasher, we made our way into the living room. The fire was going full throttle. The warmth, glow, and homey ambiance caused my heart to swell with affection toward Matt. This was possibly the best

Thanksgiving I had experienced. I was fairly certain Sophie would agree.

Sophie chose her usual spot on the couch, and Matt and I snuggled into the love seat.

"Ladies first, as usual." With a wink he pointed to the faded leather diary sitting on the coffee table.

I was madly, crazy in love with him. My feelings scared me, but also excited me. If he left me I had no idea what I would do without him. One thing I knew for sure was I would be devastated.

With excitement I reached forward and opened the diary but noticed there was a large gap between the dates. Maybe Shirley hadn't written much after she lost the baby. Well, I was glad she had picked up the diary once again to log her thoughts.

Nana's Diary: November 28, 1968

Today is Thanksgiving. I have never spent the holiday away from Robert since we first started dating. Even though we met in grade school, my parents were strict and didn't allow me to formally date a man until I was seventeen, and we abided by their rules.

At the time I thought my parents were unreasonable, but now I'm a mother, I truly understand their thinking. Daniel is a long way off from high school but that doesn't stop me from being overprotective. If I hadn't miscarried my baby girl, I'm sure I would be even more protective over her.

Not a day goes by that I don't think about my unborn child. I know it doesn't help to focus on the past but I can't help it. Daniel and I live in this big house alone. My brother and his wife are thinking about renting a room from me. I rather like the idea. I would no longer be lonely, and the money and assistance around the house would be helpful.

I receive most of Robert's checks to help pay the bills, except the small portion he keeps to buy alcohol when the men venture into one of the small towns. At first I was threatened by the thought after he mentioned the women wanting to get paid for sex, but I have to trust him and have faith. He says a lot of men cheat but he has gone to great lengths to reassure me that I am the only woman for him. I know he is a little bit concerned about me wandering as well. I'm sure that's a normal fear, but I know he trusts me and I'm not the type to cheat. Robert is the only man I've been with, and the only man I want.

It is unthinkable to consider the possibility of what I'd do if Robert didn't return home. I will face that decision if I'm forced to deal with such an awful thought. One thing I do know is I want more children. For now I have to stay strong and believe he will return despite the news being filled with talk about all the wounded and killed soldiers.

Such negative thinking on a holiday. The lonely rooms are getting to me. Daniel and I plan to visit my mother's house for Thanksgiving dinner. It almost seems wrong to enjoy a large portion of food when I know Robert will be eating limited canned food for his Thanksgiving feast.

To help my guilt, I will make him some pecan cookies this evening once we return home from Mom's house. He loves those. I will send him extra so he can share with his friends.

I know this isn't about me, but I'm depressed and need to get through the day. I pray Robert is safe.

"I wish I had known Nana," Sophie said, tucking her feet underneath herself. Either she was cold or the letters hit a nerve. I'm certain she could relate to being vulnerable and scared as Shirley had expressed in her diary. My heart went out to her.

"I know you mentioned he didn't return from the war but I want the story to end differently," I said. "I care about Shirley and Robert."

Matt rubbed my knee. "Me too." He removed his hand and opened the unread letter from the bundle. It was his turn to read.

November 28, 1968
My lovely Shirley,

Today is Thanksgiving. You'd think they would give us the

holiday off but the enemy never ceases. I'm so sick of this war. All I think about is you. You are the reason I stay alive.

I spent the morning digging trenches. Let me tell you, that is hard manual work you never want to do, especially in the rain as we did. I miss you so much that I can barely stand it. How am I going to make it a few more months? I dream about you, think about you, and miss Daniel too. From the photographs he is growing so fast I hardly recognize him. I am concerned he won't remember me when I get back.

Do kids forget their fathers when they go off to war? That would crush me.

Thanks for the scotch and cookies. I shared them with Denny and two other buddies. Your cookies put this food to shame. If I never eat ham and lima beans again I'll celebrate. Guess I shouldn't complain. At least I'm alive.

We are having music tonight to celebrate the holiday. Our parties are fun and I hope I don't drink too much. Last time it was difficult to get up early and work. I hate having hangovers.

I'm sure you can tell I'm feeling depressed. This is the first holiday I haven't spent with you since we were kids. You were my first love, my only love, my last love. Tell Daniel I said hi and give him a bear hug from his daddy. Tell him to remember me.

Love,
Your Robert

December 1, 1968
My lovely Shirley,

We had incoming today. One of our men got shot up pretty badly. He lost part of his ear and took a bullet to his arm. At least we are stationed at the hospital, so he didn't have to travel far for help. They say he's going to be okay except he's hearing ringing in his ear from a bullet skimming his head.

This week has gone by so slowly I swear it's moving backward.

At this rate it will be forever before I see you again. I had a dream about you last night. We were sitting in the living room by the fireplace, opening Christmas presents. The house was decorated as always. When I woke up, I felt safe in your nurturing arms, and for a moment I thought I was actually home. That made the pang in my heart ache even more for you. Once I return home I'm never going to leave you again other than to go to work.

Have your brother and sister-in-law moved in yet? I'm glad you'll be getting rent to help pay the bills. Maybe Mark can make the repairs needed that you mentioned in one of your letters. Again, some days I get one to three letters from you, other times I receive none. It's hard enough to get through the day, but when I don't get any letters it's really rough.

My friend Denny just received his Dear John letter today. We sat with him. He didn't cry but I could see how it was eating him up inside. The men who get the break-up letters lose hope and I've noticed they become reckless. It's as if they don't care if they live anymore. Our women are the only way some of us stay alive over here. Please never ever send me a letter like that. I know you won't but it's worth mentioning. I love you.

Like I said before, the war has a way of eating at your mind and the way you think. It's easy to allow fears to take over. I think of the day when I return home and see you at the airport. I will hug you until you are sick of me and beg me to let go. I can't wait to kiss you, to be with you.

Love,
Your Robert

"I can't get enough of reading the diary and letters," I said in awe. Real love did actually exist. My emotions were all over the place, happy yet sad, loving yet longing. I missed my mother and Emily, appreciating them instead of taking them for granted. I also fretted about Sophie leaving and possibly not living with me at Christmas. The fact I was looking forward to the holiday didn't go unnoticed by me.

If Sophie didn't return home, I was thinking about broaching the topic of adoption with her and her mother. I hadn't mentioned the idea to Matt yet, but it wasn't like we were married or anything. My mind convinced me the decision was mine to make. Still, I could mention it to him but for some reason I was putting off the discussion. I wondered how Sophie would feel about the subject.

"I'm enjoying the letters too. It's a gift, and I'm learning more about my grandfather." Matt paused, sniffed the air and frowned. "We need to check the turkey."

Without waiting for me, he stood and headed toward the kitchen. I followed behind, feeling certain the bird was fine according to my research.

He opened the oven to peek inside. "Um, we have a problem."

I placed my hand over my mouth to stifle a gulp as a burnt smell filled my nose. Maybe I had turned the oven temperature higher than recommended.

He grabbed hold of two hot pads and pulled out the dark brown turkey. The little plastic insert that indicated when the bird was done poked upward in an accusatory way. "I'd say it's done. Hand me a carving knife and we'll see what the inside looks like."

I handed it to him while holding my breath with uncertainty. I had worked so hard. It was always my mother's job to cook the turkey, baked to moist perfection. What kind of hostess was I if I burned the main course? He cut into the bird.

The crust might be burnt, the inside dryer than it should be, but possibly edible.

Matt blew on a forkful of meat to cool it off and popped it into his mouth. "This is good." His surprised tone convinced me he was being truthful.

I sighed. What a relief. I couldn't resist a taste, so I placed a small piece into my mouth. It was dry and a bit chewy. I looked up at Matt. I had messed up our Thanksgiving meal and would never hear the end of it. Unless Matt and Sophie didn't tell my family.

It wasn't hard to imagine spending my life together with him. When Sophie walked into the kitchen to check on us, my emotions spilled over into a startling sob. I was softening from years of holding back. The tears just poured out of me. Until recently, I hadn't cried since I was a child.

Matt pulled me into his arms. I gave in and leaned into his chest for comfort. Not only did I mess up our Thanksgiving, but I would miss Sophie if she left us to return home. I had to assume she would. I thought I was capable of being a foster parent and keeping boundaries to prevent more heartbreak but that wasn't the case. My heart hurt at the thought of possibly losing her.

"The turkey tastes fine," Matt said, encouraging me. He had misread the reason for my tears.

I nodded, not wanting to hold onto the pain. I wanted today to be lighthearted and fun.

With Matt and Sophie's help, I finished preparing the rest of the food. When the house was smelling delicious again, we loaded up our plates and sat at my beautiful tile table. Appreciation for the little things in life was always good. With heads bowed, the three of us held hands and Matt said the blessing.

"The turkey is good," Sophie exclaimed as she tried a bite. She shoved another large chunk into her mouth and chewed.

I noticed she had smothered the white meat with gravy. Great idea. I followed her lead and did the same. As I placed a small forkful into my mouth, someone tapped on the back door and it opened.

Shocked, I glanced up to see Emily, Keith, my mom, and Clark. A flash of panic shot through me. If they tried the turkey they would give me a hard time about it. My family was just that way.

Sophie jumped up. "Aunt Emily." She hugged my sister tight, followed by a hug to my mother.

I refrained from standing, trying to calm my insecurity about them noticing the burnt turkey. Matt grabbed my hand from underneath the table. The warmth of his touched helped me to regain control of my emotions.

"Sorry to interrupt your meal," my mom said, studying the spread.

I felt her judgment. If we had gone to Keith and Emily's house, we wouldn't have to eat dried-out turkey and pretend it was the best thing ever.

Stop. I had wanted a relaxed holiday at home with Matt and Sophie. Despite the unfortunate cooking incident, this was the best Thanksgiving ever.

Sophie returned to the table and continued to shove food into her mouth as if enjoying every mouthful.

"Your dinner smells delicious," my mom said in a genuine tone, not a mocking one.

I snapped my head upward and our gazes met. Her praise surprised me.

"We didn't mean to crash your dinner," Emily said. "The holiday isn't the same without you, so we brought dessert over."

My mouth dropped open. They came here because they missed us. "Thanks," I managed to say. Matt squeezed my hand as if to say, *see ... it all worked out.*

I stood and gave each of them a welcoming hug.

"Besides, I need your help," Emily said when we pulled away. "I'm sure Matt told you, but there is a homeless girl who needs a place to live. The police are searching for her. Jessica showed up at church on Friday for a free meal while I was volunteering."

I stared at Matt. No, he hadn't mentioned a word. He turned away from me and stared out the kitchen window. He appeared lost in the view. I wanted to ask him, but not in front of my family.

Emily leaned against the countertop and crossed her arms. "The parents gave permission for her to stay elsewhere. She is pregnant and they don't want anything to do with her or the baby."

Sophie dropped her fork and pushed her chair back with force. She made a mad dash from the room. I heard pounding footsteps on the wooden stairs. Great. This was supposed to be a positive Thanksgiving for her.

I wasn't sure if I should follow or give her time to cool down. I continued to watch Matt for some indication of why he hadn't mentioned Jessica.

He knew my passion. I was proud I had just finished the course, five nights a week of classes, to ready myself for the task of being a foster parent. Now all I had to do was have the home visit and then wait for my letter of acceptance. I didn't appreciate Matt or Sophie's attitude. I wanted the people I loved to support my dreams.

"Bring her by tonight," I said to Emily. "I'll have a room ready for her."

Chapter Nineteen

On Saturday, Matt picked Terri up for a casual lunch downtown. There was a strain between them, all because he hadn't told her about Jessica, but he hoped she would let it go. From years of dealing with his father and burying the pain of their history, Matt had become an expert at not sharing his thoughts and emotions. Especially when it concerned police matters, although he was changing. He was learning not to take things so personally and to communicate better. At least they had a few hours today to spend together.

He wanted to surprise her by keeping the restaurant a secret. She only knew it was casual and festive for the holidays.

Downtown was somewhat busy for off-season but parking was manageable near the town square. Tonight would be a different story. They'd need to arrive early for Christmas on Front Street for Sophie's choir performance. The tree lighting tradition started before the choir's show.

Terri stared at the huge tree in front of them with a perplexed look on her face. "How do they reach the top to decorate?" There was a liberal amount of oversized blue and white ornaments to match the nautical ambience of the town.

Matt laughed. "They use the ladder of the firetruck."

She thumped her forehead with her palm. "Never thought of that." She took hold of his hand as they strolled down the boardwalk along the marina. Poinsettias filled huge clay pots with a deep red that brightened the edge of the walkway.

"Normally I despise surprises but I can't wait to see where you're taking me." She rubbed her hands over her arms, likely to keep warm from the cold wind gusts, but she appeared to be enjoying the small-town atmosphere of Christmas. At least the sun was shining.

On a brick patio near a two-story restaurant called The Boathouse, a tall casual restaurant along the waterfront, Santa and Mrs. Claus waited inside a hut set up for a photo opportunity. Matt would have walked past but Terri tugged on his hand.

"Let's get our picture taken with Santa."

"For real?" She must be half crazy if she thought he wanted to pose next to Santa.

"Come on," she encouraged. The little girl in her glowed on her face, the girl who had missed out on lighthearted Christmas mornings and delightful, carefree holidays.

Guilt got him. He could stand a few minutes with Santa and then off they'd go to the restaurant. "Okay, fine."

No big deal.

But it was a big deal. She grinned like a kid with a candy cane, so arm in arm they waited their turn in the short line. When they neared the front, he turned to a nearby couple who he had gone to high school with. "Hey, Rick. Will ya take our picture?"

His petite, blonde-headed wife reached for Matt's cell phone. "I will. Rick takes horrible pictures."

"I do not," Rick said, defending himself.

Matt handed the woman his phone. "Thanks. It's our first Christmas together."

Terri's expression turned all soft and mushy.

"That's sweet. By the way, I'm Marcia," she said to Terri, shaking hands. "And this is Rick."

"Nice to meet you both." Terri smiled, apparently enjoying meeting his friends. When the line moved forward and they were next, she tugged on Matt's hand and they headed straight to Mr. and Mrs. Claus.

Matt ducked under the low wreath hanging from the hut to avoid bumping his head and laughed when Terri squealed. Santa flagged for her to sit on his knee while Matt knelt in front of Mrs. Claus. They smiled for the camera and Marcia snapped several photos. Anything to make Terri smile.

"How romantic," Marcia said, handing the camera back. She nudged her husband and Terri took a photo of them posing as well.

When they stepped away, Terri said, "I can't wait to see the photos. How about we look at them when we're eating?"

He agreed and dropped her hand as they made their way up the outside steps to the second floor of The Boathouse. The siding was made of weathered wood with clean, white trim. They pushed open a squeaky half wooden and glass door. The restaurant was a mom-and-pop kind of place with a buffet in the center, a gas fireplace radiating heat from the far wall, and a gorgeous view of the water.

"Cute," she said, glancing around.

"I thought you'd love the place. You can't beat the scenery."

They chose a table facing the window near the fireplace. He pulled off his coat and hung it on the back of the chair as they ordered two mugs of hot chocolate from Gabbi.

"Oh, Gabbi. It's good to see you again," Terri said as she leaned back in her chair.

He had to think about when she had met Gabbi before. Oh, yes. The oyster roast.

Gabbi tucked a blonde curl behind an ear. "Good to see you too. I'm looking forward to when you stop by the house to see the flowers in bloom and my artwork."

The three of them caught up for a few friendly moments before she said, "Let me get your hot chocolate, so you can warm up." She set the menus on the table and strolled off. It was special to be the only customers in the restaurant.

They glanced over their sparse menus.

Matt set his down. "I've been here several times," he explained when Terri raised her eyebrows, questioning his fast decision. "It's a relatively new restaurant. They bought out the previous place maybe a year ago."

Gabbi approached them to take their order and Matt motioned for Terri to go first.

"Just a grilled chicken salad with dried cranberries," she said.

"That should hold me over until after the festivities tonight. Sophie and Jessica are at home eating leftovers from Thanksgiving dinner."

"Sounds good," he said, but ordered a hamburger and fries. He needed something more substantial.

While they waited for their food, Terri scooted closer so they could glance at the photos on his phone together.

"Those are cute," she exclaimed. "We're practically glowing."

"They're okay."

She nudged him in the ribs. "Just okay? They're adorable."

"Okay then, but that's a woman's word." He blew her a kiss and pocketed his phone but couldn't quite hide his smile.

Gabbi brought their hot chocolate, and Terri wrapped her hands around the mug as if to allow the warmth to penetrate her fingers. The fireplace kicked on again, the heat filling the room. A Christmas tree twinkled in the far corner near the kitchen as if welcoming them personally. It was comfy inside and cold outside. Even the choppy silver water of the channel had little white caps on top.

"I need to ask you something," Terri said, sounding hesitant to create tension between them. It was probably something about their issue with Jessica.

He blew on his hot chocolate but set it down before taking a drink.

"I'm wondering why you didn't tell me Jessica was homeless, pregnant, and looking for help."

Matt clenched his jaw.

He sipped his hot chocolate to buy him some time to weigh out his response. When he finally spoke he decided to be honest. "Because it was police business and you aren't an approved foster parent yet."

She raised her eyebrows and made eye contact with him. "So what. Jessica had permission to live with someone. Isn't that enough?"

He shrugged. "I didn't know that. Terri, you can't keep getting involved with runaways until you are a foster parent. It puts my job at risk."

She turned toward the mesmerizing flames dancing in the fireplace. "So this is about you then?" Her voice stayed soft but she'd put him on the spot.

He paused, then shook his head. "It's about everybody involved."

Terri sighed and turned up her palms. "What's your issue about me helping out troubled girls?"

He stared out at the water. "No issue here. Just the law."

He didn't want to ruin their romantic date but didn't have a choice. He turned back toward her and inhaled a long breath. "There are more things about my past you don't know."

"Tell me then."

Not wanting to get into it there, he said, "Let's just say I have bad memories from my father bringing kids home to stay with us. I used to resent it."

Underneath the table he noticed her playing with her paper napkin and imagined she was practically shredding it.

"Just curious. What does that have to do with me?"

From the sound of her voice her patience was growing thin, but he blew on his hot chocolate out of habit and then took another slow sip.

"Well?" she asked, her tone a bit edgy.

"It doesn't. It's my issue, not yours."

"Well, you should know that Jessica moved into one of my rooms upstairs." She drained the last of her mug and wiped off her mouth with a paper napkin.

He stared at her with disbelief, certain she was making a mistake. "I hope you made the right choice. It's a lot easier when you go through DSS. Trust me on this." He needed to confess the truth about his past but now just wasn't the time.

Gabbi brought their food and set the plates in front of them. Neither spoke as they picked up their forks and began eating. He was disturbed by their discussion but didn't want the conversation to ruin their meal, so he left the topic alone. But at some point he'd have to come clean about his childhood.

The afternoon flew by too fast, and they switched their topic of discussion to Sophie's event tonight. She had worked hard learning the songs and he was proud of her.

I stepped from the shower and towel dried off. I had no idea what to wear for the outdoor event except something warm. I went to my closet, chose an off-white, knit pullover sweater and jeans along with a pair of boots.

I wondered if Sophie was nervous. I was proud of her for participating in choir every Wednesday night, for sticking with it. Either Matt or Jenni drove her to help me out, which I appreciated. Matt planned to meet us tonight on the boardwalk next to The Boathouse restaurant, stating he wouldn't miss it for anything. Unfortunately, Jessica wanted to stay in her room instead of joining us.

I was somewhat uncomfortable about leaving her alone, trusting her in my house since I barely knew her. But then again, if I wanted to foster kids I needed to trust them, not that I had anything of high monetary value lying around. The girls were trusting me with their lives, so it was a two-way street. I needed to protect them, take care of them, as well as trust them.

I climbed the steps and knocked on her door to check on her before we left. When she didn't answer, I knocked again.

"Come in," she said with a flat voice. The counselor said her behavior was normal under the circumstances.

And I understood why she would feel that way. "Sure you don't want to come with us? It's going to be fun."

She shook her head.

I took a chance and touched her shoulder. She didn't withdraw, a positive sign as far as I knew. "Why don't you want to go?"

"I have other things on my mind." She rolled away from me and onto her side. "If you haven't noticed, Sophie and I don't get along all that well."

I made a mental note to talk to Sophie. I wanted her to be welcoming to anyone who stayed with us.

"Why is that?"

"Because I don't like her."

I withdrew with shock. "Why?" I found myself wanting to protect Sophie, but I tried my best not to grow more defensive.

"She's an annoying little girl who thinks she owns this place."

Jessica reached for her ear buds, about to shut me out. "Besides, she reminds me of my irritating sister. I just want to be left alone, have this baby, give her up for adoption, and move on with my life."

I stared at her, unsure of what to say. "Oh, honey, things are going to be okay." I was glad we had a counseling appointment scheduled for Monday. The psychologist, having said Sophie was making wonderful progress in therapy, was chic, young, and friendly. With that in mind I thought the kids would bond well with her, so I had signed up Jessica too. It was expensive but well worth it until I eventually got help from DSS.

Jessica didn't answer. Instead she plugged her ears to dismiss me. The music was loud enough I could hear it through her ear buds.

I made my way back downstairs. I wish I could help Jessica more. Lost in thought, I retreated back into my bathroom to finish applying my makeup. I tried to shift my thought and tap back into the excitement I had earlier about the choir. I looked forward to hearing Sophie sing.

With my evening classes, I hadn't been able to listen to choir practice. From what I heard Jenni say, Sophie's voice sounded angelic. Tonight I would finally experience firsthand her passion for singing.

I finished my hair and makeup, then joined Sophie in the kitchen. She was decked out in the red and white festive Christmas sweater I had bought her, a white scarf, and a lopsided Santa hat. I pulled out my cell phone and snapped several pictures.

"Stop!" she complained, holding her hand in front of her face. "You aren't going to embarrass me tonight, are you?"

"Of course not," I said, snapping another picture as soon as she removed her hands. I dropped my cell phone into my purse. "I'm proud of you. You've shown a lot of dedication."

Sophie rolled her eyes, clearly uncomfortable by my outpour of support.

We drove downtown where groups of people strolled along the sidewalks bundled up to brace against the cold. Even though we had arrived early, I had a difficult time finding a parking place. The busy streets were festive, the black ornate lampposts decorated in white lights shaped like boats, shells, and seahorses. Never had I thought I would enjoy the down-home living here as much as I did.

"Why don't I drop you off at the town square and I'll battle with parking?"

Sophie's eyes widened. "No!"

I glanced at her, surprised. "You okay?"

She stared out the window.

I took that as a sign she was more nervous than I thought. Lucky for us, I found a parking spot a few blocks away on a dark, side street. We stepped from the car with a gust of wind catching us. I buttoned my long, black wool coat halfway and pulled on a red, hand-knit hat I had bought at a charming boutique downtown. I went back the following day and bought the matching gloves that I now had stuffed in my coat pocket. It looked as though I'd be using them before the night ended. This winter proved to be unusually cool. I had hoped to avoid the cold weather when I moved here. Not so. The other day I heard someone say the local weather station predicted snow this year, indeed rare for this area.

We strolled through the dark street and turned the corner. People flooded the sidewalks, illuminated by streetlamps, heading in the direction of the boardwalk and Front Street. Thrilled I had found a remote parking space, I didn't mind the walk if it meant not dealing with this crazy traffic. The plethora of people venturing out for Christmas on Front Street amazed me, the community involvement touching.

When we arrived at the town square, Sophie froze in place.

"You'll be great. Try to have fun," I said, offering encouragement in an area I had no experience. Singing for a group of people had never been my thing, though I didn't blame her for being nervous.

"I can't do it." Sophie shrunk visibly in her coat. Snowflakes fell into the night, lightly blowing in the filtered light cast by the streetlamps. The tiny white flakes landed on her Santa hat and dotted the brown locks of hair poking out from underneath.

Surprised by the snowflakes, I glanced around. Was it really snowing? A puff of white erupted from the upper deck of The Boathouse. Sure enough, I spied a snow machine.

Familiar Christmas music played from speakers dispersed around the square. Streetlamps lit the boardwalk along the water's edge with sparkling white Christmas lights lining the top edge of the wooden barrier fence overlooking the marina. Several boats, decorated by a variety of colored lights, rocked in the boat slips. The reflections of the lights zig-zagged across the black water. The cool air smelled of a mixture of salt and fish.

Carley approached Sophie. I straightened my back in order to protect her emotionally from the school bully.

"Let's go. The others are waiting," Carley said, jumping up and down and wrapping Sophie in a hug.

My jaw dropped. Apparently I had missed hearing about their newfound friendship. I planned to ask her about it in private once we were home.

Sophie waved at me. "See you soon, Aunt Terri." She ran off with the girl I had perceived as the enemy.

Matt approached. He slid an arm around me and placed a light kiss on my lips. "Was that Carley?" He stared after the girls who had disappeared in the crowd.

I nodded, unsure of what to say.

Emily approached us, a surprised look on her face when she saw our display of affection. She was arm-in-arm with her handsome, sweet-natured husband, Keith. I always thought I wanted to find a caring man with Keith's personality, and I had. I snuggled into Matt more.

Matt and Keith exchanged handshakes.

Matt slid his arm from around me. "Sweetheart, I need to run." He pointed to two police officers standing near the stage. "I want to catch up with them. Be back in a bit."

"Sure." I planted a quick kiss on his lips. "I'll be waiting in this vicinity."

"Okay, honey." He hurried off in the crowd.

I loved the terms of endearment he used today.

Keith smiled at me, offering his silent approval.

"Sweetheart? Honey?" Emily asked with a curious inflection in her tone.

I shrugged but the smile on my face remained.

Emily and Keith kept me company while the crowd packed tighter together to watch the tree lighting. A couple squeezed in next to us, pushing Emily closer to me. I didn't move, and to my surprise, she didn't back away. We were making progress.

"Good evening," a man said into the microphone from the stage. "Thank you all for coming out tonight. We promise you'll enjoy the tree lighting ceremony almost as much as listening to the youth group from the Goodwill Baptist Church."

The crowd clapped and a few people whistled.

The man spoke for a few minutes before they began the countdown. I glanced around for Matt but didn't see him.

"Ten, nine, eight ..." he said. By the time the crowd counted to one with the announcer, Matt showed up at my side. He slipped his gloved hand into mine. As the tree lights popped on everyone clapped. It amazed me how much light they put out.

A group of men behind us whooped out loud.

"Now get ready for the best Christmas music you'll hear this year," the announcer said. The crowd cheered.

I spotted Sophie in the back of the choir. She stood taller than the other girls, but while they were smiling, her eyes were wide with fear. The music began playing "Rudolph the Red-Nosed Reindeer." Their voices were soft, young, and sweet. I choked up, not expecting to get emotional. The crowd hushed to listen.

They sang several of the usual Christmas songs, but what surprised me most was when Sophie approached the microphone.

She sang a solo. Yes, a solo! She had never mentioned anything about singing "Silent Night" alone. No wonder she had been nervous. Her voice sounded like an angel greeting us with open arms as she welcomed us to sleep in heavenly peace. Her voice floated through the night, rich yet light, strong yet smooth.

Once again my emotions caught in my throat. Tears dampened my cheek. A flashback to the day I saw movement in the woods and found a runaway child hiding in my cottage reminded me of how much she had grown on her journey of discovery. She was maturing into a fine, adorable girl. Love filled my chest to maximum capacity, a big surprise to me, as I watched her sing. Between her and Matt, I was learning how to love beyond my wildest imagination. Shirley and Robert's story had taught me to let down my guard, taught me that real love did exist if you opened your heart to be receptive.

I turned my head slightly to take in my sister. She watched me closely, witnessing my emotional breakthrough. To my surprise she stepped forward, opposite Matt, and wrapped her arm around my waist. I was used to a family who refrained from giving hugs. I swear I just about absorbed her touch like a thirsty sponge.

Sophie's angelic voice filled the air, touching more people than just me.

After the song finished, Emily removed her arm. The crowd roared with applause. I'm sure I clapped the loudest but couldn't help notice the spot on my waist Emily had touched. It tingled with warmth and felt like home. But it cooled off too fast. I longed for her embrace, but wasn't brave enough to wrap my arm around her. The fear of rejection won out.

A stream of light from the nearest spotlight emphasized Sophie's red cheeks before she stepped away from the microphone, but I doubted anyone else noticed.

My mom and her husband, Clark, squeezed in next to us, pushing in close to me now that Emily had moved away. Mom didn't hug me—not her style—but I enjoyed her presence.

"Mom," I said, "you missed hearing Sophie sing."

"Oh, I heard her." She grinned and her gaze turned all soft like a proud grandmother. "We were standing over there." She pointed to a large poinsettia in a clay pot off to the side. "We couldn't find you at first."

"I'm glad you made it. She's been practicing hard." I bit my fear of rejection in half and leaned into my mom, touching shoulders with her. I deemed her safer than showing affection to Emily. The worst thing she could do was pull away. I embraced a new, empowered *me*. Another girl stepped up to the microphone and began singing "Rockin' Around the Christmas Tree."

Matt began to sing and I joined in. I lost myself in the magical moment of the atmosphere with the snowflakes blowing lightly in the breeze. The tree lights glowed, the boat lights twinkled. The quaint event almost overwhelmed me with a sense of belonging.

I had made this town my home, made new friends, and I finally belonged somewhere.

Once they sang the last song, the crowd cheered. We waited for Sophie to return as people began to disperse. Jenni and Claire, along with their husbands, approached us. Overjoyed by their support, I knew she would be too.

"Wow, Sophie is amazing," Claire said with awe. "She's a drop from heaven itself."

A surge of pride bubbled up inside me.

"I agree! I'll tell her you said that." I glanced around at all my friends and family standing nearby. What wonderful people. All those years I had missed out on this and never knew.

The men gathered together while the women stood closer. I watched my sister carefully to gauge if she had a problem with me talking to her friends but she had no reaction. I hadn't realized until now how much pressure I had felt about my decision to move here.

Now that Matt preoccupied himself with the other men, no longer allowing me to snuggle into him for warmth, a chill caught me from the breeze blowing in off the cold water. I fastened the remaining buttons on my coat and crossed my arms.

We chatted about the choir, church, and Christmas until Sophie bounced up next to me with Carley in tow. They were hormonal, unpredictable teenagers but I found it difficult for me not to resent Carley due to all the stress she put Sophie through. Then again, it wasn't my place to judge people, especially teenagers.

I hugged Sophie. "You were outstanding." My voice softened and I knew she believed me.

She shrugged off the compliment but I suspected she soaked up the positive feedback, something I bet she didn't receive much of at home.

It was too cold to stand outside chatting since the warmth from the crowd had dispersed. We said our goodbyes and made our way to the truck.

"So you and Carley are friends now?" I tried to hold my question but couldn't. Sophie's sense of confidence soared. She was no longer the scared, defensive girl who blamed herself for everything. Instead she sang a solo in a Christmas choir and befriended a bully she had fought early on in school. Talk about huge progress.

"Yep. Detention made us work out our problems."

At least detention had helped. "I have to know. Why was she so mean to you, and how did you forgive her?"

Sophie shrugged. "You know, we actually have a lot in common. Carley has to move around a lot because her dad is in the military. She told me she resented having to change schools all the time. She took it out on me because I reminded her she might have to move away soon, and she has friends here now and wants to stay. She didn't want to make friends with me in case I have to move again."

I flashed a glance her way. I could barely see the features on her face but could make out a hint of a smile. She was a good girl in so many different ways.

She continued on. "I learned you're supposed to try to understand people more so you can forgive them."

I smiled with an overwhelming sense of pride. "I'm proud of you, Sophie. Sometimes that's hard to do."

"Ya know, I can almost forgive my stepfather," she said, her voice sounding thick.

I wanted to know more, and now was a perfect time to ask. "Has he ever hit you?" I wasn't sure she had told me the truth early on when I first found her living in my cottage.

Out of the corner of my eye, I saw her shake her head. "No, but I don't trust him. He gets so mad for no reason."

I drove up the driveway where a vehicle waited in the dark with the lights off. Chills ran down my arms.

My cell phone rang and made me jump.

"Are you expecting someone?" Matt asked, his truck slowing to a crawl, and then to a hard stop behind us.

"No."

Sophie shrank against the backseat. "It's my mom."

I sat upright. What did the woman want?

Matt parked behind me. He closed his door and stepped up to mine. When I opened my window, a gush of cold air filled the car.

He placed his hand on my shoulder to keep me rooted in place. I was ready to argue to keep Sophie.

His hand pressed down on me. "Stay calm. We don't know what she wants." His voice grew soothing and quiet and caused me to inhale a long breath.

He was right. Nothing ever benefited me from losing my cool. And I held sudden gratitude for his occupation, which used to scare me.

"Sophie, have you talked with your mother lately?" Matt asked, glancing around me and into the back seat at her.

I noticed in my rearview mirror that Sophie had slumped down against the seat.

"She's your mother," I said in a surprisingly calmer voice than I felt. "You can talk to her anytime you wish." The logical side of me spoke with clarity despite my heightened anxiety. Matt's calming presence helped.

From underneath her wispy bangs, mashed from the knit hat, Sophie's half-hidden eye gaze met mine. "Mom called me. She wants to bring me bags of snacks, some clothes, another stuffed puppy I like to sleep with."

My mind darted back to the huge stuffed bear with the floppy ear on her bed upstairs.

Despite her height, Sophie was still so young, so vulnerable. The image of her sleeping with stuffed animals touched me. Her mother showed manipulation at its finest.

I needed to find out what she wanted. I opened my door and pushed past Matt. He moved out of my way but I knew he watched my every move. He caught up with me, and I reached for his hand so we presented a united front. I appreciated his protective nature.

Sophie's mom stepped out of her vehicle. She opened the back door and retrieved four garbage bags crammed full of items.

Sophie remained in my car. Her lack of enthusiasm to see her mother screamed at me.

"Good evening, ma'am," Matt said as he offered to take the bags from Judy.

"Hope you don't mind I brought Sophie some items to hold her over."

Hold her over from what?

"No worries," I said with the intention of being carefree but my voice sounded strained. "Sophie mentioned she had talked with you."

I contemplated inviting her into the house but my home was my safe haven, my territory. I didn't mean to come across as rude but her unplanned visit surprised me. And I despised surprises, especially of this caliber.

"Thank you for the items," Matt said. A bag almost slipped from his arms but he managed to reposition it. He didn't dare leave us alone together to bring the items inside.

"I wanted to see her. I miss her."

Warning bells clanged in my mind.

"Ralph says to let her stay here. She ran away and will do it again." Judy shifted from one leg to the next, and then back again. "I want her to come home."

I stiffened, unsure of what to say.

Matt recovered first. "Sophie is doing well here. She's making friends, has good grades in school."

I found myself starting to love Sophie, caring for her ... well, and keeping her safe. Such a simple thing, yet so complicated for Judy and Ralph. I refrained from speaking the truth, so as not to make matters worse. Then I added at the last minute, "She's involved with the church choir." There, we made a case for why Sophie should stay with us. But she wasn't my child.

Sophie approached us but stayed close to me.

I swallowed hard. I wanted to adopt her but reasoned now wasn't the appropriate time to discuss my idea.

Chapter Twenty

I swiped white paint across the cabinet. We hadn't painted much of it yet, but the little bit we had helped to lighten up the room.

"I want to talk about last night first." Matt set down the paintbrush he had just picked up. The cabinets weren't going to paint themselves, but I agreed. We needed to talk.

How was it possible Sophie had taken such a tight hold on me? Between the two of them, love seeped into me and filled the empty cavities of my heart.

Matt leaned against an unpainted cabinet. "Her mom agreed to allow her to stay with you, for now. You know as well as I do it's possible she'll change her mind."

I looked away.

He tipped my chin upward toward him, not allowing me to shut out the pain.

"I can't stand the thought of her returning to that verbally abusive situation, or that mess of a house." I sniffled and he pulled me into his arms. "She deserves better."

I snuggled into him, his chest warm and reassuring. I absorbed the comfort he offered.

"I agree. We have to let the system work." He pushed a strand of hair over my shoulder. "The legal system stinks but her mother has the right to take her home."

"What if that man hurts her this time?" There it was, my deepest fear. "I know what it's like to live without a father's love or support. I can't offer that to her, either, but I can offer her a loving, safe place to live."

"I know, honey." He squeezed me into his arms more. "Have faith. I don't know how, but everything will work out for the best for everyone involved."

How did he have such unwavering trust?

I pulled away, uncomfortable with the emotions he stirred up within me, uncomfortable with coming across as needy for requiring his love to help me through my upheaval of emotions.

I stepped back and dipped my paintbrush into the white paint, my classic attempt to distance him. My belly knotted with anxiety and I wanted to paint the cabinets in record time to expend my energy. To my relief, he didn't try to stop me.

We worked on the project all day with success. The cabinets were turning out better than I had hoped.

By late afternoon he sighed and set his paintbrush in the sink. "I can't believe we finished. Now all we have left is to paint the doors."

"I can finish them after work tomorrow since I no longer have class." We washed out our brushes in the sink next to each other using soap and water. "I hope Sophie is here for Christmas." Why I brought up the topic again frustrated me.

His facial features turned stiff. "Me too."

Once we finished washing the brushes, I reheated leftovers and we ate with Sophie at the little table in the kitchen. Jessica refused to join us, so I had brought dinner up to her. The dark enveloped us and I missed seeing the view. "What do you say we read the diary and letters tonight as our reward for finishing the frames of the cabinets?"

"Yes!" Sophie said, pumping her fist in the air. "I've been meaning to read them on my own but between homework and choir, I haven't had a chance."

"It's a date as long as I'm allowed to make the fire." He enjoyed using the fireplace, not having one at his home. I'd only been there one time, much smaller compared to this house. He had said more than once he thought it the perfect size for a bachelor.

"Absolutely. As far as I'm concerned, making a fire can be your job. Let's clean up the dishes and we'll get started on the most fabulous nonfiction love story I've read." The diary and letters had given me hope and a life I didn't know existed until I started reading them.

We loaded up the dishwasher in record time, and as Matt and Sophie made their way into the living room, I climbed the steps to Jessica's room to check on her. To my surprise, she had her door open.

"Hey, there," I said, sitting down on the edge of her bed. "We're going to make a fire and read some letters from Matt's grandfather. He was a soldier in Vietnam. Want to join us?"

She shook her head.

I chewed on my lower lip to bite back my concern. "It's good for the baby if you get some exercise and move around."

She glanced up at me.

"We'd love to have you join us." I knew my argument held some weight but I didn't know if she would bite the bait.

"Fine." She climbed from the bed and followed me downstairs.

I saw Sophie watching her but she moved over to share the couch.

While Matt stacked wood and ignited a roaring fire in the fireplace, I turned on the Christmas tree lights. So unlike me. I then found a cozy spot on the love seat.

Sophie turned on background Christmas music. As I sang along here and there, I marveled at how I used to despise this time of year.

"It's been far too long since we've read these," I said, retrieving the beloved items from the shelf underneath the coffee table. I passed the letters to Matt, who sat next to me. I scooted closer to him on the love seat, while Sophie curled up on the far corner of the couch, her favorite place, and Jessica sat upright, squished in the opposite corner to avoid touching Sophie.

I explained the storyline to catch Jessica up to speed. "I have to warn you that Robert didn't make it home from the war. But the love between them is evident, as you will see."

"Yeah," Sophie said to Jessica. "I feel like they are my grandparents and I don't even know them."

Jessica nodded and appeared interested.

Matt untied the frail rope holding the letters. "You first?"

"Absolutely." I placed the old diary in my lap and turned to where my bookmark flagged the page with the familiar writing. Nana was fast becoming family.

> *Nana's Diary: November 30, 1968*
>
> *The house took me a while to decorate for Christmas alone. My brother helped me put up the tree, and he placed my favorite tree topper where it belongs. It wasn't the same as sharing the fun with Robert but he's doing what he needs to do in Vietnam. Anyway, my grandmother had left the topper to me when she passed away. It's special and a piece I will treasure always.*
>
> *I decorated even more for Christmas than usual. Somehow the decorations make me feel like Robert is here with me. It makes me feel alive. Plus, Daniel loves it. He can't wait until Santa comes to visit Christmas Eve. His favorite part, of course, is ripping open the presents Christmas morning in front of the tree and warm fire.*
>
> *This year, instead of having a family get-together at my house, we plan to go to my mother's. It will help take my mind off the fact Robert isn't here. I can't wait until he returns. I have imagined that scenario in my mind over and over again. The first hug, the first kiss ... well, you get the idea.*
>
> *In the meantime, I'm going to take one day at a time and bake cookies for him.*

After reading about the tree topper, I tried not to feel guilty for not liking it. I'd never had one growing up, plus I found the cracked paint distasteful. Matt didn't dare mention the subject. I set the diary down so he could read the letters and settled myself back against him. There were more letters than entries in the diary, so I tried to savor them by only reading one or two.

> *December 10, 1968*
> *My lovely Shirley,*
>
> *The nights are cooling down, thank goodness. I want you to know that this war challenges me to be a better man almost daily. The language they use around here is something awful. It challenges me not to talk like that with them. I don't think they*

much notice, but even if they did, I don't need to talk bad like that. I want to stay a good man for you.

As I write this I can hear the thump thump rumble of a helicopter overhead. Evac is probably bringing in more injured. Off in the distance I hear guns. I'm so grateful I'm not in the bush.

As usual, thanks for the cookies and scotch. I can eat the cookies in almost one sitting but I try to spread them out over a couple of days. The scotch I drink at a slower pace.

I wrote you this little poem. I hope it doesn't sound stupid.

The rain is a pain and the nights are long
So I lie on my cot and write you a song
It's just the usual love letter
And I will try to do better
If I could tell you how much I love you
And have you believe me
I would get home much faster if they'd let me be
Shirley, my love, you're the only woman for me

I love you. Give Daniel a hug and a kiss from me. Here is a kiss for you. Yes, I kissed this letter.

Love,
Your Robert

December 16, 1968
My lovely Shirley,

I can't help but think of you as our anniversary nears. Christmas is so special to me, especially Christmas Eve. When I close my eyes I can picture you standing there all dressed in white in front of the Christmas tree. You were the prettiest bride in the world.

I want you to know I plan on being there with you next year for Christmas and every one of them after that. I still have our wedding photo with me. It's next to my cot where I can see it every night when I go to sleep. I give you full credit for the reason I'm still alive, for I have you to return home to. I also miss Daniel more than I can possibly explain.

As I fall asleep in a few minutes here, I can almost smell your cookies baking in the oven. I can hear Christmas music playing in the kitchen as you cook. Goodnight, my bride.

I love you and please kiss Daniel hello.

Love,
Your Robert

"Oh, wow," I said with sudden realization, bouncing upright off the couch. "That's why Shirley loved Christmas! It reminds her of Robert. I mean, they got married on Christmas Eve. How romantic."

Matt looked up from folding the letter. "I never knew why she loved Christmas so much. Now it makes sense."

I shrugged at the thought.

"What?" Matt asked.

"I appreciate Christmas more after reading Shirley's diary."

"The Christmas myth," he said, smiling wide as if to say *I told you so.*

"And that's why I shrugged. My appreciation has nothing to do with a myth." The thought brought up a scary idea. According to the legend, I was supposed to marry by Christmas. No way. I shook my head in protest.

He barked out a rumble of laughter. "And I understand why you shook your head. Who knows? You might have to marry me."

My jaw dropped. He laughed harder but smiled in a way that unnerved me.

Chapter Twenty-One

Today was an important day. Tense, but necessary, I had an appointment with DSS for a house inspection, the final step in the process to becoming a foster parent.

I zipped around and organized every last bit of my home. Thank goodness Sophie cleaned her room and organized it, and added the final touch with her large bear in a rocking chair and the smaller one on her bed. But as I glanced in Jessica's room, I panicked. She was at school but had promised to straighten it. She left the bed unmade, clothes on the floor, and the nightstand cluttered. I couldn't believe I trusted her word to clean up. The social worker would arrive any moment.

I went into overdrive and tidied up. I shoved loose clothing into the hamper and pulled the bedspread up and flattened it out. I arranged the pillows at the head of the bed and placed the teddy bear I bought her on top. I didn't have a chance to straighten the nightstand when the doorbell rang. I had adopted the backdoor policy from Matt, so no one had entered through the front door since I bought my house.

I darted down the steps and stopped at the entryway just long enough to catch my breath. I closed my eyes for a moment to say a quick prayer, took a deep breath, and then opened the door. Ms. Phillips, my teacher and caseworker from DSS, stood in front of me, wearing a black skirt and a red knit sweater with a colorful red, green, and white holiday scarf draped around her neck. Her black rimmed glasses sat low on her nose as if she were already judging me. Compared to her dressy appearance, I felt too casual in nice jeans and a top.

I stopped my critical thinking before it grew into full-blown insecurity and stood taller as I invited her inside. A gush of cold air followed her in, fitting for her personality.

I reached out and offered my hand. "It's nice to see you again." I hoped she didn't notice I was shaking.

"You as well." She extended hers but didn't return my smile.

I led her to the kitchen and offered her sweet tea or water but she declined, frowning as if I were trying to bribe her. She set her briefcase on the table and dug out a clipboard with a form attached. For the briefest moment, she stared out the window at the gorgeous view of the golden marsh and bright blue water but didn't comment.

Her report made the difference between being a foster parent or not, but I needed to have faith. Too bad Matt worked today, though. He always reminded me to trust the process and there wasn't a thing I could do to change the outcome. Remembering his words did make me feel calmer. I had taken the morning off for this appointment, so I needed to relax and let the lady do her job.

Ms. Phillips stared over the rim of her glasses at me. "I'm going to walk from room to room. I'll let you know when I'm finished."

In other words, I wasn't to follow. She had put me in my place and left me in the kitchen to fret. I sat at the table, drawing in calming breaths as I stared out at the peaceful view.

I imagined her in the family room analyzing the smoky smell of the fireplace, or noticing I hadn't removed the ashes, evidence we had a heartwarming fire last night. The Christmas tree lights were on and the house felt homey and festive thanks to Matt and Sophie, who helped me decorate. Then I imagined her in my bedroom judging it and I tried not to feel violated. What was taking her so long? The seconds ticked away ... the minutes dragged by.

Finally, I heard footsteps on the stairs. If she dinged me for Jessica's cluttered nightstand, then so be it. I thought back to the first day I purchased this home. I appreciated the progress we made with the restoration, appreciated Matt's hard work. I needed to tell him again.

Footsteps sounded overhead. More seconds, more minutes hung in the air.

Finally, Ms. Phillips' footsteps echoed on the steps as she headed back downstairs. I remained at the table and let her come to me. She entered the kitchen and placed her clipboard back inside her briefcase and closed it without a word.

I could no longer stand the silence. "How did I do? Did the house pass?"

She looped the strap over one shoulder. "You'll get a letter in the mail." She made her way through the hallway to the front door and let herself out before I could open it for her.

"Thank you for the visit," I called behind her, determined to remain positive and polite. I wondered how long it would take to receive my acceptance or failure letter stating my fate. Ten weeks of classes, tons of paperwork, inspections, and a health exam would be worth it if DSS accepted me. All I wanted was to give girls a fighting chance in the world.

Until I received the letter, I needed to keep active, easy enough to do with all the remaining items on the checklist yet to finish before the holiday party.

The rest of the week Matt showed up in the evenings to work on the house. He had no idea how to get all this finished. He found himself even grinding his teeth at night because he wanted more than anything to have the house in as best shape as possible for his family. Terri tried to help where she could but the remaining projects were tedious and making him edgy. Instead of trying to talk sense into him, she busied herself making dinner for everyone.

Frustrated with a stripped screw, he slammed down the screwdriver onto the countertop. "I'm never going to finish all this before Christmas."

The tension between them tightened.

"The house is fine as is," she said in a light tone meant to remove pressure from him. But it didn't. Her nonchalance made things worse.

He exhaled a forceful breath. "No, it's not fine. I wanted one thing, to restore this house to original condition for one last hoorah with my family on Christmas Day. Is that too much to ask? I mean, it's been one problem after another."

She remained quiet. Smart lady, allowing him to vent. Dang, he didn't even like being around himself right now. "Nana deserves this one last hoorah," he explained, trying to rationalize his fixation of completing the never-ending repair list.

"I fully support your quest to restore the house and have your party here, but Shirley no longer cares what condition the house is in. I have to ask, who are you doing all this for?"

He locked his attention onto her and she stopped dicing the vegetables.

"What's that supposed to mean? Of course I'm doing it for my family." He crossed his arms and bit his lower lip to hold back from saying something defensive.

"I'm just asking because your Christmas get-together is supposed to be fun, not stressful." She placed her hand over her lips. "I can't believe those words escaped my mouth. I have never thought of Christmas as fun. Ever."

He should have acknowledged her comment but didn't. "You don't understand." He held his hands up high and glanced around the kitchen. "I had a goal and I'm falling short."

She blinked rapidly. "You never fall short, Matt. Look at all you accomplished."

"I'm not a quitter." He sighed hard and kept his arms crossed over his chest. "And before you suggest hiring a contractor to help, just know I'm fully capable of finishing my own projects."

She stared at him. "I never accused you of being incapable of anything. If that's how you feel ..."

He turned his back to avoid saying something he shouldn't and picked up the screwdriver.

She stormed out of the room and he heard her feet slapping on the steps as she headed upstairs.

Matt used force with the screwdriver but the screw remained stubborn. He stopped, looked up and inhaled a deep breath. He tried again and, to his surprise, it loosened with ease.

"Amazing," he mumbled to himself. The next one loosened just as easily.

"Matt!" Terri screeched from upstairs. "Matt! Come quick."

He dropped the tool on the countertop and ran toward the stairs. He took two at a time and reached the top but had no clue where to find Terri.

"What's wrong?" he said huffing from the fast sprint up the steps.

He glanced around, trying to find her, and peeked into Sophie's room. Terri lay sprawled out on the bed with Sophie's small stuffed animal wrapped in her arms, the huge teddy bear missing. A succession of muffled sniffles filled the otherwise quiet room. Sophie had decked out the bedroom with Christmas decorations from the attic but she wasn't there.

"Terri?" he asked in almost a whisper.

She continued to cry. He walked over to the bed and laid his hand on her back. "What's wrong? Where's Sophie?"

She cried harder.

He glanced into the open closet. Vacant, as in all of Sophie's clothes and overstuffed bear were gone. His belly clinched into a tighter knot, like one of the tangled fishing lines from his neglected fishing poles in his shed. He had no idea how she left the house with that huge bear without anyone noticing.

He bent over to look underneath the bed. Dumb idea. As if she'd be hiding there with all her clothes. Terri sniffled again, so he sat on the bed next to her. "Hon, it's going to be okay."

She glanced up with tears streaking down her cheeks before she stood and ran to the window. "There is no sign of her. She ate breakfast this morning as if nothing bothered her. Come to think about it, she was rather quiet." She whirled around and darted down the hallway toward Jessica's room. Matt stepped into the hallway, straining to hear what Terri said, but waiting to intercept her when she made for the stairs.

"Jessica, have you seen Sophie?"

He couldn't make out Jessica's response other than brief and muffled words. Terri darted out of the room, passed by him with her eyes wide from frantic mode. Her feet pounded down the wooden stairs and he gasped when she slipped in her stocking feet. Her hand snaked out as she grabbed onto the railing and continued to make her way downstairs.

Quickly, he followed behind her and caught up in time to see her open the kitchen door and run out of the house without shoes. He let her have her moment but glanced out the window to witness her running to the cottage, yelling out Sophie's name, and then pulling open the door.

When she sank to the ground he knew Sophie wasn't there either.

He stepped outside and made his way to Terri without her noticing. He wrapped his arms around her, running his hands over the back of her hair to soothe her, but she didn't seem to notice.

He left her to make a phone call from his truck, then sat on the driveway next to her to let her cry it out. This woman made him feel protective and stirred deep feelings inside him.

Through sobs she finally said, "How could she run away?" She looked up at him but only a dazed expression stared back.

"I'm sorry, Terri." It sounded lame but he didn't know what else to say. "This used to happen to my dad. He'd get attached to them, but would be devastated when they ran off." The memories of his painful past returned. His emotions shut off to shield himself from all the hurt.

She narrowed her focus on him.

He tried to shake off the visions of his father pouring out his sorrows when he lost a battle to save David, his favorite kid, yet closing off his emotions when it came to Matt.

He didn't want Terri to hurt the same way. "Honey, I don't mean to sound cold, but in my experience, that's what runaway kids do. They run away."

She pulled back and gaped at him. "Really? Sophie's gone and that's all you have to say?" Terri dragged in a breath as if someone had wrapped their hands around her throat, trying to choke her. She squeezed her eyes shut.

He tried to push through the pain to offer her hope but his past stood in the way like an army. "I know you care for her, and so do I. But like I said, we had runaway kids when growing up. They always ran off and we always found them." He tried to pull her into a hug but she recoiled. "My guess is she'll go back home," he said in a too calm voice. "Let's drive around and look for her."

She pulled away and he sensed she had erected her own emotional wall. "Please leave. I need to do this on my own."

He stood there, his feet refusing to budge.

"Go," she said with pinpoint precision. "I can't do this." She flagged an accusatory index finger to include them both.

My world had just caved in around me.

I shut my eyes tight because I couldn't watch Matt go, but yet I demanded that he leave. A little knife jabbed my heart and twisted around in a circle.

His truck's engine revved and gravel crunched as he drove off. A wave of anger, panic and fear washed through me like a flood.

I was tired of defending my mission to help runaway kids, tired of explaining myself. I planned to embark on my passion as I saw fit. And right now I needed to drive around and look for Sophie. I imagined her cold, scared, and upset. Besides, I wanted to do something to release my annoyance and agonizing emotional pain. I stood there, my anger draining out of me, replaced by tears streaming down my face.

Good thing Jessica couldn't hear me crying. I sat down on the gravel driveway in the exact spot where Matt's truck had been parked, crossed my legs and cried. I balled up my fists only to release them in defeat moments later. The chill of the evening dug into me but I ignored the raw cold. The smell of burning wood filled the night air. It should have given me solace but didn't.

The familiar critical voice inside my head reminded me I wasn't good enough to love. My father proved that when I was in the second grade.

People I loved always left. Or more like it, I pushed them away before they left on their own.

Once I cried it out, I remembered everything wasn't about me. What about Sophie? Where had she run off to? I prayed for her safety.

I went back into the house to collect my keys and purse, then called up the steps to inform Jessica I'd be back soon. Unfortunately, I had a flashback to this morning, so I jogged upstairs instead. She hadn't moved from the sprawled out position on her bed. I didn't mention Sophie's disappearance because I didn't want to upset her.

When I reached the car, I drove around for almost an hour without luck. I had bouts of tears but managed to keep it together enough to drive. I even drove past her mother's house but no lights were on inside, and I didn't want to chance knocking on the door in case I found myself alone with Ralph. Besides, no one looked to be home.

I was mad at myself for not seeing this coming sooner. Again, I doubted my ability to be a decent foster parent.

I had no idea how long she had been gone. I thought back to this morning, in my rush to get ready for work, I had left her to eat with Jessica at the table. It wasn't unusual that the girls didn't talk to each other and the animosity between them had intensified.

Sophie had gotten into the habit of riding the school bus every day. I hadn't checked on her when I got home because Matt showed up moments after I walked in the door after work. How could I not check on the kids?

What a good foster parent I would be, or a mother, for that matter.

Sarcasm was an ugly thing.

Not sure why I hadn't thought of calling Sophie's mom earlier, but I called now. There was no answer, so I left a brief message, not wanting to give the details over voicemail.

By the time I returned home, it was well past dinnertime. I no longer wanted to finish cooking the meal I had started preparing earlier, so I heated up leftovers. I began to cry again at the empty place settings at the table. When I called Jessica down, she immediately asked about Sophie.

I had no idea what to tell her.

I stared at my plate. "She left. Her clothes are gone."

Jessica snapped her head up. "As in she ran away?"

I shrugged. "Apparently so." I swallowed hard and pushed my food away.

"What are we going to do?" Jessica sat in her designated chair but didn't touch her plate. "I didn't like her all that much but she showed up here first."

Her honesty surprised me. "What's the problem between you two?"

"I dunno." Jessica picked up the fork and shoved a small forkful of food in her mouth. Before she finished chewing she said, "She had some fantasy you were going to adopt her."

I inhaled a sharp breath. "She wanted that?" We had never talked about it but I had planned to discuss my plans with her to gauge her interest.

Jessica nodded. "She didn't like sharing you with me."

As if I wasn't determined before to find Sophie, I was now.

I had a decision to make. Did I want to make a small impact on several kids, or a huge difference with one? If I asked the question that way, the answer became obvious, but I felt bad for all the girls out there without help, like Jessica.

Saturday morning rolled around and I had no idea who to reach out to. Nervous but eager to find out if Sophie had returned home, I picked up my cell phone and again called her mom.

The phone rang several times before she picked up. When she answered, she sounded apprehensive.

I explained the situation and asked if she'd seen Sophie.

"You lost my kid?" Her scratchy, deep voice held a touch of anger.

"Lost," I repeated, trying not to grow irritated by her accusing me of negligence even though her words were true. "No, she left."

The woman inhaled a long breath and I visualized her smoking a cigarette. "I left her in your care and trusted you."

I wanted to retaliate by saying if she had been a responsible mother I wouldn't have Sophie in the first place, but I refused to allow her to drag me into an argument. Testy, I needed to get a grip if I wanted any chance of having Sophie stay with me again. Her mom held all the power.

"Have you seen her? Did she return home?" I asked with a touch of vulnerability in my voice.

"Nope. She won't come back here." The woman coughed in the phone. "She ran away once. She ain't comin' back."

I sighed. I could only imagine Sophie lying in the cold, under a bush somewhere, trying to stay warm. "Please call me if you see her."

"Sure thing." The phone clicked without Sophie's mom saying goodbye.

The call did nothing to ease my fear.

I drove around for close to an hour without a glimpse of her.

When I returned home, I invited Jessica to join me downstairs to read the diary and letters as a distraction but she declined. She lived to stay in her room and play on her phone. At least she remained connected to her friends.

I sat in my usual place on the love seat, staring at Matt and Sophie's empty spots. I tried to ignore the pain their absence caused and not let thoughts of them haunt me. I held the familiar diary in my lap as if Shirley comforted me, loved me. What a mess I had made of my life. I had experienced my dream of having a loving family and now they were gone. Vanished. Both people I loved in the same day.

I set the diary on the coffee table, unsure of my ability to handle delving deep into Shirley's thoughts, and instead pulled the letters onto my lap.

December 24, 1968
My lovely Shirley,

Today is Christmas Eve. Happy anniversary, sweetheart! Oh, I can't even begin to tell you how much you are on my mind. Do you remember our first date? Frank had a boat and a bunch of us went over to Pony Island to find the wild horses. You found this huge shell and I carried it around the island for you because it was heavy. It was love at first sight, and one of the best days of my life other than our wedding and Daniel's birth.

We are going to have a party tonight to celebrate Christmas Eve and just know in my heart I will also be celebrating you. Our marriage has survived so far and will stay that way. You are the only one for me.

I thought our weather in North Carolina felt mild at Christmas but I'm sure it feels cold compared to here. It's cool, much, much cooler, than during the summer, but in comparison to home, it's quite mild unless it rains. When it rains here, everything gets flooded and turns to mud. It's raining a lot more now than it did. One day we had incoming and spent some time in the muddy trenches. Denny tries to be funny and to keep up people's morale but sometimes even he is depressed. That makes it harder to tolerate the trenches. A bullet hit one of my other friends and he died instantly. What a really sad day.

I hope you can fly to Hawaii to meet me for my R&R. I'm grateful that the Marines do this for us. Just think, I can wrap you in my arms again and I don't have to wait until I get home.

Again, I love you. All I want to do is to make it home, alive and well. Tell Daniel I love him and please send me pictures of the family opening presents.

Love,
Your Robert

I sat curled up on the love seat feeling sad for Robert. It must stink to spend the holiday in Vietnam without Shirley and to lose a good friend to a pointless war. And I thought I had a rough life. It didn't feel right reading the letters without Matt but I had to do something to distract myself. I decided to read another one.

December 25, 1968
My lovely Shirley,

Today is Christmas day. Can't this war give us the day off? We work seven days a week and I'm sick of it. I want to be at home watching Daniel open presents in front of the Christmas tree while he's dressed in his pajamas. Is that so much to ask? Why did I ever sign up to be here? How am I going to make it 148 days more without you? That might as well be a 1000 days.

I'm sorry. I don't mean to bring you down. There is nothing you can do to help me, so I might as well make the best of it. At least I'm warm and dry. I admit I drank too much last night at our party and I'm feeling it today. I would love to be able to crawl back into bed. These early mornings are rough on a Marine. We have these crazy inspections. Why? I think they have nothing better to do right now during the holidays. There are no decorations here. It's just another day at war in 1968 Vietnam, fighting a useless war we can't win.

I'm going to end this letter now before I get you depressed too. I haven't gotten any letters from you in a while, but then again, no one has gotten them or I would be concerned you found someone else. I know you wouldn't do that. I love you and please tell Daniel Merry Christmas.

Love,
Your Robert

February 14, 1969
My lovely Shirley,

Happy Valentine's Day, honey. I know how important this day is for you and wish I was there with you. I love and miss you so much. Just think, in 98 days I'll be home with you in my arms.

I'm so disappointed you couldn't visit me for my R&R. I wish we had someone other than your mother to watch Daniel, but I hope she feels better soon. It sounds like she was really sick. In the meantime, I will keep dreaming about holding you in my arms.

And thank you for the chocolate chip cookies. I think they saved my life on more than one occasion. After all, the men want to look out for me and watch my back because I share my cookies with them.

Love you with all of my heart. Give Daniel a big hug from me.

Love,
Your Robert

Even if I wanted to, I couldn't stop reading. I chose another letter from the now thin pile, and it didn't take long to read until only two letters remained. I wished Matt sat next to me but I had to accept the ugly fact that our relationship was likely over. I stared at the Christmas tree, remembering the three of us digging through Shirley's boxes of decorations and enjoying ourselves. I glanced at the missing tree topper I hadn't wanted. Maybe I had been too rigid, too set in my ways.

I shook the memories away and pulled out the next to last letter. I never wanted them to end.

> *May 7, 1969*
> *My lovely Shirley,*
>
> *It's getting hot again but I have only fifteen days left of this hole and so far I've stayed alive. I am glad I'm leaving because I don't think I could take another summer here.*
> *This morning I woke up thinking I held you in my arms but it was my shirt. I know you don't feel anything like a shirt but I've been gone so long I can barely remember how great you feel in my arms. When I get home I promise I'll never let you go again. We can stay in bed all day long and all night. Just know I will want to hug and hold you a lot. Maybe we can make another baby when I get home. Want another baby, Shirley?*
> *I have to go. I am needed. I love you.*
>
> *Love,*
> *Your Robert*

The final letter awaited being read. I contemplated savoring it by procrastinating but the temptation gnawed at me. At the same time I couldn't bear the thought of finishing the last letter. I never wanted them to end, but yet I fought the urge to race through it to see what happened.

I got up to refill my glass of water, use the bathroom, and then settled back down into a tight corner of the love seat to mentally prepare myself.

May 18, 1969
My lovely Shirley,

I'll keep sending my letters to you, but I'll be home before I receive any more of yours. I'm almost free! Almost home! The first thing I plan to do will be to hold and kiss you. I dream almost every night about holding you again. I wish these next few days would hurry up and speed by.

Vietnam is starting to get crazy but not much is happening where I'm at. Again, God is looking over me.

I'll be headed to Da Nang tomorrow. All I need to do is get on a plane and fly out of here. Once I'm home I will have served my time, fulfilled my sense of duty. Never, ever will I go to war again and leave you and Daniel at home. I am going to scoop you into my arms and hold you forever. I love you so much! I will see you soon, love of my life. You are the only woman for me. Think about the baby thing. Wink.

Love,
Your Robert

How cute that Robert wanted to have a baby. Then it dawned on me as to why the letters stopped. In a mad panic, I rushed to read Shirley's diary. I flipped to the last page.

Nana's Diary: May 22, 1969

Today is the worst day of my life. I received the news that every military wife fears. I'm too upset to even cry. My mind is in a swirl and I have to hope they identified the wrong body. It wasn't possible someone had shot Robert a day before he stepped on a plane to return home. Life is so unfair!

I've had many dreams of hugging him close at the airport. I imagined him in his uniform, looking handsome as always. I want to kiss his lips, his cheeks. I want to feel safe again in his arms. How am I supposed to tell Daniel his father isn't coming home after all?

Last night we hung Welcome Home signs in the kitchen and living room. I tore them off the wall and shoved them into the trash can.

They said he was heroic, that he saved his friend Denny from being killed. He crawled out of the safety of the trench to help his injured best friend, and to carry him back to the trench. He passed Denny down to someone, but before Robert hopped into the dirt hole, a round of bullets hit him.

I love my lost hero. Robert, you will forever be the love of my life.

I sat in stunned silence, tears dripping down my face. My hollow soul felt like a scooped-out pumpkin being carved with a sharp knife. If only Denny hadn't been injured then Robert would have boarded the plane the following day. Daniel would have had a father to raise him, and Matt would have known his grandfather. It was unreasonable for me to think that way. Fate had its own destiny.

The lights on the Christmas tree twinkled as if Shirley and Robert wanted me to know they were together forever now. No wonder Shirley loved Christmas. I remembered she had met someone soon after her husband died and had married on the following Christmas Eve. I knew she had wanted more kids. Without a doubt she had never loved her new husband to the extent she loved Robert, a once-in-a-lifetime love. She had said so in her diary. Matt had been the only grandson related to Robert. I inhaled a sharp breath. Until now, I hadn't comprehended that Matt's father was Daniel, the son of Robert, the boy I had read about in the letters. I now understood why Shirley willed her house to Matt instead of one of his cousins.

My heart grew heavy with missing him. No wonder Matt loved this house so much, and why he had such a difficult time selling it to me.

The rest of the weekend I moped around. I barely saw Jessica because she insisted on hiding out in her bedroom as usual. I had failed her as well. My life had fallen apart in a blink of an eye, and I had no idea how to turn my situation around.

Chapter Twenty-Two

My cell phone rang, jerking me out of my miserable thoughts.

"You need to call him," Emily said after I explained to her what happened. "You keep everyone at a distance. If you want love, you need to open up."

I hated to admit she was right, but fear grabbed hold of me and refused to let go.

I swallowed hard. A single tear dripped down my cheek. "I *have* learned how to love people and let them in. I'm sorry for all the hurt my emotional distance has caused you."

"I appreciate you saying that but this isn't about me. This is about you, about Matt. Sophie even. I'm not sure you realize how afraid of commitment you are," she said in one long breath.

"No, I'm not afraid any longer," I said, defending myself. "I care about Matt and Sophie. If I didn't, I wouldn't have allowed them in my life, and I wouldn't have taken Sophie in."

Emily breathed into the phone for a long moment. "Think about it, Terri. You let Matt in to a certain degree until things got tough. Then you abandoned him, which is what Dad did to us."

There was the knife again, twisting around in circles in my broken heart.

"And Sophie. Sure, you were kind to give her a temporary home. That's not a real commitment, Terri."

"I'm trying to be a foster parent. That's a huge commitment."

"It's a start," Emily said in a softer voice. "What about adoption? Have you thought about that instead of being a foster parent?"

I sucked in my breath. "I have thought about it but her mom would never agree."

"Have you asked?"

I shook my head into the phone as if Emily could hear my answer.

"Matt's hurting too." Emily's voice grew softer, almost a whisper. It gave me a pang of grief, a sad longing.

I lowered my head and closed my eyes. The last person I wanted to hurt was Matt. I found the love of my life as Shirley had with Robert.

"And what about the Christmas party?"

I hadn't given the party any thought until now. He had worked so hard, and I had no idea what to do. I would honor my commitment. Ha! See, I could commit! But the way things stood between us, I felt uncomfortable being with him and his family on a cozy holiday.

Cozy? I wondered when my negative opinion of Christmas had changed. I suspected Shirley's diary had something to do with it.

"I don't know," I said without getting into the details.

"With the tension between the two of you, it would be awkward to have it now. I can't say I want to be a part of that."

Great, I would be alone with his family. Honestly, perhaps it was best if Emily didn't come to the party, but I planned to make sure my mother still wanted to attend. I needed an ally.

After we disconnected, I spent the rest of the afternoon wandering through the house, lost. As usual, Jessica hid out in her room. She just wanted a warm place to stay, and food. In exchange, she had chores but she completed them when I wasn't around.

I wanted to reach out to her but she wanted no part of developing an emotional bond with me. Her baby was due in two weeks. I tried to discuss the situation with her but she refused to talk about the details.

My cell phone rang. *Matt.*

I about swallowed my tongue. I thought about letting the call go into voicemail so I didn't bawl on the phone, but my finger clicked on the answer button. Chances were good he wanted confirmation about the upcoming party in a week.

"Hello?" I asked tentatively.

"Hi, Terri." His voice deep and sexy, he sounded sad. "I hope all is well with you."

We talked niceties for a moment before he said, "My contacts came up zilch for any information on Sophie, so I drove out to her house to see if she returned home. I thought you'd want to know."

I inhaled a sharp breath. "Was she there?"

"Yes."

Her mother had never let me know. I breathed in to calm my nerves, my mind filling with several questions.

Before I could ask, he said, "It's not a good situation. She was out in the yard but ran inside when she saw me get out of my patrol car."

"How did she look?" I wasn't sure I wanted to know the answer.

"Well," he hesitated. "She was barefoot, wearing a short sleeved shirt without a coat, and bringing the trash to the end of the driveway."

I waited for him to continue. My intuition screamed that he had more to tell me.

"Terri, she had bruises on her arms." His voice sounded thick with emotion.

I gasped. A surge of anger shot through me. "What? That jerk grabbed her?" I forced myself to inhale several more long breaths and slowly released them to calm myself down.

"I knocked on the door but no one answered." Matt sounded as angry and as upset as me. "Long story short, I called DSS and they brought her in. They had a quick hearing and the judge ruled to place her in custody of social services."

A lump tightened in my throat. I loved Sophie so much I didn't want to think of her stepfather hurting her. "Good for you. What a relief."

"Yeah." He paused for a moment, the silence on the phone deafening between them. "Terri, she's safe now."

"But I'm not an approved foster parent yet." It about killed me to imagine Sophie with another foster parent, but at least she was safe, as Matt had said.

"I thought you should know."

"Thank you."

More uncomfortable silence.

"What about the party?" he asked, sounding hesitant.

"I will uphold my agreement."

I swear I heard him exhale from relief. "I appreciate it. I will buy the food and stop by Christmas morning to set things up. By the way, keep an eye out on the weather. A snowstorm is moving this way."

"Snow? In Big Cat?" I hadn't checked the weather on my phone lately. The coast rarely saw snow.

"Yes, and it's going to be a doozy. You have a generator, mostly for hurricanes not snow, but it will only run the refrigerator, the heater, and a few outlets. I suggest filling up the tubs with water so you can flush the toilets. Make sure you use containers for drinking water."

I had to be the least prepared person in this area for a snow storm. Occasionally Raleigh got inclement weather, but I had city water then and had lived in an apartment instead of a house.

"Thank you." At least he cared enough to warn me. Before I found the courage to apologize for asking him to leave that horrible day, he said goodbye and hung up. I sat there with the phone pressed to my ear. I wanted to hear his voice again, to see him, to snuggle him.

Unmotivated to work on my holiday checklist, I pulled on my coat and opened the door. Sure enough, a cold burst of winter gushed inside. With my hands in my coat pocket, I walked down the gravel driveway to retrieve my mail. I usually made a habit of collecting it as I drove up the driveway after work, but I hadn't bothered today, nor had I gone anywhere all weekend. Guess I was sulking and feeling sorry for myself.

I pulled open the mail box. As if by miracle, the only letter inside was from DSS. I held my breath and opened it with shaking hands while standing on my untraveled road. I scanned the words on the page in search for approval.

My gaze stopped. I yelped.

We are happy to inform you … Congratulations … I was now an official foster parent. I wanted to call someone, tell them my good news, but everyone except my mother was upset with me. I could call Matt back but it didn't feel right. I wanted to tell Sophie my good news but she no longer lived with me.

I glanced at the time, disappointed the offices would be closed. Now in a position to help, I had no idea how to find her.

In the meantime, I decided it best to drive to the grocery store to stock up on batteries, water, bread, and milk for the upcoming snowstorm, but when I arrived, the shelves for those items were bare. I ventured to another grocery store and fought the crowded parking lot. The items on my wish list were out of stock there as well. I bought canned food that Jessica and I could eat, but cold soup and vegetables sounded disgusting. I grabbed a plethora of unhealthy junk food, although not the best choice for a pregnant girl.

It dawned on me that I barely remembered how to start the generator. I also wished I had ordered a pile of firewood but had forgotten to call for a delivery. It might get awfully cold if the electricity went out and I couldn't start the generator. I stopped by the hardware store but there were no flashlights left on the shelves, although I owned enough candles to open up a candle shop. I bought more matches and a lighter. At least there were water containers left and I bought two, along with a snow shovel for the steps and salt. The checkout lines were long. I had no choice but to wait.

When I returned home I yawned, amazed by my level of exhaustion. Between preparing for the snow storm and the drama surrounding Sophie along with work, no wonder I felt tired. But I couldn't stop now.

I stacked the food items on the counter for easy access and had Jessica clean and fill the water jugs, and then I gathered the candles to put them in a localized area in the living room. I was as ready as possible, considering the store ran out of the main items I needed. I could only pray I got the generator started and we had plenty of gas since I had no clue what containers to fill or even how to top them off. I dug through the junk drawer and found a confusing owner's manual for the generator and tried to study it.

The following morning, I put a call in to DSS. I wanted to foster Sophie if possible. I had to leave a voice mail and wait for them to call me back.

At work, the weather remained the main topic of discussion with my patients. With the roads likely turning bad, it would be a couple of days before they'd be passable for me. In the South, especially at the coast, we didn't have much in the way of snow-removal equipment or salt trucks. I educated my patients who used oxygen on how to use the emergency tanks if we lost power.

Thankfully, I got off work early. As I busied myself carrying the last few remnants of wood inside, my cell phone rang. I almost didn't hear it dinging in my coat pocket, and didn't recognize the phone number.

"Is this Terri McMillan?" a friendly woman asked.

"Yes?"

"I have a request to place Ms. Sophie Yates in your care. Are you willing to take her, and if so, can we bring her to you late this afternoon?"

My prayers had been answered. I had to fight yelling "Yes!" into the phone. "Absolutely. Any time is fine." I wanted to ask about her but decided to wait to see for myself. I'm sure she had been through a lot.

"Thank you for your help," the pleasant social worker said, so unlike Ms. Phillips.

"It's my pleasure." I disconnected and jumped up and down. I was about to see Sophie again.

After I calmed a bit and could think rationally, I wondered if I had enough food in the house for another mouth to feed. I drove back to the store in search of anything edible for a teenager that would hold her over.

I returned home, carrying in bags of groceries for the second time, when a small maroon car pulled into my driveway. I hurried inside, dropped the bags onto my table, and then ran outside to greet Ms. Phillips as she stepped from the vehicle. Sophie climbed out, wearing her original baggy blue coat, her hair a tangled mess, but she looked wonderful to me.

I wrapped my arms around her as she kept her face lowered. I planted several kisses atop her head as we both started crying. I held her tight, never wanting to let her go.

Ms. Phillips' mouth turned upward. She looked much prettier and years younger when she smiled. "I see you both are happy to be back together."

Through tears, I said, "Yes we are." I smiled at her with newfound appreciation. "Thank you for bringing her back to me."

"I had my concerns at first, but my only goal is to ensure Sophie has a proper place to live. I now see you two are perfect together." She grinned while she opened the car door to the backseat and pulled out a plastic bag of clothes. I despised that she had no choice but to pack her belongings in a bag instead of a suitcase. She passed it to me before she retrieved the familiar oversized bear with its one floppy ear. No telling everything that stuffed bear had heard or seen over Sophie's lifetime.

I invited Ms. Phillips inside, embarrassed that my kitchen looked like a junk-food store.

She studied the supplies stacked on the counter and the bags on the table. "I see you are prepared for the storm coming in tonight."

"They moved it up to tonight?" I really needed to listen to the weather more often.

"Late night, early morning. It's supposed to be bad, which is unusual for our area."

I set Sophie's belongings on the table next to the grocery bags. Ms. Phillips scooted out a kitchen chair and positioned the bear upright, the stuffed animal sitting at the table like a human.

Sophie ran out of the kitchen. I heard her sneakers slap against the hardwoods as she darted up the steps.

"Again, thank you for bringing her home," I said. Ms. Phillips had no idea the relief I felt by having the child back in my house.

"Thank you for taking her, and for being a foster parent." She opened the back door and a gust of wind blew in. "And stay warm."

Jessica appeared at the doorway of the kitchen. "If it's okay, ma'am, I'd like to go back with you. I'm the reason Sophie left in the first place."

Ms. Phillips stepped back inside and closed the door.

I swallowed hard. "Jessica? You are welcome to stay here." Even though I made a decision to only foster one child, Sophie, I had committed to helping Jessica until the baby arrived.

"It's okay, Terri." She wrapped me in a hug. "I'm only here short-term but Sophie belongs with you."

Surprised by her wisdom and affection toward me, I smiled but a tear slid down my cheek. This was the first time she had initiated any physical touch with me since her arrival.

"I want to help you," I said, sad by her desire to leave.

"I'll be fine," she said with more confidence than I knew she had. She turned toward the social worker. "Please bring me with you."

The woman raised her eyebrows at me.

I nodded. If Jessica wanted to leave, I understood. "If you are comfortable telling me, I'd like to know why you changed your mind about staying," I said, unable to come up with a reason why the girls didn't get along.

Jessica's expression grew serious. "Sophie is jealous. She wants to be your child and feels threatened that you want to foster other kids."

I had no idea what to say.

"Did she tell you that?" I asked after I had a moment to think about what Jessica had said.

She shook her head. "Not in so many words but it's obvious. This is her one chance to have a loving home and she doesn't want to share it with other foster kids. I get it. I really do."

I understood too.

"I'm sorry, but you're welcome to at least stay here until the baby arrives."

"Thanks, but Sophie deserves a family who loves her. I'll be fine," she said again, as if to try to convince me.

I actually believed her. "I want to know when the baby is born and that you're okay. If you need anything, just call me. Promise?"

"Promise."

"Run and get your things," Ms. Phillips said as she pulled out the nearest kitchen chair and sat, as if anticipating a long wait.

Jessica returned soon after, carrying the suitcase I bought her instead of carrying her items around in a bag as she had when she arrived. She hugged and thanked me, and then left with Ms. Phillips.

I watched them leave, a tear running down my cheek. I had never been a person who cried until I met Sophie, Matt, and then Jessica. I had been given a taste of family life, a sense of belonging I had never experienced before. And I loved it. I wanted Matt back.

Once they pulled out of the driveway, I swiped my hand across my cheek before I jogged upstairs to see Sophie. I reached the top step and stared at her closed door. I had a flashback to the awful day I found her missing. I pulled myself together and knocked.

"Come in," she grumbled.

I cracked it open and peered inside. She sat cross-legged on her bed with a blanket spread across her. I noticed a bruise on her hand, peeking out from underneath her long-sleeved shirt. Matt said she had bruises on her arm. She saw me studying her and turned away.

I perched on the bed next to her and ran my hand across the top of her hair. I had so many questions but was afraid to ask just yet. I opted to love her instead.

"I missed you." She didn't answer but I heard a sniffle. "You should know that I made an important decision."

Normally I would have considered Matt's opinion on such an important topic, especially since my realization that he was *The One*. But ... without him here, I needed to do what was right for Sophie, and for me.

She peeked up at me through snippets of long hair. Without a doubt, I wanted her in my life forever.

"I decided not to be a foster parent after all." At her alarmed expression, I smoothed the back of her head once more. "I mean, I won't be taking in other kids. You're welcome to stay here as long as you want."

She let out a long sigh. "For a minute I thought you were saying ..." She didn't finish the sentence.

"Never, honey." I placed my hand over hers, rubbing the back of it with my thumb. "I got to thinking. Instead of helping several kids a little bit, I'd rather help you a lot." I paused, considering how much to tell her. "I love you. If your mom agrees, and you of course, I'd like to make you my daughter."

Her head tilted. She held hope in her expression. "What do you mean?"

"I'd like to adopt you." I held my breath, unsure of how she felt about the subject. All I had to go on was what Jessica had told me.

Sophie scooted closer and snuggled into me. When she placed her head on my shoulder, my emotions unwound in a fast spiral. She was the vulnerable, scared little girl I once was when my daddy walked out on us.

Chapter Twenty-Three

I awakened to the howling wind. The chill from outside seeped into the house, despite the heater running nonstop.

Not wanting to crawl from my warm spot in the bed, I slid deeper under the covers and pulled the comforter up to my chin. Muted pings of ice hit the windows. Forget going back to sleep with a winter storm raging.

I dragged myself from bed and opened the plantation blinds to peer outside. It was still pitch black. I saw nothing except pellets of sleet bouncing off the glass. With a layer of sleet falling, the roads were going to be slick. I hadn't canceled my home health visits yet because I wanted to see firsthand that snow and ice were actually going to slam the coast.

I wrapped a warm fuzzy blanket around me and padded into the kitchen where I turned on the porch light. I leaned over my tile table to look out the window. Mr. Weather had painted the backyard white with ice. The light revealed coated trees with a shiny gloss. I knew from the ice storms we had in Raleigh that pine trees didn't hold up well before the branches started cracking. Fallen limbs caused power outages.

I backed away from the intense winter scene to crank up the heat, not that raising the thermostat helped much since the unit ran nonstop. I really wanted a warm fire but it was probably a good plan to save the wood I had.

I wished Matt were here. His peaceful influence calmed me, and the storm had me on edge.

I glanced at the time … only four in the morning. Oh, come on. Why was I up so early?

I slinked back to bed as I listened to the gusting wind. The chimes hanging from the magnolia tree clanged wildly as if mangled into one big tangled knot by a hurricane. I wished I had remembered to take them down. I crawled underneath the covers, still warm from before. I lay there for an undetermined amount of time before I dozed off, only to awaken when grey light seeped through my window. I hadn't closed the blinds after I had peeked outside at the winter wonderland.

"Terri?" Sophie's whisper filled the quiet of the house except for the sound of occasional creaking caused by the wind. "Are you awake?"

I held open the covers on the empty side of my bed to welcome her. "I'm awake. It's too cold to crawl out of bed." But the steady hum of the heater had stopped. That didn't bode well for us.

She climbed in next to me. "It's cold in here."

"The electricity must have gone out." I scooted under the blankets more, pulling them over Sophie too, dreading the inevitable need to fiddle with the generator. According to a handwritten note I found in the manual, it ran the heater and refrigerator, as Matt had said. That still meant we had no running water. Suddenly grateful I filled the tubs to flush toilets, I was thankful Jessica had filled the containers for drinking water.

The house grew colder. Winter engulfed us from beyond the windows. From my warm spot buried under blankets, I glanced outside. My view of the marsh now consisted of a frozen paradise. The trees wore at least two inches of snow on their branches.

I groaned, facing the fact I needed to climb from my toasty spot to mess with the generator and to start a blazing fire in the fireplace. Reluctantly I rolled out with my feet hitting the ice-cold floor. I chose sweat pants, a thick sweater, and wool hiking socks to light a fire first. The dark Christmas tree, without the twinkling lights I had grown to love, faced off with me in silent accusation for forgetting to order firewood. How lonely.

A stack of wood surprised me inside the cold black hole of the fireplace. Matt amazed me in his thoughtful ways. I lit the kindling, the fire roaring to life.

Smoke started to fill the room. The chimney flue!

I coughed with vigor but managed to stick my hand up into the chimney to fiddle around until I found the handle. I pushed on it but no such luck. The battery-operated smoke detector went off, the ringing unbearable as smoke filled the room.

Sophie joined me, coughing as well.

"What's going on?" a deep voice called out behind me.

I turned to see Matt hurrying toward Sophie and me. I had never been so happy to see him.

He knelt down beside me and shoved his hand up inside the chimney. Metallic scraping sounded from inside as well as the fire alarm piercing through the dark house. The smoke tinged my nose with its rancid smell.

Matt grunted and the handle gave. "Got it." He closed the glass doors to help with guiding the smoke up the chimney.

I wrapped my arms around his backside. "I'm so glad you're here."

He scooted around to face me. "I'm glad you're both all right. When my electricity went off, I remembered you've never started the generator before."

"Apparently I don't know how to make a fire either." I kissed him with all the love I held for him.

"Yuck." Sophie shielded her vision and ran toward my bedroom, likely to return to the warm bed. "You know, I can hear you still smooching," she called out, laughing. "Gross." I knew she wanted to just give us a hard time and didn't mean anything by it.

"Where's Jessica?" he asked me.

Briefly, I explained what happened, keeping my voice low so Sophie wouldn't overhear me. I didn't want her to know the reason Jessica left, didn't want her to feel bad and blame herself.

He nodded but didn't say anything, likely following my lead to keep things quiet. "Let me attend to the generator," he said, standing there with his coat dusted with ashes and his hand on my waist. "The faster we get that going, the quicker we'll have heat. In the meantime, you might want to put on warmer clothes."

His protective side filled me with love. I watched him leave the room and heard the back door close. Without a doubt we needed to have an in-depth conversation to discuss what happened between us. I knew better than to disregard problems, something my relationship with Emily taught me. If we ignored them, at some point we would have a huge pile of problems to stumble over.

"You love him, don't you?" Sophie leaned against the doorway of my bedroom with her arms crossed.

I nodded. I braced myself for an argument. She hadn't kept her jealousy toward him hidden.

"I think you should marry him." She smiled.

My mouth dropped open. "Marry him?" I never thought I'd hear her say those words. "You've had a change of heart?"

"It's obvious you both love each other." She kept her arms crossed.

I wasn't sure if she resisted the idea of Matt and me together, or if she was cold. I decided it was the latter.

"We argued for a reason," I explained. I hadn't felt supported with my dreams, even though now I had changed them. The truth? I hadn't been exactly supportive of him, either, knowing what he went through as a child and why he had a bad taste in his mouth about the whole foster process. If I had faced the situation head on, instead of taking things personally, we could have avoided the entire argument.

"It was all because of me," Sophie said, sounding older than her thirteen years. "I didn't make it easy for him to like me."

I stepped toward her. "Oh, honey. It wasn't your fault, but mine. Matt adores you as much as I do." She let me wrap her in a hug.

The warmth radiating from her began to thaw out my limbs. "We need to put on warmer clothes until the house heats up." I steered her toward the stairs so we both could change. I entered my room and found my yoga pants to wear under my sweat pants and a short-sleeved exercise shirt and sweater to layer. I put on my coat and gloves too, noticing the temperature in the house dipped to a chilling fifty-eight degrees.

When Matt returned, generator humming, we both nestled in front of the fireplace. Sophie bounded down the steps bundled up to join us.

"It won't take long to warm up the downstairs," he said.

I remembered reading that the generator operated the lower-level

HVAC unit and not the one upstairs. No worries, and Sophie had a place in bed next to me, if needed.

Apparently a few electrical plugs in the living room worked as well, so I moved the cords around to allow us to spend the day in front of the fire next to the twinkling Christmas tree.

"We need to have an electrician update some of the older wires. The list is never ending," he complained.

We. As in we were a team, not as if he were trying to take over my house. What an epiphany.

Before long, the house heated up and we removed our extra clothing. Between the generator doing its job and the fireplace doling out cozy warmth, the good life had returned.

"Let's finish reading the letters and diary," Matt said, sitting in his usual spot on the love seat.

I looked up wide-eyed. "I hate to break the news to you but I finished reading them."

He swirled around in the love seat to meet my gaze. "How could you do that without me?"

"Ummm," I said, not wanting to admit my temporary depression when we weren't together. "Curiosity about how the story ended? I hoped for a different outcome for Robert."

"I understand. And I wasn't here." He held out his hand for the letters. "But I need to finish reading them."

I passed the letters to him, knowing they were going to upset him as they had me.

"I want to hear the rest too," Sophie said, having invested her emotions into listening to them as well.

I mentally prepared myself for heartbreak all over again.

Matt read the letters aloud. When he said the last line, he turned his face away from us. I knew he didn't want us to see his tears.

My own tears were running down my face. Hearing Robert's innocent hope of holding his wife when he stepped off the plane, and then the letters stopping, left a hole in my heart.

Sniffles came from underneath Sophie's pile of blankets on the couch. I got up and sat next to her, wrapping my arm around the lump of blankets to offer support.

"I need to read the diary." Matt's voice sounded thick with emotion.

"I understand the desire," I said.

He plucked the diary from its resting place on the coffee table and began to read Shirley's last written words. When he finished, he left the room upset, saying he needed to check on the generator.

I let him be. He needed to gather his emotions.

Sophie climbed from her safe spot next to me to run up to her room.

I sat alone with my gaze on the flickering fire. From my peripheral vision, I enjoyed the beauty of the sparkling Christmas tree. I had the distinct feeling Shirley was here with me in spirit, telling me everything was okay now. The family I so wanted had returned.

When Matt rejoined me on the love seat, I noticed his eyes were red.

"I got my wish."

I glanced up. "What wish is that?"

"To know my grandpa on a personal level. When Nana remarried, I always thought of Grandpa George as my grandfather, but I had always wondered about Grandpa Robert."

"That was a special gift your grandmother left behind for you to find."

He nodded. "I never understood why she loved Christmas so much, and never knew she got married to my grandfather on Christmas Eve in this house. It makes sense now why she decorated heavily each year. It was because he never returned home and she was thinking about their anniversary."

I agreed with him. "It must have been hard on her."

He nodded. "We have a special kind of love like they had." He paused for a moment, his Adam's apple moving in his throat. "We need to talk about what happened between us."

No better time than the present. "You're right."

"There are some things you need to know about my past," he said in a quiet voice.

I settled into his arms. "There are some things you need to know about me too, but you go first."

He tilted his head at me. "Just know I love you." He kissed me with a gentle touch.

My heart grew so warm within my chest it could heat the entire house.

"As you know, my dad is the pastor of the church where Sophie sings. Growing up we took in runaway kids, and also had half the neighborhood at our house most of the time." He inhaled a slow, jagged breath. "On the surface, people thought our home life was perfect. But the truth? What a nightmare."

He captivated my attention. I pulled away to listen and watch him but kept my foot touching his leg to keep the connection between us.

"One of the kids who stayed with us, David, sold drugs. Known by other kids, not by my parents," he explained. "He bullied me because I wouldn't help him sell them to my friends. Over time I learned how to stand up to him. One day I had to get in his face and threaten to tell my dad."

He paused, his gaze distant, reliving the past.

I remained quiet but enthralled with his story.

"The kid ran away and my dad fumed. My mom said she failed to help David too, but my father blamed me. I got punished, having to do extra work around the house with his disapproval of me obvious. Although my father never laid a hand on me, his anger and disappointment were far worse. David came back within the week but this time he set me up. I got busted for possession of drugs."

I sighed, unsure of what to say.

"The police got involved, my dad mad once again, and my mother cried a lot. I tried hard to win his love, but honestly, I've always struggled with feeling like a failure in his eyes."

Confused I said, "I don't understand. Why?"

Matt inhaled a long breath. "It started when I was a kid. He wanted me to go to college, to do well in school, so I could get a professional degree. My grades were never good enough, and being a cop wasn't the professional job he wanted for me."

"Being a cop is heroic." But I no longer feared his occupation. I respected him and prayed he'd always return home safely.

Matt shrugged. "He doesn't see it that way."

"Did he say that?"

Matt shook his head. "No, maybe I just felt his disapproval. I still do. Now that I think about it, I remember he once said that his own father didn't want him to follow in his footsteps and become a pastor like him. You think he'd understood how rotten judgment feels."

"Being a pastor is an important job too," I said. "So his own father criticized him for following in his footsteps, and yet your father did exactly the same thing to you." Then I sat up taller. "Wait a minute. Daniel's father died in Vietnam."

"He considered Grandpa George his father. My dad has no memories of living with Nana alone while his dad was at war."

"Wow." I leaned in closer. "I'm just saying, we tend to push our own issues onto our kids. Apparently he behaved in the only way he knew how because his stepfather treated him the same way. I wonder if he thought he showed his love by wanting a better life for you than he thought he had."

Matt stared at me. "Although that doesn't explain why he defended a boy who set me up. I mean, he assumed I was guilty. Even after I told my mother the truth my dad still acted angry with me."

"Or angry that he misjudged you." I placed my hand on his. "Have you talked to him about this?"

Matt shook his head. "No, time passed and we've both ignored it over these years. You're right, though. It's past time. I'll call him, maybe after Christmas."

"Don't wait too long." I didn't want to nag, but after my own experience with my family, I regretted having not addressed things earlier.

Matt didn't respond but from his long sigh I knew he heard what I meant. It would be nice to have some of this resolved before the holiday party, so father and son could enjoy each other.

I wondered how his father felt when Matt sold this house to me. Matt mentioned before how he didn't want to have the family Christmas here. Was it because of the tension between them, or nostalgia?

"Was he upset when you sold Nana's house?" I decided to go ahead and ask.

Matt shrugged. "I thought so at first, but no. I thought he wanted to hold onto the past, but once I explained to him about how this house deserves a family of its own instead of renting it out like I'd been doing, he said he understood. Sure, he wished we kept it in the family, although no one stepped up to take responsibility. Anyway, I held onto my own misbelief about my dad. After I met you and Sophie, I learned how to let go emotionally and accept what love and family means."

His raw emotions touched me and I said, "You and Sophie have taught me about love too. Apparently, I had emotional barriers up my entire life until I experienced what family is truly about."

We stared at each other. The amount of electricity zipping between us was enough to light every house in this area.

"You've been through a lot too," he said.

I didn't want to focus on me. "Back to David and the drugs. How did you resolve the issue? What made you tell your mother the truth?"

He closed his eyes for a long moment before opening them. He gazed at the Christmas tree as if to draw strength from Shirley. "At first I was afraid to come clean with the true story, fearful the kid would retaliate against me. But my mother knew I was hiding the truth."

I scooted even closer to him, drawn to his gentleness, his story, and to offer support.

He didn't look at me. "She explained the importance of being honest and said it wasn't right for me to take the fall for someone else. Apparently David had hidden them in my room. The police had heard about someone selling drugs from our house. When they searched my room they found them, and I got busted."

"I'm so sorry."

He nodded. "My mom has her ways of getting me to confess. I ended up telling the police everything. And Nana always believed in me. She never wavered."

He paused, dragged in a long breath, and released it as I waited.

"The boy got in trouble, but no charges pressed for me. And never again did we take in runaway kids. Of course, I felt like my father blamed me for this too."

I shook my head with realization. "That's why you were cautious and protective of me when I took in Sophie to live with me. And why you didn't tell me about Jessica."

"Yes. It wasn't the right thing for me to do, Terri. I understand now and shouldn't have let my experience clash with your plans. I wanted to protect you from possibly going through what I had, and that wasn't fair to you."

This time he looked me directly in the eyes.

"These kids are hurting and can be manipulative by no fault of their own. They're a product of their environment and as tough as it is on them, it's hard on the foster parents too. I saw how my dad invested himself in the kids, even over his own, and they disappointed him by running off or getting into trouble."

I sighed. "I understand. What little experience I've had with Jessica and Sophie certainly showed me its rewards and losses. When Sophie ran away my heart plummeted, and when you told me you expected it, I became angry with you because you were right and I didn't want to hear the painful truth. You weren't trying to be mean, you were reacting to what you'd experienced."

"I'm sorry about coming off as being mean. I want to support all of your dreams." He squeezed my hand and then held it. "If being a foster parent makes you happy, then I will help any way I can. We can do it together."

My insides practically melted in a pool of liquid at my feet.

"Not all the kids were difficult. I've kept in touch with a few to this day."

I stared at him, feeling all dazed and yummy. He was talking in terms of being a united front. "Thank you for forgiving me and my rush to judgment. I wasn't very considerate about how my goals collided with your painful past."

"And I'm sorry for not being supportive of your dreams as I should have been. From now on I'm all in, and I love you."

"I love you too." I pressed my lips into his, and when I pulled away, I realized I hadn't told him my decision yet about fostering and adopting Sophie. If her mom agreed. "There's something you need to know too."

"What's that?"

I swallowed hard. I never liked sharing my vulnerable side with people. But Matt was safe. I cleared my throat. "When Sophie ran off, my heart went with her, as it did when you left. I had a decision to make. I could either help several kids to a smaller degree by offering them a safe place to live, a routine, someone who cared about them, or I could make a huge difference in the life of one child. Foster kids aren't just lost, they are hurting and in need of love too. They have wounds that need healing and that's not the easiest thing to do. So I've decided to focus on one child instead of a house full of kids. I love Sophie as if she were my own. I plan to start the adoption process if her mother agrees."

He blinked several times before a smile slid across his face. "That's beautiful. But you're certified now as a foster parent. Are you going to postpone that?"

"At least until Sophie grows up, goes to college. Who knows, maybe I'll change my mind again but it's nice to know you'll support me."

"Absolutely. Terri, you're a smart, loving woman. It's why I care so much for you and whatever you decide is fine by me."

"So you support my decision to adopt?"

He nodded. "Yes, I care about Sophie very much."

I had met my soul mate.

"I'd still like to carry on with combining our family Christmas, mine and yours together, for the best holiday get-together this house has ever seen. Nana would be proud," he said with a wink.

The lights flickered, the electricity popping back on.

"See, Nana agrees." We both laughed at his comment. To us, the magic of the holiday was real in our hearts.

"I'll need to make a couple of phone calls first." I needed to convince my family all was right with us. "What about the weather?"

"What about it?"

I flicked my hand toward the window. "If you haven't noticed, the roads are covered in snow and ice."

He shrugged. "No worries. We have two days left. It will clear."

"Haven't you seen the forecast?" All week the temperatures were supposed to hover around freezing. "People here aren't used to driving in it and will probably want to stay home."

"That's where you're wrong. The roads will be clear for Christmas."

Without much in the way of equipment for snow removal, I doubted his optimism, but I didn't want to argue the point.

"Trust me," he said. "We're having the party."

Chapter Twenty-Four

O n Christmas Eve we spent most of the morning cleaning house. The sun started melting the icy tire tracks on the road and by noon it heated up to whopping thirty-two degrees. I suspected it would all freeze up again tonight and prayed it warmed up enough tomorrow to melt it away for good. To my surprise, I really wanted to have this party.

That afternoon, the three of us worked in the kitchen. I made a pecan pie, following Shirley's handwritten recipe from a notecard Matt had loaned me. He stood over the stove, simmering homemade lasagna sauce. Sophie put together appetizer trays, a vegetable one and two different cracker trays, one with cheese the other with onion dip. The three of us made a great team.

Christmas music played from a nearby speaker and I no longer cringed as I listened to the holiday tunes.

"I hope this pie is edible. You know what I did to the turkey," I said, Matt moving out of the way as I shoved the fancy pie plate into the oven.

He laughed. "Your turkey was delicious, and I've become a fan of extra crispy skin." He winked then continued. "The caveat with pecan pie is you have to make sure the crust doesn't burn or the pecans. I'll help if you want."

"Absolutely," I said as I closed the oven door, a bit relieved. "Let's monitor it together."

He chuckled, grabbing me from behind, kissing me lightly on the neck. "The pie will taste great. Just relax."

"Relax? Parties aren't my thing." But I was changing my mind very quickly.

Sophie put the trays in the refrigerator. "Anything else I can do? I kind of wanted to binge-watch Christmas movies but that's okay. I never really got to watch many of them and Carley shared her favorites."

Thrilled she and Carley had become good friends, I loved how they were peas in a pod and would be able to help one another. Her father, now stationed for the long haul, planned for her to finish her schooling here. I believe these girls would develop a strong friendship, and it would benefit them throughout their lives.

"You know what, Sophie? I wish I could watch them too." But I had too much work to do to get ready. Besides, I usually avoided holiday movies, but shocking to me, I now had a hankering to watch a charming Christmas love story. I glanced at Matt as he layered a deep red baking dish with cooked lasagna noodles, ricotta cheese, sauce, and a layer of shredded cheese and parmesan.

"Go for it," Matt said. "I'll watch the pie. We're just about finished with everything anyway."

I smiled and winked at him. "You'd make a good wife."

He blushed. "How about a good husband?"

My cheeks burned hot. Was he being playful, or feeling me out on the subject once again?

Throughout the day the snow melted slowly on the roads, revealing pavement in large sections. However, my yard still hung onto the gorgeous icy winter. I wasn't sure if Matt's family would want to drive tomorrow, but I knew my family planned to arrive by early afternoon.

I had a special surprise for Sophie's Christmas present. I couldn't wait to give it to her but it depended on the safety of the roads.

Matt's cell phone rang and interrupted my thoughts.

He stared at the phone. "Excuse me for a bit, Terri. My dad is finally returning my call."

The *talk*. I left the room to give him privacy and went to join Sophie in the family room to watch a movie. I hoped Matt and his father found a way to work out their differences. If I'd learned anything lately, albeit the hard way, I'd swear good communication was the key to inner joy and successful relationships.

Before long, the sweet aroma of pie filled the house and I heard

Matt open the oven to remove it while he continued to talk to his father. I smiled, knowing he had my back and always would.

I curled deeper into the plush sofa pillow. When the movie was almost over, Matt joined us in the living room. I wanted to hear what happened but when I paused the movie, he motioned for us to finish.

Once it ended, I climbed out of my cozy spot on the couch. "Be right back," I said to Sophie as she clicked through a long list of movies to watch when I returned.

Matt and I walked into the kitchen and sat at the table. He smiled and I held out hope he had a productive discussion with his father.

"Well?" I asked, unable to restrain myself any longer from knowing the details.

"I tried to word everything just right but in the beginning he got defensive."

Sure, that didn't surprise me really. Most people did when confronted, even in a gentle way. I imagined his father felt a bit guilty with the whole matter anyway.

"We talked, discussed, got frustrated, and apologized." Matt glanced at the time. "All in all, I'd say it didn't take that long, considering we've had this rift for years."

I nodded. "And?"

"And you were right. He didn't understand why we weren't close and never knew how I perceived the whole thing, as a kid and now. Long story short, he lost his father to the Vietnam War and tried to surround himself with kids to help."

I pressed my hand into my mouth to restrain a gulp. "Everything makes so much sense now."

Matt nodded. "And he acknowledged me but figured out something I hadn't."

"What?"

"Without understanding it at the time, he resented me too because I pushed back against what he wanted to accomplish. We talked it out and made up." Matt let out a long sigh.

"Really? Amazing, the beautiful closure you received." But one thing still didn't sit well with me. "Did he apologize for believing David at the time, not realizing what effect it had on you?" I really wanted to know, plus I thought Matt might benefit from talking it out.

"Yes, he thought I knew he loved me. He recognizes now he'd been devoting too much of his time to the other kids and neglecting his family. He takes the blame for our strained relationship."

I didn't know what to say. But it did convince me, more than ever, that my decision to raise Sophie without interference from other kids was the right one. I would hate to put such a burden on a child as Matt's dad had done to him unintentionally. I just wanted to wrap her in love and offer her a carefree, enjoyable life.

"Anyhow," he continued, reaching for my hand. "I told him I understood, and that you'd pretty much figured everything out. He's glad I met you, and I told him I am too." He winked and I held onto his hand tighter. "So, we forgave one another and decided we wanted to be more involved in each other's lives. I think that's a really good start and we're in a positive place. Thanks to you."

I jumped up and wrapped my arms around him. He stood and pushed his chair back, squeezing me into a tight embrace. "If you hadn't encouraged me to talk with him, I doubt I would have."

"Oh, Matt. I'm so glad it worked out for the best. I'm learning life is too short to be separated or angry from the ones we love." Now they could relax and enjoy each other as they moved their relationship forward in a positive, constructive manner, not to mention enjoy the holiday party we had worked so hard to create. And it was a lesson to me to not hold grudges, to get things out in the open, whether it hurt or not.

He kissed me and I swear my toes curled. I loved this man more than I had ever loved anyone my whole life.

We spent the rest of the day being comfortable in front of the fireplace watching movies. So far this was my favorite Christmas yet. Before long, we said our goodbyes until the big party day tomorrow.

On Christmas morning, I padded to the front window in the dining room and glanced out. The roads were mostly clear, thank goodness, and the sun gleamed across the bright white yard. We were having a white Christmas.

When I snuck out of the house to meet Clark's daughter driving up the driveway, I could see my breath in the cold air, but the streets were almost clear. I said thank you, took Sophie's present, and hid it in the cottage.

Sophie woke up an hour or so later and we sat at the table, finishing breakfast and waiting for Matt. I enjoyed the frosty scenery and the Christmas music playing, along with the warm feeling inside of me. It was a first.

We talked some about school and about the choir. It turned out she wanted to sing on Sundays at the church, and Carley wanted to join her. Lately, the girls were practically glued together.

"Do I have to wait to open my presents?" she asked, squirming in her chair at the breakfast table. "I can't stand it. Carley says she gets to open at least one when she first wakes up."

I hated to ask her to wait. "Sorry, I know it's hard but we'll open gifts as soon as Matt arrives. Promise. It won't be much longer." I picked up my cell phone to call him when I heard his truck pull into the driveway.

"He's here!" She ran to the door, opened it, but didn't venture out in the cold.

Matt walked inside, bringing sunshine in with him along with an armful of presents. Sophie jumped up and down. "Merry Christmas, Soph. Wanna put the presents under the tree?"

"Yes!" She struggled but managed to carry all the gifts in one armful into the other room.

I abandoned my cereal bowl to meet him at the door. I slid my arms inside his coat and kissed him, so happy to have him back in my life.

"Merry Christmas, sweetheart." He bent down and kissed me, holding me in his arms for a tender moment.

Sophie ran back into the kitchen. "Can we open presents now? Please!"

What a great first experience of a proper Christmas morning, so I couldn't ask her to wait any longer. I planned to make it the best one possible, full of love and warmth. "Absolutely."

She bounced up and down as we made our way into the living

room. I couldn't believe how many presents Santa had piled under the twinkling tree. I swear Shirley's presence blessed us.

"First, I need to make a fire," Matt said, glancing at us both for our reaction. "It's part of my childhood tradition."

I loved the heartwarming idea of opening presents to flickering flames with Christmas music playing. In some ways this was a first Christmas morning for me too, one I planned to enjoy instead of resist as I had for years.

When we each found a comfy spot to sit and call our own, I said to Sophie, "Why don't you be Santa and pass one present to each of us." As a kid I used to hate opening one gift at a time, but now I understood why my family adopted the tradition. Everyone could enjoy watching the others open their presents with delight.

Sophie handed Matt a present, then me, and then herself. She shook the red and silver one with the perfect ribbon curled around the package. Matt had outdone himself.

"You want to go first?" I asked her.

She bit her lower lip and ripped open the package. "Oh!" She held up a new stuffed animal, the cutest brown dog. "I love him!" She squealed while hugging her toy. "Thank you so much, Matt." She crawled over to him and wrapped her arms around his neck before she sat back in her heaping nest of messy wrapping paper.

"You're welcome, honey." Matt smiled as if he appreciated seeing Sophie's excitement and joy, the best reward of all.

Matt nodded to me. I held a long and small package, wrapped in shiny green paper with another elaborate curly bow on top. I had no idea what to expect, so I tore off the paper with new excitement. I found it heartwarming that the man I loved had picked out something special just for me.

"Ohhh," I exclaimed when I glanced inside. The prettiest silver necklace ever gleamed back at me, so dainty and feminine with a silver heart charm and a small diamond in the center. "This is gorgeous." I wasn't sure how to handle my overwhelming emotions. No one had ever bought me such a lovely gift. I leaned over and wrapped my arms around him. "Thank you."

"You're welcome, sweetheart. I hope you like it." The love in his eyes shown bright and I fought back tears of joy.

"I love it." I removed it from the box, lifted up my hair to allow him free access to latch it around my neck. "I plan to wear it always."

I hadn't been sure what to buy him for Christmas, so I bought him the best smelling cologne I could find. I had fun sniffing the different bottles at the store. One of my girlfriends from Raleigh and I used to go into the cologne store at the mall and pretend we were there to buy for the boyfriends we didn't have. I swear we used to spend thirty minutes sniffing different scents and imagining the man we'd buy for. Now that dream had become a reality.

Sophie handed me a present. I glanced at Matt, knowing full well Sophie wasn't able to buy me anything. He smiled and winked.

I ripped open the paper. "Oh!" I opened a beautiful soft leather diary and ran my finger over one of the white-on-white roses embossed at the top of each page.

I leaned forward and hugged Sophie tight. "Thank you. I love it."

She stayed in my arms for a long moment before she spoke. "You're welcome. I thought you could write in the diary to leave behind your memories too. You know, like Nana did."

I stared at Sophie, touched by her thoughtful gift. "What a wonderful idea. Finding Nana's diary was a special treat for me, one I'll never forget."

"Actually, that's the first time you've called her Nana," Matt said with a smile and a wink of approval.

I finally let my emotional wall crash down around me and embraced love and family.

Sophie glanced at Matt. "Maybe you could write Aunt Terri, I mean, Mom ... love letters too, just like your grandfather did."

Mom. The word choked me up. Although I wasn't her mother yet, when the adoption went through I planned to be the best mom ever. I had a brief conversation with Sophie's mom last night and she had agreed to let me adopt her.

"Thank you, Sophie. You know the happiest moment of my life will be once the adoption becomes official." I wrapped her into a tight hug and didn't let go for a long minute.

"And I'd be honored to write your mom love letters like Robert." Matt motioned Sophie over and we folded ourselves into a group hug that started out emotional at first until it turned silly and became a tickling match.

I'd never had such a fun Christmas morning in my life until today and couldn't wait for more Christmases to come.

After we finished unwrapping our presents, the paper covered the floor of the family room, mostly because I resisted the temptation to clean up as we went as my mother had always insisted. Instead, I announced I had a special gift waiting for Sophie. I excused myself and left the house to retrieve her present from the cottage. I couldn't wait to see the look on her face.

I opened the door, picked up the precious bundle, and carried it into the house. When Sophie saw what I held squirming in my arms, she screamed with delight.

I handed the brown puppy, with one floppy ear, over to her. She started to cry as the dog licked her face.

All girls needed a puppy to love.

"It will help you through the troubled times of teenaged years. I also plan to adopt two of the wild horses from Jenni's grandmother to fill our field. I will hire a trainer to help us since I know next to nothing about riding. But I want us to learn together."

"Are you for real?" Sophie squealed again, and wrapped me in a hug around the puppy in her arms. The puppy licked me on the chin.

Matt and I cleaned up the mess in the living room while Sophie played with her new best friend. The joy I saw on her face filled me with my own sense of pleasure so deep I realized I was already a mom.

We finished cleaning the room and left Sophie to play with Cookie, the name she chose for her puppy.

As we entered the kitchen, I said, "By the way I got a call from Ms. Phillips, the social worker, last night after you left."

Matt raised his eyebrows. "Is something wrong with Sophie's placement?"

I shook my head. "No, but Jessica had her baby and is doing well."

"Good for her," he said as he kissed my cheek and then my lips while he mumbled. "Did she give the baby up for adoption?"

I kissed him long and deep before I answered. "She did. Everything went as planned. The baby arrived two weeks early but both are healthy."

"Yet another Christmas miracle," Matt said as he held me close. "Don't panic, but we have a lot to do this morning."

I raised my eyebrows. "Isn't everything finished?"

"Mostly," he said as he pulled the huge dish of lasagna out of the refrigerator and set it on top of the stove. He turned on the oven and placed the lasagna inside.

"Is everyone still coming?"

He grinned like a boy. "Of course. The roads are fine. The snow is only on the grass, so technically it's a white Christmas." He started singing "White Christmas" and pulled me into his arms to nuzzle my neck. I giggled as his lips tickled. When he finished singing, he said, "This is a special day. I've never in my lifetime had a white Christmas before."

Special didn't even begin to describe our Christmas. "I've only experienced a white Christmas once years ago in Raleigh. The dusting of snow lasted for an hour but we considered it a white Christmas."

He snuggled me close. "Well, it's definitely white out there. Maybe it's more of Nana's Christmas magic."

I smiled up at him, no longer resisting the truth of the legend. "Maybe." I kissed him softly on the lips.

Sophie cleared her throat to announce she entered the kitchen. With reluctance, Matt and I pulled away from each other.

"I think Cookie has to go to the bathroom," Sophie said.

I had a proud moment, seeing her dressed in her boots and coat, ready to take care of her pet.

"Oh gosh, I left the leash and collar in the other room. Hang on, Sophie."

When I returned and hooked the leash on Cookie's collar, Sophie carried her outside and set her on the grass. As we watched them through the window, we chuckled at the adorable puppy as she mouthed and played with the snow. When they came back inside the puppy collapsed at Sophie's feet while she pulled off her boots. But as soon as Sophie left the room to remove her coat and store the items in the hall closet, Cookie followed.

Adorable. Cookie made the perfect companion.

When they returned, Sophie asked, "What's left to do?"

Matt pulled out several items from the refrigerator. "Can you pour chips into bowls, stack the cups, and set the flatware on the counter along with the pies?"

"Sure thing." She got to work opening chip bags and began to whistle. It was important to involve her in the makings of the festive occasion.

He glanced at me. "Can you check over the house to make sure it's ready and keep an eye on the lasagna while I carry in more wood?"

"Yes sir, task master," I teased while he lightly tapped me on the rear. "And thanks for bringing your wood after my epic failure to order more."

"You'll pay," he said and winked.

Electric energy shot through me. I had to be the luckiest woman alive to have him back in my life.

"How so?" My voice raised an octave, or several to be exact. He smiled but didn't answer and instead bundled up to head outside to his truck. I ignored Sophie's dramatic display of pretending to gag at us.

I turned up the Christmas music, singing along as I replaced hand towels in the bathrooms and made sure we had an ample amount of toilet paper available. Still singing, I turned on the vacuum for a once-over on the hardwood floors. As I turned around, I gulped as Matt stood there in the hallway with wood in his arms, grinning at me.

The morning flew by. Not long after I showered and changed into a red sweater and slacks our guests began to arrive.

Holiday music filled the air as my mom walked in. She removed her festive red coat and gloves and handed them over to me. I left the room, feeling light and happy for the first Christmas ever, and set her belongings on my bed. When I returned, there were three more people in the kitchen. Matt's uncle, his wife, and their older son were laughing and joking. We moved the party into the living room around the Christmas tree. The pile of coats began to accumulate into a mound on my bed as more people filtered in.

I noticed the smile on Matt's face when his father and mother entered the kitchen. His dad glanced around and whistled. "Nice job on the house. It looks even better than when Nana lived here."

Matt's face glowed with pride. Today was a new beginning for them. They'd finally gotten over their differences and I could only imagine how much better life would be for them both.

I found the amount of people standing around chatting in my house a pleasant experience for me. Everyone wore smiles, having fun. The decorations hung along the mantel, a basket I found in the attic held pinecones on the hearth, and candles glowed with warmth. A pleasant aroma of lasagna wafted through the rooms as it baked. Candy canes even dangled from the limbs of the Christmas tree. Without a doubt, I knew Nana's spirit was with us, and she was happy all of her family gathered together at last in one place.

We had decided to invite friends as well as both families. Matt said his relatives were so appreciative to just be back in the house to celebrate Christmas, they didn't mind who I invited. The more the merrier.

Even Jenni and Scott were here with their adorable babies. They brought their friend, Gabbi, my next-door neighbor. I held a newfound belief that no one should spend Christmas alone, and I found it amusing to see her at the punch table laughing and talking to Chip Baker, one of Matt's cousins. The romantic side of me wanted to see them get together and find the same joy I had found with Matt.

My sister opened the kitchen door and entered with Keith. She was here! From the surprised expression on her face, I knew she experienced the same reaction to the roomful of cheer as I did.

I approached her, glad to let our rocky past melt away. "Merry Christmas." I squeezed her into a hug. She hesitated for a moment but returned the embrace. It was the first time in years but a long time coming. I had finally arrived home.

When I drew back, I noticed the smile on her face. I hugged Keith too, then took their coats and added them to the mound on my bed.

I stepped from my room and quietly observed the mingling group of festive people. We had pulled this off, Matt, Sophie, and I. Although I had been resistant for most of the preparations, the work was worth the reward. If I had known the pleasure upfront, I might have been more enthusiastic from the beginning.

Matt gathered us around the tree in front of the fireplace. "Let's sing 'O Come, All Ye Faithful.' Can someone turn off the lights?"

The flames of the fireplace flickered across everyone's faces, the candles glowed, the tree twinkled. To my surprise, we all held hands. I held Sophie's and Matt took hold of mine, gazing at one another as we sang.

Tears sprang to my eyes. Even though I missed this all my life, I had the blessing now, and for that I was thankful.

When the song finished, we all clapped.

"I want to make an announcement," Matt said, claiming everyone's undivided attention. Bing Crosby's "White Christmas" played softly in the background. Matt lowered himself to one knee and took my hand in his.

I gulped, fighting off tears. To most it might seem too fast, but Matt and I were meant to be together. There had never been a real doubt in my mind.

"Terri, I love you more than I've loved anyone ever. I want to spend my life with you and Sophie." He paused and swallowed hard as if fighting off his nerves. "Will you marry me, be my wife?"

The room blurred. I saw no one but the loving man kneeling before me.

My throat burned from unshed emotions. "Yes. Yes I will." Tears spilled down my cheeks.

He slipped a glittering diamond onto my finger. It fit with perfection.

Everyone clapped as he stood, pulling me into the best kiss of my life. I nestled my cheek close to his and we held each other. Family joined us with one big hug and congratulatory words but I barely heard anything anyone said. My mind swirled in bliss.

"Nana's Christmas magic worked," one of his uncles said loudly enough that I heard him.

"But they aren't marrying before Christmas," someone else said, a woman.

"Engagement counts," another female voice said, possibly my sister's.

Matt pulled his cheek away. "Let's get married in this house like Grandpa Robert and Nana did?"

I grinned. "I love that idea."

Sophie scooted next to me and I squatted down to hug her in earnest. Matt then joined us saying, "Sophie, do you want to be my daughter too?" She leaped onto him, wrapping her arms around his neck as the sound of joy filled the room.

What a surprising and heartwarming Christmas.

As we prepared dinner, Emily approached me. "Congratulations, Sis."

"Thanks." We hugged for the second time in one day. My heart filled to full capacity.

"You two are a wonderful match."

I knew I glowed from the inside out. "I appreciate that. I plan to never let him go again."

I glanced down at my ring. Never had I thought I'd be engaged or be married. The Christmas magic worked its blessing and I met my soul mate. I had left the pain of the past behind me and would marry my best friend.

The End

Made in the USA
Columbia, SC
28 November 2021

49956119R00167